"WHY WON'T YOU MARRY ME?" DOUG DEMANDED.

"I've been married once," Jody replied. "It's not an experience I care to repeat."

"And why is that?" His eyes flashed dangerously, and Jody felt a tremor of the old fear taking hold of her.

"You know my reasons better than anyone, Doug. And don't look at me like that. You're scaring me."

"I'll look at you any way I want. I'm mighty angry right now."

"That's the same expression Larry used to have on his face before . . ."

Doug uttered a harsh oath. "You said you had put all that behind you. I thought that after last night—" He paused and looked at her. "You don't trust me, do you? You think I'll hurt you like Larry used to."

"You're Larry's brother. How do I know you're not the same?"

"I'd never treat you the way he did!"

"How do I know that?" Jody cried in anguish, turning to run through the door.

CANDLELIGHT ECSTASY SUPREMES

A VERY SPECIAL LOVER

Emily Elliott

A CANDLELIGHT ECSTASY SUPREME

Published by
Dell Publishing Co., Inc.
1 Dag Hammarskjold Plaza
New York, New York 10017

Dell ® TM 681510, Dell Publishing Co., Inc.

Candlelight Ecstasy Supreme is a trademark
of Dell Publishing Co., Inc.

Candlelight Ecstasy Romance®, 1,203,540, is a registered
trademark of Dell Publishing Co., Inc.

ISBN: 0-440-19315-X

Printed in the United States of America

March 1986

10 9 8 7 6 5 4 3 2 1

WFH

To Our Readers:

We are pleased and excited by your overwhelmingly positive response to our Candlelight Ecstasy Supremes. Unlike all the other series, the Supremes are filled with more passion, adventure, and intrigue, and are obviously the stories you like best.

In months to come we will continue to publish books by many of your favorite authors as well as the very finest work from new authors of romantic fiction. As always, we are striving to present unique, absorbing love stories—the very best love has to offer.

Breathtaking and unforgettable, Ecstasy Supremes follow in the great romantic tradition you've come to expect *only* from Candlelight Ecstasy.

Your suggestions and comments are always welcome. Please let us hear from you.

Sincerely,

The Editors
Candlelight Romances
1 Dag Hammarskjold Plaza
New York, New York 10017

CHAPTER ONE

Doug Ford killed the engine of his rented car and stared for a moment at the small church where his brother's funeral service was to be conducted. Dear God, he thought, he had wanted to come home, but why did it have to be for this? He took a cigarette from the pack in his pocket and lit it. The service was not for a while yet, and he was in no mood to greet all of his and Larry's old friends and accept their condolences. Damn, why had it been Larry? Doug wondered. Larry, the one who had so much promise in the beginning, dead at the age of thirty-four, his car wrecked into a bridge abutment, enough alcohol in his bloodstream to more than qualify him as drunk.

Doug inhaled a lungful of smoke and rolled down the window of the car. The sharp December wind stung his cheeks, reminding him that south Texas was colder in December than San Diego, where he was presently stationed with the navy. He blew the smoke out and watched as an elderly woman got out of her car and made her way up the steps to the church. It was old Mrs. Borrer, he realized, the woman who had taught them both in the first grade. Tears stung the back of Doug's eyes, and he blinked quickly. He had never quite gotten over the notion that a man doesn't cry, even when his heart is breaking.

Doug finished his cigarette and checked his watch. Seeing that it was time to go inside, he locked the doors of the car and walked slowly up the stairs of the old stone church, willing his hand not to tremble as he pulled the door open and stepped inside. It smelled damp and musty, just as it had smelled when he was a boy. He made his way down the aisle to the casket, waiting for a moment while Mrs. Borrer and another elderly woman viewed the body. Barbaric practice, he thought as he stepped up to the casket and stared down at the lifeless face of his younger brother, handsome even in death.

Tears stinging his eyes again, Doug turned from the casket and sat down in the second row on the right, one of the rows reserved for the family. Under other circumstances, he would have sat in the first row, but he had no desire to sit beside Larry's widow, if she even bothered to come. *This is her fault,* he thought bitterly as he stared at the elaborate arrangement of flowers on a stand next to the casket. *Every bit of this is Jody's fault. Does she even know Larry is dead? Does she care?*

Tearing his eyes away from the flowers, Doug let his gaze drift around the church, looking for familiar faces. He didn't see many, just Mrs. Borrer, Tim Smith, one of Larry's old friends from high school, and the dark-haired woman playing the organ. Doug thought a minute and identified her as Marilyn White, Jody's cousin. She had been in Larry and Jody's wedding. As Marilyn played an old hymn with aching sweetness, Doug wondered what Marilyn now thought of her cousin, who had left Larry to run around with a man in San Antonio. He could hardly believe it when Larry had written him last year, telling him that Jody had up and left him and had taken their son with her. Doug had written him back im-

10

mediately, telling Larry to take Scott from her, but Larry had not done that. His letters had become fewer and farther between but had alluded to the wild life he was leading; Doug could only assume that he was trying in his own way to get over the loss of his faithless wife.

This is all Jody's fault, Doug thought again as the pallbearers filed in and sat down in the rows across from him. If she hadn't cheated on Larry, if she hadn't left him, this never would have happened. Where was she, anyway? At that moment a side door opened and his sister-in-law, Jody Ford, stepped into the sanctuary, her young son clutching her hand. Dressed in dark blue, her soft dark hair pulled severely away from her face, she looked every inch the grieving widow. Doug's midsection tensed as he responded involuntarily to her pure, madonnalike appeal. Oh, couldn't looks be deceiving, he thought as she and Scott walked into the sanctuary. Jody spoke to Marilyn at the organ, and Marilyn nodded as Jody and Scott walked toward the first pew. Jody spotted Doug and looked down into his eyes.

"Hello, Doug," she said quietly. "Thank you for coming today."

Doug willed himself not to show the disgust he felt toward Jody. "It was all I could do," he said simply. "He was my brother and I loved him."

Jody nodded and appeared to be holding back tears. "I know. I loved him too." She sat down and clutched her son's hand tightly in her own.

You little hypocrite, Doug thought bitterly as he stared at the prim chignon on the back of Jody's head. Love him? She didn't know the meaning of love. He gazed at the back of her neck, remembering how lovely she had been on her wedding day twelve years ago. She hadn't been much more than a girl

11

that day, fresh out of high school and as pretty as could be, with smiling dark eyes in her sweet, gentle face. He had envied his brother, and had half wished he had met Jody first, although he had been genuinely happy for Larry. Today he wished with all his heart that Larry had never met the cheating little bitch.

As Marilyn ended the hymn, the door to the back opened again and a tall, fair-haired man with piercing black eyes entered the sanctuary. Doug stared in amazement as a slight smile curled his lips. It had been fifteen years since he had seen that face or those black eyes staring into his, but he would never forget Hunter Templeton or the way the man had fought to keep him and his buddies alive when a shell hit their boat in Vietnam. It had been a number of hours before help had arrived, and by a sheer act of will, Hunter had managed to keep Doug and two more of his fellow sailors alive until their injuries could be treated. Somehow Doug was not surprised that Hunter had gone into the ministry.

Hunter stepped up to the pulpit and opened his Bible. " 'Let not your heart be troubled, believe in God, believe also in me,' " he began slowly.

As Hunter read the familiar passage, Doug glanced at Jody. Her face was pale but composed, and as Hunter finished the passage, she reached up and wiped a tear from her face. *How does she do it?* Doug asked himself incredulously. *How can she sit there and pretend that she is grieving?* He tore his gaze from Jody and stared at Scott, expecting to see grief on the boy's face. Scott's face was impassive, bearing no signs of sorrow. Doug wondered momentarily what the boy was thinking, but his attention was drawn from the boy when Jody stood up.

Hunter moved to one side as Jody stepped in front

of the pulpit. Doug watched through narrowed eyes as her trembling hands gripped the sides of the podium, but her voice was clear and strong as she sang the first notes of "The Old Rugged Cross." He could only stare at her as her clear, strong soprano voice filled the church. He had forgotten she could sing that well.

Doug looked up into her tired, sad face. She wasn't the happy, smiling young woman she had been on her wedding day, but she was still lovely. Gentle, dark eyes shone out of a classically oval face, and although Jody wasn't a showstopper, she was beautiful in a quiet way. Doug lowered his gaze and stared at her figure critically. She was much too thin these days; her once-soft curves were now reduced to angularity. Maybe her boyfriend liked her that way, he thought sarcastically as Jody started the second verse. Doug's lips thinned into a grim line as he vowed not to return to California with his bitterness burning him up inside. Maybe Jody Ford could pull the wool over the eyes of New Braunfels, but he knew the truth about her, and he had every intention of confronting her with it before he left. He was going to tell her just what he thought of a woman like her, and he was going to make sure she knew exactly who he held responsible for Larry's death. He knew that what Jody had done wasn't really any of his business, but Larry was his brother, and Doug had loved him. He felt as if he owed it to Larry to let Jody know that it was *her* fault that Larry was dead.

But as Doug stared at the woman behind the pulpit, he had to acknowledge that she was an attractive woman. Too damned attractive, in that prim little dress of hers. He felt the involuntary tightening of his midsection again and had to admit that, had the cir-

13

cumstances been different, he would have been very attracted to this pale, fragile-looking woman.

Jody made her way back to the pew and sat down beside Scott, grateful that she had gotten through the solo without breaking down. She had come close a few times when she had seen tears on the cheeks of the ladies in the church, but she had willed herself to finish the song. In earlier, better days, Larry had loved for her to get out her guitar and sing to him, and in spite of the way her marriage had turned out, she had wanted to sing for him one more time.

Hunter stepped back up to the pulpit with the notes he had made with her last night and read the formal facts of Larry's life, but Jody's thoughts kept drifting back to her husband and the years they had spent together, to the things that would not be mentioned at the funeral today. Even after two years, she still found thoughts of her marriage disturbing, and she wondered if there was any way that she and Larry could have managed to get help or put their marriage back together. But even Hunter and Marilyn, when she had finally been honest with them about Larry, had encouraged her to leave him, and Hunter had offered to help her pay for a divorce. But for reasons she couldn't understand herself, she had never gone through with one, and so this week she had become Larry's widow, even though she hadn't really been his wife for a very long time.

Jody half-listened to Hunter's sermon as he talked about how Larry simply hadn't been able to cope with the pressure and disappointment of losing the family ranch three years ago after four years of drought. The congregation was going to assume that Hunter was talking about Larry's drinking and the way he had died, which was fine with Jody. Only she,

14

Scott, Marilyn, Hunter, and the counselors at the women's shelter in San Antonio knew the truth about how Larry had reacted to losing the ranch. She didn't want it to be known that Larry responded to that pressure by hitting her and finally driving her away from him in fear. After the third time, when he had broken her nose and chipped her two front teeth, she had known that, for Scott's safety as well as her own, she had to leave him. She had stayed in San Antonio for two months, letting her nose heal and having dental work. She then faced Larry one more time, telling him flatly that if he didn't let her have their antique store and get out of town, she was going to press charges against him. Since Larry knew that Marilyn, who was a deputy sheriff, would have arrested him on the spot, he got a job in Houston and had never come back, although in the back of her mind Jody had always been afraid that he would.

Jody glanced over at the open casket. Larry was tall and blond, with thick wavy hair and a dimple in his chin; he had been the golden boy, the most handsome boy in school, and she had loved him dearly for many years. Jody's eyes filled with tears and she sniffed back a sob. Why couldn't things have been different for them? Why had he turned cruel? Jody wiped the tears from her cheeks and admitted to herself that a part of her still loved Larry, in spite of what he had become, and her heart grieved for how their lives might have turned out if Larry had been different.

But Larry hadn't been different, she reminded herself, and that part of her life was over now. As Hunter signaled the pallbearers, Jody straightened her shoulders. She had put all this behind her and had gone on and made a good life for herself and Scott and was trying within herself to undo the psy-

15

chological damage that Larry had inflicted on both of them.

Hunter led the congregation in a closing prayer and nodded to Jody. She and Scott stepped up to the casket and looked at Larry briefly before one of the pallbearers closed the lid. The congregation filed out, leaving Jody and Doug and the pallbearers in the church.

Marilyn Templeton stepped up to Jody and put her hand on her shoulder. "They'll carry out the casket now, and you and Scott will follow it out," she said quietly. "Is there any other family?"

Jody nodded. "Doug is here," she said as she gestured to the second pew. "He may want to ride with us." She turned toward him. "Would you like to ride in the limousine with me and Scott?"

Doug blinked and shook his head. "I have a car here," he said. "I'll drive it in the procession."

"There isn't going to be a procession," Jody said. "The cemetery's just down the street."

"Then I'll walk," Doug replied.

Jody turned away from Doug quickly, her fingers trembling just a little. Although Doug had said nothing wrong, she could sense a feeling of hatred for her coming from him. But why? Why would he be hostile toward her? What had she done to make him feel like that?

Jody stepped up to Scott and Marilyn. "He doesn't want to come," she told Marilyn quietly.

Marilyn's eyes narrowed, and Jody knew that her cousin was mentally comparing Doug with Larry.

"Whatever," Marilyn said.

Jody took Scott's hand, and together the two of them followed the casket out of the church. The pallbearers loaded the casket into the hearse while Scott

16

and Jody got into the limousine. The other mourners started walking to the cemetery.

Jody smiled gratefully and moved over as Marilyn got in the car beside her. "Thank you," she said quietly. "I would hate for the only family to be Scott and me."

Marilyn shook her head. "You have a more generous spirit than I do," she said. "If a man had treated me like Larry treated you, I wouldn't care if his family limousine was empty."

Jody smiled slightly. "I don't believe that for a moment, and neither do you. After all you've gone through yourself, you've been the most loving, giving woman this town has ever had." Marilyn had recovered from the tragedies of her only child's death and her husband's desertion almost five years ago and two years later had married Hunter Templeton, taking on the role of minister's wife with graciousness and enthusiasm.

"But I've received a lot too," Marilyn said softly as the limousine pulled into the cemetery and stopped. They got out of the car and stepped under the canopy, where the casket was not sitting. Jody sat down in one of the three folding chairs provided for her, Scott, and Doug. Scott sat to one side of her and Marilyn motioned for Doug to take the third one. He did so, not looking in Jody's direction, but Jody could feel his hostility again, the same way she had felt Larry's hostility when he hit her. Dear God, was Doug mad at the world right now, or was that hostility for her? she wondered. But why should his attitude surprise her? He was Larry's brother, wasn't he? They were similar in other ways. Why shouldn't they share the same violent temper?

As Hunter stepped up to the casket, Jody sneaked a look in Doug's direction. Yes, he was very much like

17

Larry. They shared the same fair hair and green eyes, and the shape of their faces was similar. But there were differences too. While Larry had tanned easily, Doug was fair, and long years of exposure to the sun of the high seas and tropic ports had taken their toll on his skin, tanning it some and weathering it far past the thirty-nine she knew him to be. And while Larry had been well-muscled and tended to put on weight, Doug had a leaner strength. Doug did not have Larry's smooth handsomeness, since his features were rougher and less well-defined. He seemed to be a rougher man than Larry, and if Larry had been as cruel as he had, what could a woman expect from a man like Doug?

Jody shivered slightly and turned her attention to Hunter as he started to speak. He read a psalm and said a prayer before he picked up a handful of dirt and sprinkled it on the casket. *Ashes to ashes, dust to dust,* Jody thought as Hunter bowed his head in a benediction. Jody stood as she, Doug, and Scott were surrounded by old friends who had come to pay their last respects to Larry. Her responses automatic, Jody shook hands and introduced Doug to Larry's friends, many of whom were obviously uncomfortable, not knowing quite what to say to a widow who had been an estranged wife. Jody did her best to put them at ease, accepting their condolences and words of comfort and inviting them to her house for something to eat before they went home. She noticed that Doug seemed to be bitterly amused by the awkwardness her friends felt around her.

Finally, the crowd around Jody and Doug thinned, and Marilyn appeared at Jody's elbow. "Are you ready to go back to the house?" she asked.

Jody nodded as Hunter joined them. "Thank you for everything, Hunter," Jody said, squeezing the hand he extended to her. "You've been just wonderful."

Hunter engulfed Jody in a huge bear hug. "Oh, Jody, Marilyn and I wish there had been more we could have done to help you, both now and before. Sometimes we felt pretty helpless. We'll be over to the house just as soon as we've checked on Rachel. She's trying to take those first steps, and she's probably run the babysitter ragged." Hunter stopped and looked at Doug. "I know you're Larry's brother, but don't I know you from somewhere else?"

Doug nodded. "Hue, 1968. You saved my life."

"Of course," Hunter said as he extended his hand. Doug shook it and put his hands back in the pockets of his overcoat. "But I hardly saved your life. I just kept you awake until the medics could get there." Hunter drew Marilyn toward him. "Doug, this is my wife, Marilyn. Or are you old friends?"

Marilyn nodded and looked at Doug, her face expressionless. "I remember you from years ago," she said. "I'm sorry you had to come back for this."

"So am I," Doug said. He could feel that Marilyn didn't altogether like him, and it irritated him a little, since she had no reason to feel that way.

Jody picked up a small vase of flowers and held them out to Marilyn. "Would you like these for Bobby?" she asked. "We have so many."

Hunter took the vase of flowers and put his arm around his wife. "Thank you," he said as Marilyn's eyes grew misty. "We'll see you at your house." They walked toward the small grave on the other side of the cemetery, where Marilyn's little boy was buried.

Doug was puzzled by Hunter and Marilyn. Surely the minister couldn't have approved when Jody left Larry for that other man, yet he was comforting her with the familiarity of a dear friend as well as a minister. Did Hunter and Marilyn know the whole story, or had Jody pulled the wool over their eyes, just as she had everybody else's? He was becoming more and more puzzled. Was Jody such a good actress that she had fooled everybody? Or was there more to this than he realized? He didn't know the answer to that yet, but by the end of the evening he would, even if he had to drag it out of Jody. He had a decision to make, and he had to know exactly what had happened to Larry's marriage before he could make it intelligently.

Jody turned to Doug. "Would you like to come back to the house?" she asked quietly. "The town has sent more food than we can eat in a week."

"I'll be there," Doug said abruptly as he turned from them.

Scott looked up at Jody with fear in his eyes. "He looks like Daddy," he whispered. "He sounds just like Daddy too."

Jody swallowed. "I know," she said. "But he isn't Daddy, Scott. Daddy's gone."

"I'm glad," Scott replied, his young voice shaking with hatred. "He made you hurt."

Jody shuddered. "Don't feel that way, Scott," she pleaded. "I don't want you to feel that way about your own father. Can't you even be a little sorry he's dead?"

Scott turned mutinous eyes on her. "No," he said. "And no one's ever going to hurt you again, Mom. I'm going to protect you."

A small smile touched Jody's lips. "I love you, Scott, you know that?" she said as she ruffled his hair. "We better go on back to the house."

The limousine delivered them to the old Victorian home that she and Larry had bought the second year they were married. The driveway and the street were full of cars, and Jody suddenly regretted inviting all the mourners back. She would have loved to be by herself for the rest of the evening, but instead she was committed to another several hours of friends and family talking, eating, and wondering behind her back just what had gone wrong with her and Larry's marriage. Jody had never told anyone in New Braunfels the truth about Larry except Hunter and Marilyn, and Larry's death had resurrected all the gossip that had circulated when he had left town and she had returned. At the time, she had been emotionally wiped out and the gossip had left her unmoved, but now it made her uneasy and a little resentful, even though she realized that there was no way to stop her friends from wondering.

Jody left her coat in the front closet and went into the kitchen. "Is the food holding out, Iva?" she asked as her neighbor cut a pound cake into slices.

"Jody, you have enough food here to feed an army," she said. "Don't you worry about the food. Marilyn and I will take care of it. You just go in there and sit down."

"I'd rather be helping in here," Jody admitted. "I'm just about out of polite chatter."

Iva's face softened in sympathy. "It's only for a little while longer," she soothed. "Then you can be alone."

Hunter poked his head through the back door. "Marilyn will be here in a minute. Can I take a plate of food over to the babysitter?"

"Sure thing," Jody said as she found a paper plate. She piled it high with food and handed it to Hunter. "What did Rachel get into?"

Hunter winced. "She pulled all the books out of the bottom shelf in my study and ate four pages of my notes on Ezekiel."

"I wonder if they were as dry as they were the last time you preached them," Jody teased. Hunter laughed and shut the door behind him. "I guess I better go on out there," she said to Iva. "I hope they don't stay long."

Jody entered the living room just as Doug pulled open the front door. Their eyes met, and Jody again shivered at his grim expression. She reminded herself that Doug would be gone soon and that he couldn't hurt her like Larry had.

Jody picked up a glass of tea and sat down on the couch. She watched Doug warily as she talked with Larry's old friends and made sure they had enough to eat. Doug served himself a plate of food from the buffet and had just settled himself in Larry's recliner when Hunter and Marilyn came in. Marilyn went straight to the kitchen to help, but Hunter served himself and made a beeline for Doug. He sat down on the footstool beside the recliner and the two of them were soon reminiscing about their days together in the navy.

Jody got some food, but between the strain of the funeral and the uneasiness she felt about Doug, she couldn't force it down her throat. She drank another cup of tea instead and carried the half-eaten food to the kitchen.

Marilyn glanced at the plate and sighed sympathetically. "Nerves?" she asked.

Jody nodded as she dumped the uneaten food in the trash. "I don't know why, but Doug's making me nervous," she said under her breath.

Marilyn looked at Jody perceptively. "Frightened of him?" she asked.

Jody took a breath and nodded. "I know it's silly, but he is Larry's brother, you know. And Larry looked at me like that the last time he hit me."

Marilyn shuddered. "I don't think it's silly at all. If I had been through what you have, I'd be scared too. We'll make sure you're all right tonight."

Jody looked at Marilyn with a question in her eyes. "Before, when you were married to Robert, I know you weren't happy. Did he ever . . . was he ever cruel?"

Marilyn shook her head. "No. As lousy as that marriage was, Robert never raised his voice to me, much less his fist. All men aren't like that, you know."

Jody looked through the crack in the door at Doug. "Maybe not, but that one is," she said. "Have you eaten yet?"

Marilyn admitted that she had not, and Jody steered her toward the dining room table. Marilyn sat down on the chair closest to Hunter while Jody wished several friends who had to drive back to Houston good night. She visited with others for the next hour or so, her natural graciousness masking both her tiredness and her growing uneasiness around Doug. The only thing that kept her uneasiness from turning into outright fear was Marilyn's assurance that they would make sure she and Scott were all right.

Finally, the last stragglers said their good nights and departed, leaving only the Templetons, Jody, Scott, and Doug. Jody glanced from Hunter to Doug and was surprised to see Doug smiling openly at Hunter and laughing at some shared joke from the past. So he wasn't like that with everybody, she thought as she picked up a stack of dirty paper plates and carried them to the kitchen. It was just her. Was there something about her that inspired hostility in men?

"Come on, Hunter, help Jody and me get this mess cleaned up," Marilyn said as she handed Hunter a

23

plastic trash bag. She turned impassive eyes on Doug. "Would you like some more tea before you go?"

In response, Doug stood up and started gathering up dirty paper dishes. "I'll help you clean up, and then I need to talk to Jody before I go," he said smoothly.

Jody turned her startled gaze on Marilyn, who in turn turned uneasy eyes on Doug. Marilyn knew something, he thought grimly. Either she was trying to protect her cousin or she knew something more than he did. Whatever it was, he had to find out the truth about Jody and Larry before he left here tonight, so he could decide what to do about the note. He stuffed the paper plates into the sack and gathered up another handful.

Hunter looked from Jody to Marilyn, his face impassive. "Jody, why don't you put Scott to bed while we clean up here? He's had a long day."

Jody willed her hands not to tremble as she saw Scott up the stairs. She waited while he put on his pajamas and brushed his teeth, and together they said his prayers. She tucked him in and kissed his forehead. "Good night, honey," she whispered.

"Has Uncle Doug gone yet?" Scott asked.

Jody shook her head, hoping she didn't sound as frightened as she felt. "No, he's still here. He wants to talk to me for a minute."

Scott wrapped his arms around her neck and hugged her tightly. "I mean it, Mom. I'm never going to let anyone else hurt you."

Tears stung the back of Jody's eyes. "Thank you," she said, wishing fervently that Scott really could protect her.

She came down the stairs slowly. The living room was clear, and she could hear the sound of the dishwasher coming from the kitchen. She found Marilyn and Hunter in the dining room, dishing up the last of the leftovers. "Would you like to take some of this?" she asked. "I know how hungry Hunter gets when you're working nights."

Marilyn nodded and selected a couple of the casseroles. "I'll stay if you want me to," she said under her breath.

Hunter looked from Jody to Doug, who was sitting on the living room couch. "I don't think you have to do that," he said quietly. "She'll be all right, Marilyn. Besides, you have to go on duty in an hour."

Marilyn shot him a dirty look, but Hunter gently steered her toward the door. "We'll talk to you tomorrow, Jody. Are you going to the store?"

Jody shook her head. "The reading of the will is tomorrow. Beatrice will be at the store until Thursday." She held her hands tightly in front of her to keep them from shaking. "Thank you again for everything."

Marilyn let Hunter steer her out the front door. "I'm right across the street if you need anything," she said loudly enough for Doug to hear. Doug's lips thinned slightly as Jody shut the door behind the Templetons.

She sat down in the chair across from Doug, willing herself to meet his gaze. He stared at her for long moments as they sized one another up. He was big, he was angry, and he was not trying to hide it. Jody trembled as she remembered what a man in his state of mind could do.

"I have to know the truth about you and my brother," he said finally. "Why the hell did you cheat on him?"

25

CHAPTER TWO

Jody stared at Doug in shock. Was that why he had been so hostile toward her? Did he really think she had cheated on Larry? Numbly, Jody shook her head back and forth. "I never cheated on your brother," she said through stiff lips.

"I don't believe that!" Doug snapped. He got a letter out of his pocket and waved it in her direction. "He said so right here. He said that you cheated on him, that you left him and went to San Antonio to live with a man."

Jody shook her head again. "No, Doug, that wasn't the way it was, not at all," she said firmly, though her voice trembled a bit. "I did go to San Antonio, but I never stayed with a man."

"That isn't what Larry said," Doug said, his voice quiet. "He said in this letter that you had left him and were living in San Antonio with a man."

"I don't care what Larry wrote you, I didn't leave him to go to another man!" Jody said as she shifted across the couch to move away from Doug. "I left him, yes, but not for the reason that you think." She twisted her hands together to keep her fingers from shaking and wondered if she should leave the house now. She had tried, that last time, to run away from Larry, but he had caught up with her before she had been able to get away.

"Then why did you leave my brother?" Doug demanded.

"Is it any of your business?" Jody asked with spirit.

"It is if you had a hand in killing him," Doug said bitterly. "Now, how about the truth?"

Jody bit her lip, the old sense of shame keeping her from blurting out the real reason. "I—we weren't getting along," she stammered. "I thought it would be better if we were apart."

Doug stared at her, his gaze piercing through her fragile defenses. She was lying to him; her nervousness confirmed it. "Not good enough, Jody," he replied. "Lots of couples don't get along at times, but they work out their problems. Why couldn't you?"

"Some problems are too complicated to work out," Jody said quietly. "Ours were, and that's why—"

"That's a damned lie and you know it!" Doug ground out, clenching his hand at his side the same way Larry had when he was upset. Jody quailed at the sight of Doug's clenched fist. "You didn't leave him because you were having problems. You left him because you wanted another man! You tore Larry's insides out, he said so in his letters!" Doug cursed the angry tears that started to gather in his eyes. "You killed him, Jody. He wouldn't have been out there drinking and driving if you hadn't left him to go to another man. Dammit, it's all your fault!"

"No!" Jody cried. "No, Doug, it was not my fault! I'm sorry Larry died the way he did, but I had nothing to do with that!"

"The hell it's not your fault!" Doug exclaimed. "You killed my little brother, Jody. You killed him the same as if you took a gun and aimed it at his heart. I loved him, Jody. He was the only family I had left, and you took him from me. Dammit, he was a good man. You shouldn't have left him! I swear, you ought

27

to have some sense knocked into you for leaving a man like that!" He stopped and sniffed, but Jody was too frightened to notice.

I'm getting out, Jody thought as she rose from the couch and made a run for the door. But a cry from the landing of the stairs froze both Doug and Jody.

"*No!*" Scott yelled at the top of his lungs. He ran down the stairs, clutching a small knife in his hands, and planted himself between Doug and Jody. Doug stared in astonishment at the whitefaced figure of his nephew, the boy's trembling fingers trying not to drop the small pocket knife, which wasn't much more than a toy. Scott looked up at him with hatred in his eyes. "You're just like him, aren't you? You're just like Daddy. You want to hurt Mom, just like he used to do. Well, you're not going to. I'm bigger now, and I'll protect her. I'll put this knife into you if I have to."

Doug stood, frozen to the spot with a mixture of horror and astonishment on his face. Jody looked down at her small son, pride and sadness mingling on her face as she moved away from the door and knelt beside Scott. "Give me the knife, Scott."

"No," Scott said as he stared up at Doug. "He wants to hurt you, and I'm not going to let him."

Jody reached out and gently pried the knife out of Scott's hand. "I was just going to get Aunt Marilyn and Uncle Hunter to help me," she said as she folded the blade back into the knife. "Remember the talks about violence we had at the shelter in San Antonio? Returning violence with more violence isn't the answer, Scott."

The boy nodded unwillingly. "But what can you do to stop him?"

Jody swallowed. "Aunt Marilyn can stop him if she has to," she said. "Scott, do you remember the other things we talked about? You said that you didn't want to be like Daddy. Or Uncle Doug," she said, casting a disdainful glance up at Doug's stiff figure. "Well, if you start threatening people with hitting or sticking a knife into them, that makes you the same as them, and you don't want that, do you?"

Scott shook his head. Jody stood up and faced Doug with a frightened but proud expression on her face. "I left your brother simply because I got tired of having some sense knocked into me," she said, her voice low and choked with hatred. "Now get out of my home."

Doug stared over at the woman and the child for a moment before he left the house, still in shock from the scene he had just been a part of. Jody had not acted guilty, he now realized, but she had been frightened, and that child would have gladly put that knife through him. What could have happened to have made them both react like that? Larry had always had a temper, he had to admit. Maybe Larry had slapped her or something when she had left him, and she and the child both thought that he would do the same.

Doug looked back at Jody's front door. There was no way she would talk to him again, and he still didn't know what had really happened between Larry and Jody. He glanced across the street at the rambling old parsonage. Hunter might know what had gone on between Larry and his wife. Taking a breath, he tried to put his hands in his pockets and realized that he had left his overcoat in Jody's front closet. Shrugging, he walked across the street and knocked on the door of the parsonage.

Hunter answered a moment later. He had changed into jeans and was holding a small, dark-haired baby girl in his arms. "Doug. We didn't expect to see you again tonight," he said as he opened the door. "Come in."

Doug stepped into the warm house. Hunter motioned him into a large parlor and sat down on the couch, gesturing for Doug to sit down beside him.

"Your daughter's beautiful," Doug volunteered.

Hunter smiled as he unwound the little girl's fingers from a handful of his hair. "Thank you, she's the light of our lives," he admitted. "Is there anything special we can do for you tonight, or is this a social visit?"

Doug moistened his lips with his tongue. "I want to know if Jody was unfaithful to my brother," he said in a rush.

Hunter stiffened noticeably, and his friendly smile faded. "No, she wasn't," he said shortly. "Not that it's really any concern of yours."

Doug bridled a little at the intended rebuke. "I think it is my business, if her leaving him was in any way responsible for his death," he said curtly. "He was my only family and I loved him." He lifted his chin a little. "Besides, I have a financial decision that will affect my nephew quite a bit in the years to come, and I need to know the truth about his mother before I make it. I've just come from talking to Jody and she wouldn't tell me anything."

Hunter's eyes grew cool. "I can assure you that your sister-in-law was not an unfaithful wife, even if that's the impression your brother chose to give you."

"Then why did she leave him if it wasn't to go to another man?" Doug demanded.

"That question isn't mine to answer," he said quietly. "I'm under ministerial confidence."

"I'm not under confidence," Marilyn said from the end of the room. Dressed now in her deputy's uniform, she stared at Doug with open unfriendliness. "And I think he ought to know exactly why she left his precious brother. Dammit, Hunter, you should have let me stay with her over there. I knew he was going to give her hell about something when you marched me out. And you did, didn't you?" she demanded. "You tore her up. You yelled at her for her supposed infidelity."

"I spoke to her about it, yes," Doug said shortly.

"She's probably terrified out of her wits," Marilyn said. She stared down at Doug with disdain in her eyes, and he felt more than a little uneasy as he stared up into the angry law officer's face.

"Marilyn, you shouldn't swear," Hunter said quietly.

"Sorry. I shouldn't be swearing at you, but this jerk probably needs it.

"Doug, Jody never cheated on your brother. She left him because he abused her."

Doug drew in his breath in a shocked gasp. "He *what?*"

"You heard me," Marilyn said. "He slapped her, hit her—*abused* her. She put up with it twice, but left him after the third time, when she got scared that he would kill her."

"I don't believe you," Doug said flatly. "You've got to come up with something better than that."

"Are you calling my wife a liar?" Hunter asked, his eyes flashing. "Now that Marilyn's spilled the beans, yes, Doug, your brother beat his wife. Three times that she admitted to. I drove her to the women's shelter myself after the third attack."

"She must have been lying to you," Doug insisted. "Dammit, Larry wouldn't *do* that!"

"And you wonder why she doesn't want to tell

31

anyone why she left him," Marilyn said to Hunter. "Your brother was a brutal bastard, Doug."

"It couldn't have been that bad," Doug said hotly. "Larry wasn't like that."

Hunter's lips thinned, and Marilyn took a small black and white photograph from the desk in one corner and handed it to Doug. "That's what your dear, darling brother did the last time he hit her."

Doug stared in horror at the bruises on Jody's face and her broken nose. "I—I can't believe it," he whispered. "Larry was capable of that?"

"Yes, he did that," Marilyn said. "She also had to have her front teeth capped. We showed this picture to your brother and gave him twenty-four hours to get out of town before Jody pressed charges and I arrested him," she added as she looked Doug straight in the eye.

"Why did he hit her like that?" Doug asked quietly. "Was it for cheating on him?"

"No, she was not cheating on him. That night I think it was because the roast was a little too well done for his taste," Hunter said flatly.

Doug looked down at the picture again, and nausea washed over him as he thought of all the unfounded accusations he had made tonight. She had already suffered so much, and he had added to her pain tonight. "Oh, dear God," he said quietly. "I thought maybe he slapped her for seeing another man or something."

"Jody was a fine wife," Hunter said. "Too good, really. She probably should have left after the second incident, but she took her marriage vows seriously and did everything she could to hold her marriage together."

"Have we satisfied your morbid curiosity?" Marilyn snapped. "Are you convinced that Jody's not the wicked adulteress your brother dreamed up? Will you leave the poor woman alone now? I think she's suffered enough from the Fords, don't you?"

"You don't have to talk to me like that," Doug told Marilyn. "You couldn't dislike me right now any more than I dislike myself. How could he have done that to a woman like Jody?" His fingers trembled as he handed the picture back to Marilyn.

"He was a very paranoid and insecure man after he lost the ranch," Hunter said. "He never quite got over the frustration and anger of losing property that had been in the family for generations, and he took it out on her. He might have really believed that she was cheating on him, or he might have just used it as an excuse to take out his frustrations on her, I really don't know. But she never gave him any reason to treat her the way he did."

"And I believed him," Doug said under his breath. "I was fool enough to believe him." He looked from Hunter's solemn face to Marilyn's. "I'm sorry," he said. "I'll say it to you first, and then I'll go tell her. I had no idea that Larry had become like that." He turned bewildered eyes on Hunter. "Why didn't she just tell me the truth?"

Hunter's face softened a little. "She was ashamed, Doug. Ashamed and horribly embarrassed. We're the only people in New Braunfels who know the whole story."

"Doug, don't go back over there," Marilyn said firmly. "I'll go over and tell her you're sorry if you like, but stay away from her. You've done enough already."

"Believe me, I'd like nothing better," Doug said. "But that's the coward's way out. I'll talk to her myself." He got up off the couch and left.

"I'm going with him," Marilyn said as she started across the room after Doug.

"Marilyn," Hunter said, his tone enough to detain her.

"But she might need me," Marilyn said.

Hunter shook his head as he cuddled Rachel. "He's not angry anymore, and even if he was, he's not the kind of man to strike a woman. He might tear her up verbally, but I can assure you that he wouldn't hurt her, and the way he's feeling right now, he would probably kiss the bottom of her shoes if it would make her feel better."

Marilyn turned doubtful eyes on Hunter. "How do you know? We never thought Larry would be cruel, but he was."

"Larry and I didn't serve on the same ship for nearly a year. I know him, Marilyn. He may be a little bossy and arrogant, but he's not cruel. Trust me. Besides, you're due at work in five minutes."

Marilyn kissed Hunter and Rachel good-bye and hurried out the door. Hunter stared after her thoughtfully as he wondered how it would go at the house across the street.

Jody's front porch light was off when Doug walked slowly up the sidewalk. He hated having to face her again so soon, especially after learning what he had about her marriage to his brother, and he was tempted to get in his rented car and leave. But he couldn't do that, not until he had dealt with the debt on the store that Larry still owed him. Besides, he owed Jody an apology, and he hoped she would accept it, although it would serve him right if she didn't.

Doug felt around for Jody's doorbell for a moment before he realized that a house as old as hers probably didn't have one. He rapped twice on the front door, waited for a moment, and knocked again more loudly. He could see a light in the living room go on and suddenly the porch was bathed in the harsh yellow glow of the porch light.

"Jody, I have to talk to you," Doug said through the door. "Open up. Please."

Jody opened the window next to the door just a crack. "Get out of here," she said angrily. "We've already talked."

"Jody, I—" Doug stammered as Jody slammed the window shut. "Jody, open the door, please! I talked to Hunter and his wife, and I—"

The window banged open again. "Do you intend to tell my problems to the whole neighborhood?" Jody demanded. "Get off my porch and go away."

"I'll tell them everything if you won't open the door," Doug threatened.

"Go ahead and tell them, then," Jody said. "It beats having some sense knocked into me."

Jody slammed the window down and leaned against the wall, trembling from a combination of fear and anger. What did he think she was going to do, let him in to finish what Scott had interrupted? She glanced fearfully out of the window and saw Doug heading back toward Hunter and Marilyn's house. Why was he going there, for heaven's sake? She started to pick up the telephone and call Hunter but figured that Doug would already be there by the time her trembling fingers could dial the number.

Jody checked the deadbolts on the door and was about to go back upstairs when the telephone rang. She picked it up cautiously, afraid it might be Doug on the other end. "Jody, this is Hunter," his familiar deep voice said. "I've just talked to Doug, and he wants to talk to you."

35

"He's already done that, Hunter," Jody said bitterly. "He's said enough for tonight."

"Jody, he didn't know," Hunter said gently. "I think you'll find his attitude much different now."

"You didn't *tell* him, did you?" Jody exclaimed. "Hunter, how could you?"

"Marilyn thought he needed to know the truth," Hunter said. "Believe me, she raked him over the coals for talking to you the way he did. He only wants to apologize, Jody."

"I don't want him over here," she said. "Scott and I have been through enough today."

"Jody, the man needs to talk to you," Hunter said. "You're not afraid of him, are you?"

"Of course I'm afraid of him," Jody said. "Wouldn't you be afraid of the brother of the man who broke your nose?"

Hunter paused. "What if I come with him?"

"What about Rachel?"

"She's still awake."

"Oh, all right," Jody said. "But just don't leave me alone with him."

"We'll be there in a minute," Hunter said.

Jody hung up the telephone and looked around helplessly. Then she turned on the porch light and soon heard Hunter's knock. She opened the door and Rachel immediately leaned toward Jody, squealing with delight as Jody reached out and took the little girl from Hunter.

"How's my favorite girl this evening?" she crooned, deliberately ignoring the man behind Hunter on the porch. "Come on in, Hunter," she said, moving aside so that Hunter and Doug could enter.

Doug followed Hunter inside, and the two of them sat down on the couch. Jody handed the squirming baby to Hunter and sat down across from them in the recliner.

"Jody, Doug only wants to talk to you," Hunter said gently.

"Haven't we already talked enough this evening, Doug?" she asked bitterly.

"No, we haven't," Doug said. "Jody, I'm very sorry for the things I said to you. Hunter and Marilyn told me what happened between you and Larry."

"I wish you hadn't done that," Jody said, looking toward Hunter.

"Why? So he could go on thinking you left Larry for another man?" Hunter asked.

"Why didn't you tell me the truth?" Doug asked.

"Would you have believed me?" Jody demanded.

Doug's ears turned red as he remembered the hard time Marilyn had had getting him to believe the truth. "No, probably not. But how was I supposed to know? Larry wrote me that you had left him for another man. How was I supposed to know that he had hurt you? I honestly believed you'd cheated on him."

"And where do you get off talking to me like you did? What business was it of yours if I *had* left Larry for another man? Who set you up as my judge and jury?"

Doug's face turned redder.

"Jody," Hunter said reprovingly.

"No, Hunter, I'm not going to let him just waltz in here and apologize for threatening to knock some sense into me," Jody said. "He scared me to death! I'm already acquainted with the Ford right hook, remember?"

Doug blanched as he remembered the photograph Marilyn had shown him. "Surely you don't think I would have really hit you!" he said in horror. "That's just a figure of speech, Jody."

"Not always," Jody said quietly.

Doug leaned forward and linked his fingers together around his knee. "Jody, you have to believe me. I admit I was angry with you earlier, but I would never have hit you. I'm not like that." He wilted at Jody's skeptical expression. "I'm not like my brother, honestly! It makes me sick to think of him hurting you the way he did."

Jody shrugged. "It's all water under the bridge, anyway."

"Jody, I'd give anything to be able to take back the things I said to you earlier," Doug said earnestly. "Please accept my apology, and please believe me when I say that I would never hurt you the way Larry did."

"I accept your apology," Jody said slowly.

Doug waited a moment, but no more was forthcoming. He and Hunter glanced at one another, and Doug could tell that Hunter thought the same thing he did—Jody still thought him capable of the same kind of cruelty that his brother had inflicted on her. That bothered him. He didn't want her to be afraid of him. "Jody, I wouldn't have hurt you, I swear. Even if I'd gone on believing that you had left Larry for another man."

"If you say so," Jody said. "Will you be flying back to San Diego tomorrow?"

"Uh, not until the day after," Doug said. "Larry's attorney asked me to be present tomorrow for the reading of the will."

"I hope you're not expecting a windfall," Jody said dryly, wondering why Doug needed to be present. Larry certainly didn't have anything of substance to leave to him.

Doug shook his head, his face softening at Jody's feeble attempt at humor. "Hardly." He reached down and tickled Rachel under her chin, and the little girl looked up at him and laughed. "Hunter, this little lady's a charmer," he said, grinning boyishly at them.

Jody stared at the transformation in him. Suddenly he seemed warmer and even appealing somehow, with some of the charm that Larry had possessed. Jody shuddered inwardly at this sudden change—an attractive Doug was more unsettling to her than a grim, angry Doug.

"Doug, do you have a hotel room?" Hunter asked. "If not, you're welcome to stay with Marilyn and me." Under other circumstances, Jody might have offered to put Doug up herself, but she wouldn't make that offer tonight.

"Thanks. I'll take you up on that," Doug said gratefully. He stood and turned to Jody. "Please, try to forgive me."

Jody stood. "I'll try."

Doug smiled down gratefully and extended his hand. Jody had no choice but to reach out with her own. His hand was hard and calloused and gripped hers firmly when her instinct was to pull away. Yet the touch of his hand wasn't at all unpleasant.

"Until tomorrow," Doug said.

Jody nodded and saw them to the door, stealing a wet kiss from Rachel before Hunter carried her out. Jody turned off the porch light and refastened the locks before she sat down alone on her couch.

Doug had thrown her off-balance when he came back to talk to her the second time. Once he had gotten over his anger, he had much of the same appeal that Larry had once had—the same smile, the same boyish earnestness that had won her heart so

39

long ago. And that made him more unsettling to Jody than he had been earlier; she didn't need to find herself attracted in any way to Larry's brother. Thank goodness he would be gone in two days, she thought with a sigh.

CHAPTER THREE

Jody sat down on the couch in the waiting room of the law firm and picked up a magazine, trying not to let her nervousness show. Last night she had not thought too much about the attorney's request that Doug be present for the reading of the will, but she had thought about it more this morning, and she had to admit that it made her nervous. Had Larry changed his will and left his share of their estate to Doug? He had been furious with her when she had demanded that he get out of town and leave the store with her. Was this his way of getting even with her for that?

The door creaked, and Jody looked up to see Doug enter the room. He smiled uncertainly and sat down across from her. "How are you today?" he asked quietly.

"Fine," she said, hoping her nervousness didn't show. "Do you know what this is all about?"

"I know some, but I think we both better wait and let Sam explain it," he said evasively. Sam Adamson had been the family's attorney for years.

Doug picked up a farm and ranch magazine and leafed through it idly. Jody tried to get interested in an article in her magazine, but her gaze kept drifting to the man across from her. He was not dressed in his suit this afternoon, but his slacks were well cut and his light green shirt almost matched his eyes. Firm muscles rippled under the thin shirt, and Jody wondered if his job in the service was highly physical. She chided herself for even caring and turned back to the magazine.

A couple of minutes later, Sue Phillips left Sam's office. "Doug, Jody, Sam's ready to see you now," she said.

Doug stood and extended his hand. "Sue, you're looking wonderful. How are you?" he asked, smiling down at her.

She blushed prettily. "I'm just fine, Doug," she said. "And you're not looking so bad yourself. Are you still in the service?"

Jody watched as Doug proceeded to thoroughly charm Sam's secretary. Larry had been able to charm women the same way, she thought uncomfortably as Sue laughed at something Doug said. Doug was just too much like Larry for her to trust him much, and as far as Jody was concerned, the sooner he was on a plane back to San Diego, the better she would like it.

Jody followed Doug into Sam's office and pulled the door shut behind her. "Doug, Jody, it's good to see you," the lawyer said as he stood to greet them. He shook hands with both of them and they sat down in comfortable chairs across the desk from him. "Thank you both for coming in this afternoon," Sam said. "I'd like to extend my condolences to both of you. It's sad to lose a loved one, and it's not easy to have to come for the reading of a will."

Sam cleared his throat and handed Jody and Larry copies of the will. Jody looked down at the bottom and saw that this was the same will that Larry had signed three years ago, when he had lost the ranch and they had redrawn their wills to omit any mention of the property. Jody breathed a sigh of relief. So

Larry hadn't changed his will, after all. She would still inherit Larry's half of everything they owned.

"As you and Larry agreed on earlier, everything goes to you, Jody. Now, let's talk about the debts against the estate."

"What debts?" Jody asked. "Did Larry start using credit cards after we separated?"

"Not that I know of," Sam said. "I'm talking about your debt to Doug."

"There shouldn't be a debt," Jody said, shocked. "Larry paid Doug off before I left him." Larry and Jody had borrowed a large sum from Doug to start the antique store, but they had scrimped and saved, and Larry had told Jody he had paid Doug back.

"He never paid me, Jody," Doug said quietly, his face expressionless. "He never even paid me any interest on the money."

"But we saved, and we—" Jody turned anguished eyes on Sam. "Where did the money go, if he didn't pay Doug with it?"

Sam flipped through a stack of papers. "Was the date on that in March?"

Jody thought a minute. "Yes."

"Then the money went to pay off one of those shyster loan companies in San Antonio. Apparently that last year, when the ranch was doing so badly, Larry ran out of credit here at the bank and went to one, trying to get enough money to keep the ranch floating."

Jody uttered a quiet curse. "He never even told me." She looked from Doug to Sam. "Are there any other assets that I can pay Doug with?"

Sam looked through Larry's papers again. "Larry had three hundred dollars in his checking account when he died. That's all he had to his name, other than his share in the antique store. Leaving you pretty well left him broke." Sam looked a little disapprovingly at Jody.

Jody lifted her chin. "That may have seemed unfair, but I became the sole support of Scott when Larry left," she reminded the attorney. "So you're telling me that there's no money left from the sale of the ranch or anywhere else to pay off Doug," she said flatly, feeling despair start to well within her at the thought of losing her beloved store.

"No, I'm afraid not," Sam said.

"What are your profits like?" Doug asked. "Could you afford to pay me in the next year or so?"

Jody thought a moment. "You want the whole lump in the next year?"

"Yes, I do," Doug said.

"Then there isn't any way," she said numbly. "The only reason we were able to save that first year is that Larry was doing all the upholstering and refinishing work. Now I have to pay to have that done, and it's cut my profits considerably. I'm just barely making enough to make ends meet." She bit her lip and turned to Doug, but his expression was implacable. There was no way he would agree to write off the loan, she realized. She would have to sell the store. "I'll put the store on the market." She turned tear-filled eyes to Sam. "Is there anything else?"

"Uh, not really. Just don't forget to notify Social Security. Scott's entitled to a check every month now."

"I'll do that," Jody said. She turned to Doug. "I'll pay you as soon as I can sell the store. Have a good flight back to San Diego. Good-bye, Sam," she said as she left the office, forcing back her tears.

She left the office, ignoring Sue's puzzled look, and got into her car. Tears streamed down her face as she thought about all the time and hard work she had put into making her antique shop a success. Three years of hard work down the drain, all due to Larry's irresponsibility. "Damn you, Larry!" she cried out as she hit the seat with her fist.

"I don't blame you for feeling that way about him right now," Doug said as he leaned down and looked in the window.

"What do you want?"

"I want to talk for a minute," Doug said as he handed her his handkerchief.

Jody wiped her eyes and blew her nose. "Is this more of your torture-Larry's-widow routine?" she asked. "You scared the hell out of me last night, and now you're taking my business away from me."

"Do you want me to crawl across the parking lot on my knees for last night?" Doug replied. "I misjudged you terribly, and I'm very, very sorry for the things I said to you."

"And what about this afternoon?" Jody asked, knowing she was being unreasonable. It wasn't Doug's fault that Larry hadn't paid him back.

Doug took a deep breath. "You're upset right now, with good reason. How about taking a few hours to calm down and then let me take you out to dinner? I have a business proposition to make to you."

"No, thank you," Jody said quickly.

"I insist that you come," Doug said firmly. "Look, I know I'm not your favorite person right now, and I understand why, but what I have to say to you will affect not only your future but Scott's too. Do you have any kind of career besides the store?"

"I worked as a secretary for a few years before Scott was born, and then I helped Larry with the ranch until he lost it. Thank God we were living in town and didn't lose our home too." She took a deep breath. "I can always go back to being a secretary, I guess."

"But you don't want to do that, do you?" Doug asked.

Jody shook her head.

"So come out with me tonight and hear me out," Doug suggested. "Do that much, at least, before you give up the store."

"All right," Jody agreed reluctantly.

"Thank you," Doug said. "I'll pick you up about seven, okay?"

Jody nodded and started her engine. She drove back to the house in a daze. A business proposition. What kind of proposition could Doug have for her? What would it involve? Would it enable her to keep the store that had come to mean so much to her? And what would Doug want from her in return?

Jody stared in the mirror as she put some blusher on her cheeks. She hadn't been out to eat with a man in a long time, and she was out of the habit of putting on a pretty dress and evening makeup. She had rummaged around in her closet and found the dress she had bought last year to wear to her nephew's wedding. It was a soft blue and was neither glamorous nor businesslike, but it would have to do. The padded shoulders and dropped waist helped to disguise her too-slender figure and gave her a fragile beauty. Jody turned this way and that, studying herself. She didn't mind herself this thin, but several people, including Marilyn, had hinted that she would look better if she gained back the fifteen pounds she had lost when the trouble with Larry started.

Jody started to twist her hair up in its customary chignon, but she heard Doug knock on the front door and hurried to answer it.

"Hello," she said, suddenly shy. Doug was standing on the porch, looking a little uncertain himself.

His eyes swept Jody's face. "You look lovely tonight," he said.

"Thank you. Come on in. As soon as I have my hair up we can go."

"Leave it down," Doug suggested. "It's so lovely that way."

"It's easier to handle up," Jody said quickly. She wanted to look as businesslike as she could this evening. "I'll only be a minute."

Jody returned to the bathroom, and with fingers that trembled, put her hair up. She put her wallet and keys into her dress purse and found Doug in the living room leafing through one of her trade journals.

"I'm ready," she said softly.

"This is interesting," Doug said as he tossed the journal back onto the magazine stack.

"I think so," Jody said as she got her coat out of the closet. Doug held it for her, his hand grazing the back of her neck and sending chills down her spine.

"Is the Arbor Haus still good?" Doug asked as he opened the car door for her.

"Better, if anything," Jody said.

"Fine. We'll go there." Doug started toward the Arbor Haus. "Where's Scott tonight?" he asked.

"He's with Hunter and Marilyn," Jody said. "I often leave him with them when I have to go somewhere in the evening."

"I would have invited him, except that we're going to be talking business," Doug said easily.

"That's all right. Scott wouldn't have wanted to come," Jody said.

"Did you talk to him this morning?" Doug asked quietly.

"Yes, but it didn't make much of an impression,"

47

Jody said. "Larry used to try to tell Scott that it wouldn't happen again. Scott's learned to distrust people."

"And I guess I didn't help matters much, did I?" Doug asked ruefully.

"No, if anything you set him back," Jody answered frankly.

Doug winced in the darkness but said nothing. They made the rest of the short drive in silence, and Jody was out of the car before Doug could open the door for her.

The management of the Arbor Haus had converted one of the stately old stone homes close to town into a cozy restaurant and tavern. Since Doug didn't have a reservation, they had to wait for a few minutes in the bar before a table was free. The waitress seated them at a corner table away from most of the other patrons, flashing Jody a conspiratorial smile as she took their orders. Doug ordered a beer and Jody a glass of rosé wine. Jody saw a few familiar faces staring at her and Doug, and she hoped he didn't notice the looks they were getting.

Doug sipped at his beer and leaned over toward Jody. "Are we the local sideshow?" he asked.

"That's a small town for you," Jody said softly. "They talked about it for months when I disappeared and then came back and Larry left."

"Do they have any idea what happened?" Doug asked.

Jody sipped her wine. "God, I hope not," she said. "That's the last thing I want all over town. It's hard enough on Scott as it is." She shook her head. "I can just hear them now—Larry's barely in the grave, and she's out whooping it up with his brother."

"Whoop, whoop!" Doug teased, grinning for a moment. Jody smiled in return and took a sip of her wine.

A table was free by the time they had finished their drinks. Jody ordered sauerbraten and Doug the beef roulade, saying that he had never found another restaurant that made it quite as well as the Arbor Haus. The waitress flashed him a flirtatious smile as she disappeared with their order.

"Are you ready to talk business?" Doug asked. "I hope we can get it out of the way before our meal comes."

"As ready as I'll ever be," Jody said.

"First off, I'm sorry you were so upset this afternoon. If you'll forgive me for saying so, I think Sam was rather tactless not to have talked to you privately about the debt."

"Sam's not noted for his tact," Jody said. "But it really doesn't matter. The bottom line, no matter how it's put to me, is that I have to sell the store to pay you back. Damn Larry," she added bitterly.

"That store means a lot to you, doesn't it?" Doug asked.

"You don't know how much," Jody replied.

"Are you doing pretty well with it?" Doug asked.

"I'm making a living, but I'm not getting rich," Jody admitted. "That first year, when Larry was running it with me, we did pretty well, because there was very little overhead. Now I have to pay to have the repair, refinishing, and reupholstering done, so my profits are down quite a bit. But it provides for me and Scott." She sipped her water. "I'll put it on the market next week, and we'll hope for a quick sale."

"That may not be necessary," Doug said slowly. "How would you feel about taking me in as a partner?"

"A what?" Jody asked.

"A partner," Doug said. "Look, if I could, I'd just write off the debt and let you and Scott have the store. But that money I lent Larry was everything I had saved for my retirement, which starts in six months. The navy will pay me a decent retirement pension, but I'd like more than that to live on. You do understand why I can't just write it off, can't you?"

"Of course," Jody said. "I'm not sure I would have even lent my retirement funds to anyone."

Doug shrugged. "You and Larry needed it worse than I did at the time. I just want you to understand that I'm not trying to be nasty about it. Anyway, rather than you selling the shop and giving me the money, why don't you take me in as an equal partner? I had planned to open a small business of some sort with it, anyway."

"I don't think so," Jody said quickly. "I'll call the realtor tomorrow."

"Hey, not so fast," Doug said. "What's wrong with the idea?"

"A lot of things," Jody said. "For one, the store's barely bringing in a livelihood for me and Scott. I can't split that in half and expect to live on it."

"I didn't plan to sit at home and collect my half at the end of the week," Doug said. "I already know a lot of carpentry and how to refinish furniture, and I bet I'm smart enough to learn how to reupholster a chair. You could save a bundle by not having to contract that out."

"But you don't know how to do old pieces," Jody objected. "They have to be done differently."

"I bet I could learn," Doug said. "Come on, Jody, you don't have any reason to object to the idea. I could be a lot of help to you in that store."

"Yes, you could be a lot of help, but I still don't want to work with you," Jody said quietly.

"Why not?" Doug demanded.

"A business partnership, especially in a small establishment like mine, is bound to be a close relationship. And I don't want to be in a close relationship of any kind with you," Jody said baldly. "Somebody else, maybe, but you're out of the question."

"Why am I out of the question?" Doug asked arrogantly.

"Because you're Larry's brother," Jody answered quietly. "That last time, when he hurt me so badly, I promised myself that I would never get mixed up with another man like Larry."

"I'm not like Larry!" Doug said quickly.

Jody raised her eyebrow. "I'm not so sure of that," she said bluntly. "I have no reason to think that you're not like him."

"Good grief, woman, what more do you want?" Doug asked. "I apologized, didn't I?"

"That doesn't mean a thing," she said disgustedly. "Larry used to apologize all the time for the yelling and then for the hitting. It got so that I could say it along with him."

"Jody, I'm not like my brother," Doug said firmly. "I would never have hit you!"

"That's not what you were saying last night," Jody reminded him. "As I recall, you said I ought to have some sense knocked into me."

"Jody, I swear, I never would have touched you," Doug protested. "I only said what I did because I was bitter about Larry dying the way he did. I wandered around for two whole years believing you had been unfaithful to him. How do you think you would react if the situation were reversed and it were *your* brother?"

51

"I hope I would have enough common sense and respect to realize that there are two sides to every situation," Jody said. "You had no right to come in with judgment passed on me, Doug, even if I *had* been cheating on Larry. It wasn't any of your business."

"All right, all right. I was totally out of line last night," Doug said, holding his hands up placatingly. "You're right—it wasn't any of my business. But I wanted to know what kind of woman you are, Jody, before I offered to go into business with you. If you cheated on your husband, the chances were good you'd cheat a business partner too."

"I think the important question here is what kind of man *you* are, Doug," Jody said. "All you've managed to show me since you've been back is that you pass judgment on others without having all the facts in your possession and that you have the same capacity for violence that your brother did. I don't think I want to go into business with somebody like that."

"Jody, I'm not like him," Doug said fervently. "Good grief, I wouldn't have hit you, even if you'd come out and told me you'd slept with half the men in New Braunfels! I would have taken my money and gone, but I wouldn't have hit you. Besides, a business partnership's a far cry from a marriage. What do you think, Jody? Wouldn't it beat selling the store and going back to typing for a living?"

Jody thought a minute. No, she definitely didn't want to go back to the drudgery of typing for a living. But could she believe Doug when he said he was different from Larry? She really had no proof that Doug was any different. But a business partnership didn't have the same kind of intimacy as a marriage —as long as they kept their relationship strictly business.

"All right, Doug," she said at last. "I can take you in as a partner, but only on certain conditions. If you don't agree to them, I'll have to sell the store."

"What conditions are those?" Doug asked.

"First, although financially you'll be a full partner, in that store I call the shots. I'll decide what pieces to buy and how they should be priced."

"Wait a minute. Shouldn't I have some say in those things?" Doug protested.

"I'm not letting a greenhorn come in and screw up a store I've spent three years on," Jody replied. She pointed to an old oak pie safe in the corner of the dining room. "What's that piece over there worth?" she asked.

"Oh, not more than a hundred," Doug ventured.

"Try five times that," Jody said. "Yet another piece might be a shoddy reproduction that you might get a hundred dollars for if you were lucky."

"I see what you mean," Doug said. "And later, when I've learned the business?"

"By then we'll both be able to judge just how good at antiques you are," Jody said, protecting herself in case Doug proved to have no business sense.

"Maybe Scott will take an interest in the business," Doug said. "We can teach him—"

"Maybe I better discuss my second condition," Jody broke in. "I want our relationship to be strictly business, Doug. Once the store is closed, I want you to stay away from me and particularly from Scott. I want you to keep your distance."

"I don't remember inviting myself to be an intimate of yours," Doug said dryly.

Jody blushed. "I didn't think you were ready to jump into my bed," she protested. "What I don't want any of is an Uncle Doug routine. I don't want you around Scott."

"Do you think that's healthy for the child?" Doug asked. "He's going to know you're working with me."

"Let's just say that I think it would be wise," Jody said. "Scott has no use for you, and after last night I don't really think you can blame him."

"I think you're being totally unreasonable to keep me away from Larry's son," Doug said bitterly.

"I'm only thinking of Scott," Jody said. "So is the second condition acceptable, or do I sell the store?"

"No, it's not acceptable, but I guess I don't have much choice in the matter, do I?" Doug asked. "All right. I won't have anything to do with either your or Scott's personal life. Does that satisfy you?"

"Yes, it does," Jody said. "When will you be coming back to New Braunfels?"

"I'll be out of the navy in June and will move back then," Doug said. "Is there a special way to reupholster antique furniture, or will the community college course in San Diego be helpful?"

"Yes, you should find the course a help," Jody said. "I'll teach you the rest of the business myself."

"Shake on it?" Doug asked.

Jody nodded. For the second time, Doug's large, calloused hand engulfed Jody's smaller one. He shook hands firmly across the table, holding her hand perhaps just a fraction longer than necessary. Jody withdrew her hand and put it in her lap, again wondering why she didn't find him unpleasant to touch.

The waitress brought their plates and set a bowl of hot German potatoes in front of them before leaving.

"Mmm, these are the best part," Jody said as she took a big spoonful of potatoes onto her plate.

Doug raised his eyebrows. Although there were more than enough for him, Jody had taken a hefty portion. "You don't diet, I gather?"

"No, I work it off," Jody said. She sampled the potatoes. "Delicious."

"I agree," Doug said a moment later, after he had tried his. "Better than any I ever ate in Germany."

Jody thought a moment. "We don't have any naval bases in Germany," she said.

Doug's eyes lit up. "And I thought I had you!" he teased. "I did go there on vacation once when I was stationed in the Mediterranean."

"I guess you've been stationed all over the world, haven't you?" Jody asked.

"Pretty much," Doug said, and over dinner proceeded to entertain her with stories about his years in the service. He told her about wild weekends onshore in New York, being stationed everywhere from Diego Garcia in the Indian Ocean to the Philippines, and about being in the North Atlantic Fleet, where it was so cold that they had a layer of ice on the deck.

Warmed by Doug's openness, Jody's wariness gradually faded, and she in turn told him about some of the places she and Larry had gone in the good days, before he had lost the ranch and their marriage had disintegrated. She described the fun they had shared traveling all over the state to buy furniture for their house, and the pony they had given Scott for his third birthday. Doug laughed and told her more stories, and Jody could feel herself growing attracted to Doug as a person, in spite of the brave speech she had made just a short time earlier. He was charming, interesting, and just plain fun, and she hadn't enjoyed herself like this in a long, long time.

Doug gazed across the table at Jody's animated face as she described Larry's first attempts to teach Scott to ride a pony. He couldn't imagine what depths Larry had sunk to to abuse a lovely woman like Jody. He wanted to touch her, yes, but he wanted to kiss her, not hurt her. He would have loved to feel her soft, smiling lips on his and to have those long, delicate arms wrapped around his neck. And she was interesting to talk to. Now that he knew she wasn't a faithless woman, he could feel himself growing more attracted to her every minute they spent together.

Doug paid for their dinner and held Jody's coat for her. They walked in silence to his car, the attraction almost electric between them. Jody could feel herself drawn to him. She wondered what his lips would feel like pressed against hers, and if his body was as hard and fit as it looked. As he leaned toward her to unlock the car door, she caught a whiff of his woodsy after-shave and the masculine scent that was all his own. She could feel the pulse pound in her neck but tried to ignore the way Doug was making her feel.

They made small talk on the way to Jody's house, then Doug parked in the driveway.

"Will you be flying back here in June?" she asked.

"No, I have a few things I want to bring back with me," Doug said, "so I'll drive. I'll write and let you know when to expect me."

"All right," Jody said. "Thank you for dinner, and for not making me sell the store."

"I'm glad to be part of an established business," Doug said.

Jody got out of the car and Doug walked her to the front porch. She stared into his eyes, not sure what to say next, and was startled by the longing and the need she saw there.

"I'm going to kiss you, Jody," Doug whispered. "I need that."

Before Jody could do anything, Doug leaned down and placed his lips against hers. She stood, frozen, as he nibbled the soft skin of her lips and held the back of her neck in one of his big hands. His touch was warm and tender, and without meaning to, Jody opened her lips and leaned closer, placing her hands on his shoulders. Encouraged by her movement, Doug curled his other arm around her waist and pulled her closer, deepening the kiss they shared with tender persuasiveness. He could hear Jody's breath rasp and feel her chest heave with each breath she took. She was as moved as he was, he thought with satisfaction as her arms crept up around his neck.

He was as hard as he looked, Jody thought in a daze as Doug pulled her against his firm, muscular body. Every nerve in her body was singing with feelings Jody thought had died in her. She kissed Doug back, seeking the warmth and the caring she hadn't had for such a long time. Together they stood for long moments, sharing the tenderness, until Doug pulled Jody even closer and she could feel the evidence of his desire for her.

Jody blinked and abruptly pulled away. "I didn't mean for that to happen," she said, her eyes wide with horror.

"I didn't either, if that means anything," Doug said quietly. It was on the tip of his tongue to make a joke about their business relationship, but he thought better of it. "I'll let you know about when I'm due in town," he said.

"Th—that's fine," Jody stammered.

"I'm driving back to San Antonio tonight," Doug said, "and flying out early in the morning." He ran his hand down the side of her face. "Until June, Jody."

"Until June," she whispered. She unlocked the front door with fingers that trembled, and sank down on the couch in the living room. What on earth was the matter with her? How could she be attracted to Doug, after what Larry had done to her? A lot of good her brave speech about maintaining a business relationship had done!

But Jody couldn't blame Doug for the kiss. He had not forced himself on her in any way. She had responded to him willingly, and that was the problem. She had once felt the same kind of passion for Doug's brother, and he had treated her badly. Jody was afraid that, if she couldn't control her feelings for Doug, she was going to end up right back where she started.

Doug hummed a little under his breath as he turned onto the interstate that would take him to San Antonio. Actually, his plane didn't leave San Antonio until late in the morning, but he hated to impose on Hunter and Marilyn's hospitality any longer than necessary. Then too, Jody might want to talk to them and wouldn't feel free to if he were there. Doug ran his hand across his lips, wondering if his faint beard had scratched her skin. He would hate to hurt her in any way, even with something as mild as a whisker burn.

Doug frowned in the darkness of the car. She had kissed him so passionately, but there had been fear in her eyes afterward. Damn Larry for his brutality! Although Jody seemed fine for the most part, she had scars in her heart from his brother's cruelty, and Doug knew that it would be a long time before she was over what Larry had done to her. He would have to wait patiently, he thought, for her to learn to accept him. Doug was surprised to find himself very interested in his pretty sister-in-law, and he hoped that someday he could convince her that he really was different from his brother.

CHAPTER FOUR

Jody wiped her sweating forehead and extended her hand. "Mrs. Miller, I definitely want these three pieces," she said. "I'll send Mario out to pick them up in the morning."

Mrs. Miller smiled as she shook hands with Jody. "I don't know which I need more—the money or the space. I hate parting with them, but Otis is moving his furniture in here next week, and I didn't know weddings cost so much more these days. Tom and I didn't have to spend anything near this much!"

"I'm so happy for both you and Otis," Jody said as they left Mrs. Miller's spare bedroom. "When's the wedding?"

"Next Saturday night. Reverend Templeton's doing the honors."

"He preaches a nice wedding," Jody said as she sat down at the kitchen table and wrote Mrs. Miller a check for an old brass bed and a matching oak dresser and washstand. "This should help some." She handed the check to Mrs. Miller.

Mrs. Miller walked Jody to her car. "It's going to be a hot summer," Mrs. Miller said as Jody made a face at the hot door handle.

"Scott and I are going to be spending a lot of time at the Landa Park pool, I can tell already," Jody said. "Thanks again, Mrs. Miller."

Jody turned on her air conditioner and drove just a little above the speed limit back to town. If it was already this hot in June, the rest of the summer was going to be miserable, just like it was the summer the bank had finally foreclosed on the ranch. It had been dry that summer too, and Larry would go outside and stare at the sky, cursing the sunny blue heavens. It was that summer that he had hit her for the first time. . . .

Jody quickly turned on the radio and made herself think about the three pieces of furniture she had just bought. They only needed a good coat of polish before she put them out on the floor, and she—no, she and Doug—would make a nice profit on the pieces. It had taken her several months, but she had trained herself to think of the business as belonging to Doug as well as to herself, and the thought of having him as a business partner no longer bothered her as it had in the beginning. If he was willing to do his share, and he had certainly seemed willing last winter, the overhead would be cut drastically and their profits should be increased.

Jody pulled up in her customary parking place on the side of the shop. She stared at the snappy looking Datsun with a trailer hitched to the back and smiled. Probably a couple of newlyweds from San Antonio buying something for their first home, she thought as she pushed open the door. She looked around, expecting to see Mario and some young customers, and instead found Doug lounging against the counter. "Hello, Jody," he said quietly. "I said I'd watch the store so Mario could go back to the workroom."

"Hello, Doug," Jody said, hating the way her breath caught in her throat. His green eyes shone brightly out of his ruddy, sunburned face. He was dressed in a blue T-shirt and jeans, and on his left arm he sported the kind of tattoo that most sailors end up with sooner or later. And he was even more attractive to her than he had been last winter, which would never do. "I—we weren't expecting you quite this soon," Jody blurted out.

"I got packed and out sooner than I expected to," Doug said, smiling at her. "I thought you could show me around the store this afternoon, if you have time, and I could spend the rest of the day finding a place to live. I can start here in the morning."

"Sure," Jody said. "But don't feel like you have to look over the store today. Find a place to live first."

"That's all right, I already have a place in mind," Doug said. "It's kind of close to you."

Jody frowned inwardly as she thought of the big old house across the street from her that was for rent, but then she remembered the singles' apartments they had opened last year that were just a couple of blocks from her and figured that that was where a bachelor like Doug planned to live. "All right, then, come this way for the grand tour," she said. "I have nearly two thousand square feet here in the front where I can show the furniture. I try to buy things in all styles and price ranges, and my customers vary from wealthy San Antonio and Austin people to young kids starting out on a budget. In fact, when I saw your car and trailer, I thought you were newlywed customers."

"Sorry to disappoint you," Doug teased.

Jody walked toward the back of the shop, conscious of Doug right behind her. This close, she could feel the warmth of his body, and that set her on edge. "Here's the combination workroom and storage room," she said as they stepped into the hot dusty room. "It's not air conditioned because of ventilation problems. Sorry."

"That's all right, I've worked in a lot of hot places," Doug said.

Mario looked up from an old iron bed that he was stripping. "Did you buy the furniture?" he asked Jody.

"I sure did," Jody said. She smiled at Mario. "Doug, Mario's agreed to stay on for a month or so, and then he's moving to San Marcos and going to college."

"That's terrific, Mario," Doug said. "What are you using to take the paint off?"

Mario told him, and they were soon immersed in a discussion about refinishing old furniture. Jody excused herself and returned to the store. She glanced out at the Datsun and the trailer. If that was the sum total of Doug's earthly possessions, she thought, he hadn't accumulated much in the last twenty years.

Doug came back a few minutes later. "Mario's going to be a lot of help to me until he leaves."

"He's a peach," Jody agreed. "Are you having your things shipped here later?"

"No, that's everything that I own," Doug admitted. "Except for my dog. I put her in your backyard for the time being. I hope you don't mind."

"No, of course not," Jody said. "But did you notice the hole in the back of the fence? A small dog could get through it."

"Oh, Goldie won't get through it," Doug said. "She's a golden retriever."

Jody's mind raced. She hoped the apartment complex was willing to let him keep Goldie there. Otherwise, Doug would have to get rid of his pet, because she wasn't willing to keep her for him.

Jody wished Doug good luck and said she would see him when he picked up his dog. But when she and Scott got home, the dog was already gone from the yard and the Datsun and trailer were parked across the street at the house that had been for rent.

"Oh, *no,*" Jody groaned as she parked under the tree that shaded her driveway. The trailer was open and half empty. Just what she needed—Doug Ford for a neighbor.

"Hey, look, Mom, somebody's already rented the Gibsons's place!" he said. "Isn't that great? I hope they have some kids to play with."

"That's Uncle Doug's car," Jody said tonelessly. "He must have rented the house."

Scott's expression went from excited to wary. He was silent for a moment, then asked, "I don't have to go over there, do I?"

"No, of course not," Jody said quickly. She got out of the car and slammed the door a little harder than she needed to. "Go in the house, Scott," she said.

"But, Mom—"

"Go in the house," she repeated.

Scott did as he was told. Jody marched across the street and knocked on Doug's door, intending to read him the riot act for moving in so close to her, but the wind was taken out of her sails when Hunter pulled open the door. He was accompanied by a big retriever wagging her tail. "Doug, it's Jody," he called over his shoulder.

"No, Hunter, I'll talk to Doug later," Jody said quickly as she started to back off the porch.

Doug appeared at the door before Jody could get away. He took one look at her angry, wary face and his own tightened in frustration. "I haven't forgotten the damned agreement, if that's what you're thinking," he said tightly as he grabbed Goldie to keep her from running out. "Down, Goldie." Goldie ignored him. "I needed a yard for my dog."

"Just so long as you remember," Jody said. She

glared at him for a moment before she went back across the street.

"Private feud?" Hunter asked.

"One of the conditions she made for taking me in as a partner was that I stay out of her and Scott's private life," Doug admitted.

Hunter smiled faintly. "You don't intend to do that, do you?"

"I sure don't," Doug admitted with determination.

Jody waited until Scott was in bed before she walked across the street and knocked on Marilyn's door. "Is Hunter closeted in his study?" she whispered when Marilyn came to the door.

"No, Mr. Jacobs had a heart attack and Hunter went to the hospital," Marilyn said. "Come on in."

"Hunter's had a lot of ministerial duty to do today," Jody said dryly. She followed Marilyn back to the kitchen and poured herself a big glass of iced tea.

"Huh? Oh, you mean helping Doug move his things in," Marilyn said. "I don't think that was in the line of ministerial duty. I think Hunter was renewing an old friendship. I heard them laughing together a couple of times, and you can bet they weren't discussing Scripture!" Marilyn and Jody both laughed, then Marilyn sobered. "How do you feel about having Doug this close?"

"I don't like it," Jody admitted. "I've accepted the fact that I have to take him in as a business partner, but I sure don't want him as anything else!"

"Does he still frighten you?" Marilyn asked.

"Yes, he does," Jody said slowly. He did frighten her, but she was more frightened of her own response to him. Living this close to him, would she ever be able to hold him at arm's length? "How about you? How do you feel about having him this close?"

"I'm not thrilled," Marilyn admitted. "I hurt like

64

the dickens for you when Larry treated you the way he did, and Doug is just too much like Larry for my taste."

"Amen to that," Jody said. "But I guess there isn't much we can do about it, short of burning his house down."

"That's true," Marilyn agreed.

Thank goodness the week was over, Jody thought tiredly as she closed the register late Saturday afternoon. The last four days had gone by unbearably slowly, as Jody had tried to get used to having Doug in the store all the time, as well as having him for a neighbor. It seemed like Doug was there every time she turned around. He was jogging by, clad in running shorts and a sweat-soaked T-shirt, when she stepped out on her front porch to get the morning paper. He was in the store with her all day long, his voice drifting in frequently from the back where Mario was teaching him the fine art of restoring old furniture. And in the evenings he was either sitting on Hunter's front porch or Hunter was on his, laughing and reminiscing about their days together in the navy. Thank goodness she wouldn't have to see him until Monday! she thought as she poked her head into the back room. "I'm locking up and taking the money to the night depository," she said to Doug and Mario. "See you Monday."

"Isn't the shop open tomorrow afternoon?" Doug asked. "It seems like that would be a good day for San Antonio business."

"Mario's sister, Beatrice, keeps it open on Sunday," Jody said. "I reserve Sunday for church and Scott. You can come in if you want to."

"What do you say we knock off, Mario?" Doug asked as he wiped his greasy hands on a rag.

"Sure thing," Mario said. He wiped his hands on his back pockets and got out his car keys. "See you Monday."

" 'Night," Jody said as Mario disappeared out the back door.

"Hunter and Marilyn are coming over for hamburgers this evening. Would you and Scott like to walk over?"

"No, thank you," Jody replied quietly. "We have other plans."

"What plans?" Doug jeered softly. "Sitting all alone in that big old house trying to avoid me?"

"As a matter of fact, Scott and I are having dinner with Mrs. Borrer," Jody said, her anger showing only in her eyes. "Since all of Scott's grandparents are dead, she's adopted him as an unofficial grandson. Good night, Doug."

Doug winced as she shut the door a little harder than she had to. He had blown it again, he thought. He had assumed she was refusing to come on principle, but she really did have other plans. Well, that was all right. He would enjoy an evening with Hunter, he would do his best to thaw Marilyn out some, and he would see Jody again tomorrow morning.

Jody stuck her head in the door of Scott's Sunday-school room. "Scott? Are you ready to go?"

Scott got up from his chair, a grin on his face. "Mom, can I sit with the Bohannons? Ryan's mom said it was all right."

"Are you sure, Suzanne?" Jody laughed. The last time the two boys had sat together in church, Ryan had smuggled in a water pistol and Scott had aimed it across the aisle at Elder Thomas, who had not been amused.

Suzanne laughed. "I frisk Ryan every Sunday

66

morning now," she said, rumpling Ryan's hair affectionately. Ryan had gone through extremely serious heart surgery three years ago and was still small and weak for his age, but what he didn't have in physical strength he made up for in pure mischief. "Sure, he can sit with us."

"Okay. Scott, I want you to be on your very best behavior," Jody warned her eager son.

Scott promised to behave for the Bohannons, and Jody entered the sanctuary and sat where she always did, about halfway down, not noticing the man who stood to one side of the vestibule. But the skin on the back of her neck prickled a little later when she heard a familiar voice at the back of the sanctuary, and in a moment Doug slid into the pew beside her.

"Good morning, Jody," he said smoothly, the glint in his eyes daring her to make a spectacle of herself by moving.

"Good morning, Doug," Jody replied evenly, though she would have liked to wring his neck. Why was the man so determined to horn in where he wasn't wanted?

"Where's Scott?" Doug asked as he flipped open the bulletin.

"He's sitting with Ryan Bohannon's family," Jody said.

"That's too bad. I was hoping to see him this morning," Doug said easily.

Jody shrugged and opened her bulletin, glancing over the list of weekly activities. Doug said nothing more, and a moment later Marilyn started the prelude music.

Normally Jody found church to be a calming and rewarding experience, but with Doug beside her she was tense and distracted. She hoped Hunter wouldn't ask her what she thought of his sermon, as he sometimes did, because she would be hard pressed to remember three words of it. She was acutely conscious of the man who sat quietly beside her listening intently to Hunter. She was attracted to him, yet at the same time she was very, very wary of him as he sat there absently creasing the bulletin the way Larry always had. And when they opened their hymnals to sing, his deep baritone sounded so much like Larry's that goosebumps rose on her arms.

Jody escaped as soon as Hunter said the benediction. She ignored the curious looks she received from some of the congregation and hastily found Scott and Ryan. "Ready to go?" she asked brightly.

Scott's expression was a little sullen as they got in the car. "Why were you sitting with Uncle Doug?" he asked.

"Because he sat next to me, and I chose not to make a scene," Jody said honestly.

"But you didn't want to sit with him, did you?" Scott asked.

"Not really," Jody said.

"I wouldn't have wanted to sit by him either," Scott said, and Jody realized that Scott was even more wary of Doug than she was.

As the days passed, Jody came to appreciate the new partner who had been more or less forced on her. Doug pitched in at the shop and made a quick study of the business. By the end of July he could refinish a piece even better than Mario could, and he could often clean them up so well that they didn't even need refinishing. He had learned quite a bit about reupholstering at the community college in San Diego, and Jody was able to stop sending that out the second week Doug was there. Her costs fell dramatically, and she and Doug were able to split a fairly generous profit at the end of the month. Jody couldn't say for sure, but she thought Doug enjoyed the work—at any rate, he didn't complain about it constantly as Larry had, and once he thanked her for keeping the office refrigerator stocked with soft drinks for him, saying they made the heat tolerable.

Doug had proven helpful in the front part of the store as well. Although he stayed out of purchasing and pricing, leaving that to Jody's expertise, he would sit at the register on the days he didn't have work to do in the back, shooing Jody out the door to find more merchandise. She spent those days scouring the countryside for antiques. If she could, she would bring them back in the truck, and if she couldn't, Doug would pick them up the next day. When she made the idle comment that she missed bringing in New York antiques, Doug got in touch with an old navy friend who lived in New York, and two weeks later a van arrived full of marvelous oak furniture that had Jody drooling for days. Jody had broken her rule about noninvolvement that day, and she and Doug had gone to the Arbor Haus to celebrate. He had not tried to kiss her that night but had shaken her hand at the end of the evening, leaving Jody perversely disappointed.

Jody hated the fact that she was finding herself more attracted to Doug. She berated herself for being a fool, reminding herself that he was Larry's brother and that Larry had hurt her, but she still felt a strong pull toward Doug. It wasn't sexual attraction, she told herself over and over, it was just that she found him a fine business partner, and she was beginning to find him a very good friend. Besides, even though she was attracted to him, he still made her very uneasy. He reminded her a great deal of Larry. Not only was there the physical resemblance, but Doug shared many of Larry's mannerisms too. His eyebrows would move closer together when he was concentrating; he held his cigarette the same way Larry used to; and then there was the way he would ball his hand into a fist when he was angry or upset, just the way Larry always had. Jody tried to tell herself that it was nothing, but that particular mannerism made her very nervous.

Jody wandered back to the workroom and peered over Doug's shoulder. "Are you even going to have to refinish that?" she asked as she looked over an elegant mahogany end table. It hadn't looked like much when she had bought it last week, but Doug had wiped away years of grime and the piece already looked much better.

"What do you think? I'm tempted just to fill in the scratches and give it a good polishing," Doug said as he wiped his brow. "The finish is really in good shape."

"Let's do that," Jody said. "It's a pretty little table."

"Yes, but it's sturdy," Doug said. "Say, will you hand me another Coke?"

"Sure." Jody came back with two Cokes and handed one to Doug. "I'm sorry it's so hot back here," she said as she sipped hers. "I'm not sure I could stand it out here like you do." It was the middle of August, and the daytime temperatures were hitting the hundred-degree mark regularly. "How do you tolerate it?"

Doug ran his hand down his damp T-shirt. "I go home and stand under a cool shower for an hour," he said.

Jody quickly pushed away the enticing mental image that Doug's innocent statement had aroused. They talked comfortably while she and Doug finished their soft drinks, and Jody returned to the front of the store. Customers were few on a sweltering afternoon like this one, and Jody had plenty of time to think while she dusted the silver and the crystal that were displayed on the shelves. She was being ridiculous, she told herself. She ought to be pleased that Doug had made no move toward her since he had come back. In a way, she was, or at least a part of her was, relieved, but at the same time a part of her was perversely disappointed too. She had honestly expected him to come on to her when he had moved so close to her and had started sitting with her in church, and she had been baffled and a little disappointed when he hadn't.

Doug finished the table and left shortly before closing time. Jody left a few minutes later, going by the bank to make the deposit on her way home. Ryan Bohannon had asked Scott to spend the night, and Jody had a salad and a delicious mystery novel ready to fill her rare evening alone.

Jody showered and put on shorts and a knit top and was just digging into her salad when the telephone rang.

"Jody, I'm sorry to bother you on such short notice, but Eileen Towns just called," Marilyn said. "She had to leave on a family emergency, and the choir director doesn't have any special music for tomorrow. Would you be willing to pinch-hit?"

"I wouldn't mind, Marilyn, but I just sang three weeks ago," Jody protested. "Aren't they going to get tired of me?"

Marilyn thought a moment. "Well, how about a duet with you and Doug? I've heard him a couple of times when he's been over here, and he has a lovely voice."

Since when had Marilyn become such a Doug Ford

fan? Jody asked herself irritably. Lately Marilyn seemed as fond of him as Hunter was. "Well, I don't know, I've never sung with him before," Jody said.

"I would think you would sound wonderful together," Marilyn replied. "Can I at least call him and ask?"

"All right," Jody said, seeing that there was no way to get out of this gracefully. "I'll come over after supper and we can go over something."

"Thanks, Jody. You're a lifesaver," Marilyn said.

Jody finished her dinner but put aside the mystery until another time. She waited until she thought Hunter and Marilyn were through eating before she walked across the street.

"Marilyn, are you ready?" she asked as she stepped inside the house.

"Come on back, Jody, Marilyn will be with you in a little bit," Hunter said. Jody found Hunter and Rachel in the kitchen, where he was valiantly trying to persuade the little girl to eat her supper. "Come on, Rachel, take another bite of potatoes. Please?"

Rachel glared at him with eyes as dark as his own. "No," she said.

Hunter tried to pop the potatoes into her mouth, but Rachel clamped it shut before he could get the food in. "Open up, Rachel," he coaxed.

Rachel shook her head firmly.

"Here, let me see if I can get anything down her," Jody said.

"Be my guest."

Jody sat down and was able to persuade Rachel to eat a few more bites. "Where's Marilyn?" she asked as she wiped Rachel's face with a wet washcloth.

"She wasn't feeling too well, so I told her to lie down for a few minutes," Hunter said. "You know how it is with her. She gets sick every night just at suppertime."

Jody raised her eyebrow. "Another baby?"

Hunter smiled gently. "I know it's a little soon, but I'm not getting any younger. Then too, after what happened to Bobby, Marilyn's overprotective of Rachel, and I think she would be more relaxed if she had two to care for."

Jody looked at Rachel wistfully. "There are times I wish Scott had a brother or sister."

"What's this about a brother or sister for Scott?" Doug asked as he came in the back door.

"Oh, nothing," Jody mumbled.

"We're discussing the fact that Rachel's getting a brother or sister," Hunter said proudly.

"Congratulations, Hunter," Doug said. He looked down at Jody's bent head and suddenly felt the absurd desire to see Jody pregnant with his child. Maybe someday, he thought, if he could ever get around the wall she had erected between them.

Marilyn poked a pale face into the kitchen. "Doug, Jody, are you ready?" she asked.

"Yes, Mommy," Jody teased.

Doug laughed and Marilyn blushed. "Keep it under your hats, will you? I don't want every sweet old soul in town calling me with advice just yet," she said.

Doug and Jody promised that they would say nothing, then followed Marilyn out to the piano and flipped through the duet book that she handed them. None of the songs looked interesting, so Jody looked through one hymnal while Doug looked through another.

Marilyn sat down at the piano and started playing an old chorus idly with her right hand. "Remember when we used to sing this one at camp?" she asked Jody.

73

"I remember that one," Doug said. He started singing softly along with Marilyn.

Marilyn added the harmony with her left hand, and Doug and Jody started singing along with her. As soon as Jody came in with the melody, Doug dropped down to harmonize with her. They finished the song, all three of them amazed at how well Doug and Jody's voices blended together.

"That was beautiful," Marilyn said.

"It's a shame we couldn't sing something like that tomorrow," Jody said.

Doug thought a minute. "Why can't we?" he asked.

Marilyn turned around. "You could, you know, if you wanted to."

"But that was just a chorus," Jody said. "It wouldn't be long enough."

"What if we did a series of choruses?" Doug asked. "All the songs we used to sing at summer camp."

"It would be something different," Jody admitted. "But do you think the older folks would like it?"

"If they liked the hippie street preacher from Austin who filled in for Hunter last summer, they'll like anything," Marilyn said. "You two can do what you want, but I think it's a great idea."

"Let's do it," Doug said.

The three of them put their heads together and thought of five different choruses that both Doug and Jody knew. They practiced together with Marilyn to get the harmony worked out, and Jody was amazed at how well Doug could harmonize by ear. On the fourth song, Doug took the melody and Jody's voice soared over his during the impassioned refrain.

Hunter leaned against the doorframe listening to them. "What do you think, Hunter?" Marilyn asked.

"They sound great, but have you thought about

what it's going to sound like on the organ?" Hunter asked.

Marilyn made a face. "It's definitely going to lose something in translation."

"Why don't I go get my guitar?" Jody suggested. "After all, if they can take the hippie street preacher, they can take anything!"

Jody ran across the street and returned with her guitar. "Hit E natural, would you?"

Jody quickly tuned her guitar, then her fingers played over the strings as she plucked out an introduction. "Now," she said to Doug as she started into the first chorus they were singing.

Hunter and Marilyn applauded them when they finished. "It sounds great," she said.

"I wonder how the congregation would like this one?" Jody teased as she played the first few bars of "House of the Rising Sun."

"Doug and I sang some in the navy that make that one sound holy," Hunter laughed.

"Hunter, remember that singer in Saigon—no, we better not talk about that, there are ladies present," Doug said.

"And you wonder why nothing that happens in New Braunfels shocks him," Marilyn whispered to Jody as she tried to stifle a yawn and failed.

"Jody, why don't we go over this a few more times at your place and let this tired mama-to-be get her rest?" Doug suggested.

Jody thought they already sounded fine, but for once she was not averse to the thought of spending time with Doug. "Sure. Come on over and we'll go over it a few times."

They wished Hunter and Marilyn good night, and Marilyn watched them cross the street together and disappear into Jody's house. "He's interested in her," she said when Hunter put his arm around her shoulders.

"No kidding. I had that figured out the first day," Hunter teased. "You don't mind, do you?"

"No, not anymore," Marilyn said. "Now that I've gotten to know him, I can see that he's nothing like Larry. But will Jody ever be able to see that?"

"Doug sure hopes so," Hunter said quietly.

Jody turned on the light in the living room. "Can I get you anything to drink?" she asked.

"Wine?" Doug suggested.

Jody poured them each a glass of wine and sat down on the couch beside Doug. They went over the choruses several times, and Jody realized that Doug had been right to want to practice them a little more. They sounded infinitely better than they had before, smoother and more sure of themselves.

"That sounds great," Doug said finally.

"Yes, we do," Jody said, grinning at her immodesty as she fingered the introduction to "House of the Rising Sun."

"Do you know the words to that?" Doug asked.

"Some of them," Jody said.

"Want to try it, just for fun?"

Jody grinned and started over. She sang as much as she knew, Doug filling in where she stumbled, and then Doug took over, singing several verses that Jody had never heard before and that brought a blush to her cheeks.

"You made those up!" she said when Doug finally ran out of steam.

"Just a little, yes," Doug admitted. "Do you remember 'The Times, They Are a-Changing'?"

"Sure," Jody said, beginning the chord sequence for that one. She remembered more of the words than Doug did, but his skillful harmony more than made up for his lack of words.

One song led to another, and by the end of the evening they had pretty well exhausted the ballads of their youth.

Finally, Jody put her guitar aside. "It's late," she said with regret. "Thank you for one of the nicest evenings I've had in a long time."

"Thank you," Doug said as he reached out. When Jody did not flinch away, he ran his hand down the side of her face. "I—we—let me kiss you, Jody." He slid across the narrow space that separated them.

She did not try to move away. Instead, she moved to fill in the small space that separated them, meeting Doug's kiss with passion that equaled his. She could taste the wine on his lips, and they touched and caressed one another before Doug wrapped his arms around Jody and held her close, cradling her delicate body tenderly lest he hurt her with his need. The tips of her breasts brushed the hard warmth of his chest through the thin barrier of clothing, and Jody was shocked at the longing she felt within her to feel Doug's hard-muscled body next to hers. She wound her fingers into the fair hair at his nape, surprised at its silky softness.

Pleased by Jody's boldness, Doug pulled the pins from her chignon one by one and ran his fingers through her freed hair. "Beautiful, just like I knew it would be," he said when Jody's face was framed with her long, flowing hair. "You look like an angel."

Oh, but I don't feel like one, Jody thought as she lifted her lips to Doug's again. She felt human, so delightfully human, and more alive than she had felt in years. Boldly, she ran her hands up and down Doug's back, every bone and muscle bringing pleasure to her as she touched him eagerly. Doug's fin-

77

gers trailed down from Jody's neck to the tip of one breast, which he stroked through the thin knit top and bra that she wore. Her nipple contracted into a hard nub of pleasure, and Jody groaned against Doug's lips at the sensation.

"Do you like that?" Doug asked.

Jody nodded, and Doug caressed the tip of her other breast until it was puckered against her shirt. Tenderly, he put his hand against her chest and could feel her heart pounding as strongly as his. She was on fire for him, as he was for her, but if he hurried things and made love to her tonight, he knew he would undo what few steps toward trusting him that she had made. He needed to take it slowly with this woman, slowly and tenderly until she was ready to become his. But a few more kisses wouldn't hurt, he told himself. Just a few more.

Jody could feel Doug pulling away from her and tried to hold him.

"No, Jody, we have to stop," Doug murmured against her lips. "If we don't stop now, I'm not sure I can stop at all."

Jody moved from Doug's arms. "You're right," she said tonelessly.

Doug leaned toward her. "You're quite a woman, Jody Ford," he said before stealing another short kiss and leaving.

Jody sat where Doug had left her, staring into space as she thought about what had just happened and tried to figure out how she felt about it. She was not horrified by their embrace, as she had been last winter, but she was baffled. She admitted to herself that she was powerfully attracted to Doug—more attracted to him, in fact, than she could ever remember being to Larry. And she also admitted to herself that Doug shared many of Larry's more attractive qualities. But did he also share Larry's less attractive personality traits? Was she attracted to another cruel man?

CHAPTER FIVE

Doug was waiting for Jody when she got to the sanctuary, her guitar case by her side. "Nervous?" he asked.

"No, why should I be?" Jody said.

"I am!" Doug admitted. "It's been years since I sang publicly."

"You'll do fine," Jody assured him.

They went in together and sat in the first pew. Marilyn winked at them before she started her prelude. "Has Marilyn always played that beautifully?" Doug asked quietly.

"Oh, yes," Jody said. "She didn't play for a while after Bobby died, and we were sure glad when Hunter got her playing again."

"Was Bobby her first husband?" Doug asked.

"No, he was her first child—the son she had by Robert Davis. He was a few months younger than Scott."

Doug winced. "Gutsy lady. No wonder she watches Rachel like a hawk."

"I'm surprised she had the courage to have more children," Jody said.

"It takes courage to start over, risking yourself again after being hurt once," Doug said thoughtfully. Jody didn't think he was talking entirely about Marilyn.

Jody made a point of using the congregational singing to warm up her voice, and when Hunter announced that she and Doug were to be the special music, she stepped up to the pulpit with confidence and spoke into the microphone.

"Use your imaginations if you would, and imagine it's night, and you're sitting around the campfire, worshipping the Lord in song."

She and Doug positioned themselves just behind the pulpit, and Jody played the introductory chords to the first chorus. Together she and Doug launched into "Will the Circle Be Unbroken," followed by "Michael, Row the Boat Ashore." Jody could feel that the congregation was with them, and by the time they had come to the last chorus, a prayerful rendition of "Kum Ba Ya," most of them looked positively rapt.

A loud chorus of amens followed them as they sat down. Jody glanced over at Doug and saw that he looked very relieved. She reached out and squeezed his hand as Hunter took his place behind the pulpit.

Doug glanced over at Jody with admiration. She had been as poised and serene as she could be up there in front of the congregation, while he had been shaking like a leaf. But he had loved singing with her, and he hoped that Marilyn would call on them again.

Doug and Jody were surrounded after church as the members of the congregation told them how much they had enjoyed their duet. Jody finally retrieved Scott from Suzanne Bohannon.

"You sounded great, Mom," the boy said eagerly. He looked up at Doug. "You, too, sir," he said gravely.

"Let me walk you both to your car," Doug said. "I have an invitation for the two of you."

Jody started to protest, but Doug took her arm and escorted her from the church. "Would you like to

81

drive out to Canyon Lake this afternoon?" he asked. "We can go swimming at one of the public beaches."

"Sounds fine with me," Jody said. It was hot, and she was willing to forgo her conditions for one more afternoon. "Scott?"

"Aw, Mom, do I have to?"

"I'd like to," Jody said honestly. "I've been working hard all week in the store while you and Ryan have been swimming at Landa Park. Of course, if you'd rather we spent the afternoon cleaning the house, I guess—"

"All right, we can go to the lake," Scott said. He looked at Doug suspiciously. "You'll be nice to Mom, won't you?"

"Yes, Scott, I'll be nice to your mother," Doug promised, wincing inwardly at the question.

Jody unlocked her car. "What time should we be ready?"

"In an hour or so, if you can," Doug said. He whispered into Jody's ear, "I love that motherly psychology you used on him!"

Jody grinned and got in the car. She fixed Scott a simple lunch and put on her swimsuit under a pair of shorts. As she adjusted the straps of her suit, she wondered if Doug found her too thin, as most people did these days, and she wondered if he would notice that the suit was cut to make her look heavier, not thinner.

She and Scott wandered over to Doug's a few minutes early. Doug answered the door still dressed in his shirt and tie from the morning. "Sorry, I just got off the phone. A good friend from San Diego left a message on my machine and I had to call her back. Say, Scott, have you met Goldie yet?"

"No, but I've seen her," Scott said as Goldie stuck her nose in his hand.

Jody stared after Doug as he disappeared into the back of the house. It was ridiculous of her to feel jealous of Doug's lady friend in San Diego, she chided herself. She didn't want him, did she?

Doug reappeared a couple of minutes later dressed in a T-shirt and cutoffs. His legs were strong and muscular, and the T-shirt did little to hide the wiry strength of his chest. "Do you like Goldie?" he asked Scott.

"Yes, sir, she's a nice dog," Scott said politely, only the light in his eyes telling Doug and Jody just how much the child liked Goldie. The dog wagged her tail and licked Scott's hand. "Mom, when can we get another dog?"

"Just as soon as Mom gets the hole in the back fence fixed," Jody said. "We had a little mutt, but she got out and disappeared last summer," she explained to Doug.

"I can fix that fence for you," Doug volunteered. "That way, you and Scott can have another dog." He patted Goldie's head. "This lady's a champion. I'm planning to breed her next spring."

Doug put the dog in the backyard, and they got into Jody's car, Doug behind the wheel. They laughed and talked on the way to the lake like any other family, and Jody found herself missing the warmth and the camaraderie that she and Larry had shared in better days. Maybe someday, she told herself, she would find that again.

Doug parked near one of the more popular lake beaches. The water was sparkling and the lake was littered with sailboats out in the distance. "I love the smell of cedar out here," he said as he breathed deeply.

"I hope the water is as cool as it is pretty," Jody said. "It's hot out here today!"

"But we won't be for long," Scott said as he pulled his shorts down his thin legs and tossed them back into the car. He let out a whoop as he got his float out of the back and ran for the water.

"I must admit I'm relieved," Doug admitted. "I thought he was going to pout all afternoon. He doesn't like me very much."

"Your first meeting with Scott was unfortunate," Jody said. She took off her shorts and shirt and stood beside Doug, painfully aware of his encompassing gaze as he took in her long legs and thin body. She blushed when Doug met her eyes.

"You look great!" Doug volunteered as he pulled his T-shirt over his head.

Jody scanned his nearly bare body. He didn't have an ounce of fat anywhere, and a thick mat of fair hair graced his chest. Jody pointed to a long scar that snaked around his side. "Nam?"

"Yeah. I got that the time Hunter saved my life," Doug said. "Are you ready to go get cool?"

Jody was more than ready, and the two of them ran to the water like a couple of kids. Scott had already floated out too far, so Jody struck out in the water to swim to him. As she swam, she was conscious of Doug keeping pace right behind her.

Jody swam to within a foot of Scott's float. "You're a little too far out," she said. "Let's go in a bit."

"How about if I give you a tow?" Doug asked Scott as he hooked one arm around the float. Scott's delighted laughter could be heard for a long way as Doug pulled him and his float toward shore.

Jody followed, and once back in the shallow water, the three of them played keep-away with a small rubber ball that Doug had brought in his pocket. When they got tired of that, Scott got on his float again, and Jody sat on the sandy beach staring out at the water. Doug swam a long way out in the lake before he came back and joined Jody on the beach. "Cooler?" he asked.

"Definitely," Jody said, acutely conscious of the attractive man beside her. Droplets of water clung to his hair and to the thick hair on his chest, and it was all Jody could do to keep from running her fingers down Doug's chest. What made him so attractive to her? she wondered as she stared out at the sailboats in the distance.

Doug and Jody alternated swimming and sunning for much of the afternoon. Scott's nose was red and his fingers puckered by the time Jody called him out of the water. They ducked into the public bathrooms to change, and Doug offered to buy them each an ice cream cone at the small ice cream parlor at the marina.

Jody and Scott leaned over the freezer in the café, looking at all the ice cream flavors they had to choose from.

"What are you getting, Mom?" Scott asked.

"The praline, what else?" Jody asked.

"I'm having chocolate chip," Scott announced.

"What are you having, Doug?" Jody asked.

"At the moment the only flavor I can see is backside of Ford," Doug teased.

Jody jumped out of the way, and Doug leaned over the counter. He selected cherry and gave the waitress their order. As they sat down at one of the little tables with Scott, Jody noticed a family coming in with a little girl who wasn't more than three or four. She was chattering nonstop to her young parents, who were trying to contend with both her and a new baby. Jody smiled inwardly at the harried parents. "Cute little family," she whispered to Doug.

"I can't remember being that young," Doug said.

85

The waitress called their number. "Mom, Uncle Doug, let me go get the ice cream," Scott said eagerly.

"Think you can manage it?" Doug asked.

"Of course," Scott scoffed.

Doug gave Scott the ticket, and Scott very proudly presented it to the girl behind the counter. She gave him two of the cones, Jody's and Doug's, and Scott carefully brought them back to the table. "Now I have to go back for mine."

The baby at the next table set up a howl, and the little girl slid out of her chair and pointed to Jody's cone. "Mine," she said.

"No, honey, yours will be here in a minute," Jody said.

The child wandered toward the counter where the girl was just handing Scott his ice cream cone. "Mine," she said, pointing to the cone.

"No, it isn't," Scott told her. "It's mine."

"Mine!" the child said, reaching for Scott's cone. She missed the cone but managed to grasp Scott's arm and jerk it downward, making Scott spill his cone on the floor.

Scott uttered a word that made Jody cringe and knocked the little girl over with his fist.

"Scott, *no!*" Jody cried as she ran for the children. She pushed Scott aside and knelt beside the little girl. "Are you all right?"

The child let out with a howl of pain as her mother ran over and scooped her up, glaring angrily at Jody. "We would have bought your son another ice cream cone," the woman snapped. "He didn't have to knock her down like that."

Doug grabbed Scott by the forearm. "You're going home where I can take a belt to your backside," he said angrily as he marched Scott to the car.

Jody was hot on Doug's heels. "Where the hell do you get off threatening to take a belt to my kid?" she asked angrily as Doug opened the back door and put Scott in the car.

"What he did in there was inexcusable," Doug thundered. "He hit a little girl, for God's sake! Didn't you see him?"

"Of course I saw him!" Jody snapped. "And why shouldn't he hit a little girl? He saw his father do it often enough. For crying out loud, Doug, hitting girls is all he knows!"

They were all silent on the way back to New Braunfels. Scott sat sullenly in the back, and Jody would have loved to know what was going through her child's mind. Doug's lips were thinned into a grim line. He glanced over at Jody and found her expression belligerent. But she was right—Scott had learned by example from Larry that it was all right to hit girls. And he had a feeling that Jody would hit him herself before she let him lay a hand on her child.

Doug pulled up in Jody's driveway. "I'm coming inside for a minute," he said as they got out of the car.

"I'll handle this myself," Jody said stiffly. "Go in the house, Scott, and wait for me in the living room."

Scott stared at them both before he went in.

"I'm sorry the afternoon turned out the way it did," Jody said.

Doug followed her to the front porch. "I mean it, Doug, you're not touching him," Jody said. "I *will* punish him, but he doesn't need to be punished with more violence. Now go home."

"I agree with you that, under the circumstances, other punishment should be used with Scott," Doug said. "But I'd like to talk to him for a minute, if you don't mind." Without waiting for Jody to agree, he joined Scott in the living room.

Jody followed him in. Scott stared at both of them belligerently.

"Scott, we need to talk," Doug said quietly.

"Hit me and get it over with," Scott said bitterly.

"Scott, I'm not going to hit you. Your mother and I agree that's not the best way to punish you. But before we do anything, you need to listen to me and you need to listen good." He sat down on the couch beside the boy. "Scott, I know you saw your father hit your mother more than once, but that was wrong. It was a very wrong thing for him to do."

Scott shrugged. "You threatened to hit her yourself."

Doug stopped and took a deep breath. "I said something I didn't mean that night. I would never have hit your mother, that night or at any other time. That's something that good, decent men simply don't do. I know your father did it, but that certainly doesn't make it right."

Doug's expression was stern as he stared down into Scott's face. "I don't care *what* the circumstances are, a boy doesn't hit a girl, and a man doesn't hit a woman. That's why your mom left your dad, you know, because he treated her wrong. And if you treat a girl or a woman like that, the same thing's going to happen to you."

"But she made me spill my ice cream," Scott protested.

"That's not the point. I don't care what she did, you shouldn't have hit her," Doug said.

"Scott, I think it would be best if you spent the rest of the day in your room," Jody said. "Take a bath and get into your pajamas, and I'll bring your supper to you."

"But, Mom, there's a movie on—"

"Tough," Jody said firmly. "Up the stairs."

88

Scott looked at both of them sullenly before climbing the stairs and shutting his door behind him.

"I didn't get through to him," Doug said.

"Did you really expect to?" Jody asked tiredly. "He's acted like this ever since Larry treated me the way he did."

"I see," Doug said softly. "Jody, I want to talk to you about Scott."

"What do you want to say? That I'm a lousy mother, that my kid's—"

"Jody!" Doug said sharply, "I wasn't going to criticize you. It's just that what I saw today worries me. Let's make some sandwiches for supper and talk about Scott while we eat. All right?"

"All right," Jody said. They made a plate of pimiento cheese sandwiches, and Jody took a couple up the stairs to Scott, who turned his back on her when she put them in his room.

Doug made iced tea and put the sandwiches in front of them on the table. Jody helped herself to one. "How long has Scott been acting like this?" Doug asked.

"Ever since he saw Larry be cruel to me," Jody said. "Scott was never unkind as a little boy, but I guess from Larry's behavior he got the idea that it's all right to hit when you're upset or frustrated, which was what happened this afternoon. Scott was upset by having his ice cream cone knocked out of his hand, and he retaliated by hitting that little girl."

"But he doesn't think it's all right for someone to hit you," Doug observed.

"Strange, I know, but it's apparently a very common reaction," Jody said. "The counselors at the women's shelter in San Antonio said that most of the children whose mothers have been abused are very protective of the mothers, yet at the same time they tend to be more violent than other children toward their peers."

"It's understandable," Doug said thoughtfully as he finished his first sandwich and reached for another. "They don't like to see their moms hurt, but they see their dads hitting a peer and they think it's all right."

"Scott was an indirect victim of Larry's violence," Jody said softly. "That child was at least as traumatized by what happened as I was."

"You need help with him, Jody," Doug said. "I'll start spending time with him."

"Oh, no, you won't!" Jody said quickly, thinking of the way Doug had hauled Scott out of the ice cream parlor. If she hadn't stopped him, Doug would have taken his belt to the child.

"Why not?" Doug asked imperiously.

"We have a deal, remember?" Jody said.

"To hell with the deal!" Doug said. "We're talking about a child who needs a man's influence. What's so terrible about having me around him?" he demanded.

"I'm not so sure you'd be any better for him than Larry was," Jody said. "You were ready to knock fire out of him yourself."

Doug flinched as though she had slapped him. "All right, if that's the way you feel," he said stiffly. "Thanks for the sandwiches." Jody's remark had hurt him badly, and he didn't even bother to try to hide it.

Jody stared as Doug slammed out of the house. She had not missed the hurt on his face when she had said that he was no better for Scott than Larry had been. Even though that was the way she felt, she could have expressed herself more tactfully.

Jody cleaned up the kitchen and got out the mystery that she had put away the night before, but as

90

the evening wore on she felt more and more guilty about what she had said to Doug and the way she had said it. He had only been trying to help her with a difficult situation, and she had thrown his offer back in his face. The hurt expression he had worn on his face when he left her house kept haunting her throughout the evening, and she finally put down her book and slipped upstairs. Scott was asleep, so she ran across the street and knocked on Doug's door.

Doug and Goldie answered the door. "Hello, Jody. What can I do for you?" Doug asked too politely.

"Can I come in and apologize?" she asked softly.

"Come on." Doug pushed open the screen door, and Jody followed him to the living room. She sat down on the only chair in the room and Doug sat down cross-legged on the floor. "I'm planning to get furniture, but I'm just getting started."

Jody glanced around at the once-elegant room. With the right furniture, it would be lovely again. "This place has a lot of potential," she said. "But that's not why I came over. Doug, I'm sorry I hurt you this evening. I should have never said what I did."

"Why not, if that's the way you feel about me?" Doug asked bitterly.

"You scared me, Doug! You didn't think. Scott did something wrong, and you were all set to lay into him! And you would have if I hadn't stopped you."

"Yeah, I might have given him three half-hearted whacks and sent him to his room for a little while," Doug jeered. "Real brutality."

"I didn't know that," Jody said. "For all I knew, you intended to really let him have it."

"Jody, there's a big difference between discipline and violence," Doug pointed out. "I wouldn't have been cruel to your child, but I *would* have disci-

91

plined him. And he needs discipline, Jody. Every kid does, no matter how traumatic his background."

"I know, but under the circumstances, even a mild spanking's too much for Scott," Jody argued. "That only reinforces the idea that hitting is all right. He had to be punished in other ways."

"Oh, I agree," Doug said. "Now that I've had some time to think about it, I can see why you're so opposed to his being spanked." He paused for a moment. "Was Larry ever cruel to Scott?"

"He didn't hit him the way he did me, but yes, Larry spanked him a lot. And he never told Scott why he was getting a spanking, nor did he ever talk to him afterward about his future behavior. It got so that the spankings didn't even faze Scott. They just made him sullen."

"Then I guess Scott really shouldn't be spanked," Doug said thoughtfully. "It sounds like my brother really did his child in emotionally. Have you ever thought of having Scott talk to someone about this?"

"Who would he talk to?" Jody asked.

"A psychologist or a counselor—someone who's trained to talk with children who have suffered traumas."

"Oh, I'm sure that's not necessary," Jody said quickly. "Scott's not emotionally disturbed or anything like that."

"Still, don't you think it might be helpful?" Doug pressed on.

"No, I don't," Jody said flatly. There was nothing wrong with her child that time wouldn't heal, she thought.

"Well, have you reconsidered my offer?" Doug asked quietly. "Would you like me to spend a little time with Scott?"

"Doug, I appreciate the offer, but I don't think so," Jody said as kindly as she could.

"You still think I'm as bad as Larry, don't you?" His tone was bitter.

"No, you're not bad at all," Jody said. "At least, I don't think so. But Scott's not your responsibility, Doug. He's mine, and I've got to cope with him the best way I can. I don't want Scott to have to start dealing with two authority figures, especially when you and I disagree, as we did today, on how best to deal with him."

"So good old Uncle Doug's supposed to just keep his distance, huh?"

"I'm not going to foist you off on Scott," Jody said. "He doesn't even like you."

"That could change," Doug said. "If he got to know me—"

"Doug, please try to understand," Jody said softly. "I appreciate your offer more than you'll ever know, but bringing you into Scott's life right now just isn't what he needs. He resents you terribly, and he'll only be more difficult for me to handle if I force a relationship between the two of you."

"Suit yourself," Doug said. "But I'm telling you, Jody, you're making a whale of a mistake."

"That's a chance I'll have to take," Jody said. "I'll see you tomorrow."

She walked back across the street, but instead of going inside, she sat down on the front steps and stared up at the full moon. She had not been entirely honest with Doug this evening. She admitted to herself that Scott's feelings about Doug weren't the only reason she had refused his offer. She didn't want to

93

get any closer to Doug herself. She didn't want him any more involved in *her* life than he already was. She still didn't trust him, though his kisses set her on fire.

CHAPTER SIX

"Scott! Hurry up or you're going to be late for school," Jody called up the stairs as she put two pieces of bread in the toaster.

"Coming, Mom."

Jody cracked three eggs into a bowl and stirred them up while the butter melted in the skillet. "Scott! We have to leave in fifteen minutes," she called again as she poured the eggs into the pan. In just a couple of minutes they were yellow and fluffy. "I swear, that boy's going to be the end of me some-day," Jody murmured. *"Scott!"*

"Yes, Mom?" Scott asked from right behind her.

Jody jumped and almost dropped the skillet. "You sure came down quietly."

Scott pointed down at his new sneakers and grinned. "Sneaky soles."

Jody laughed and handed Scott his plate. "Make quick work of it, we have to leave in a couple of minutes."

"I don't want to go to school," Scott complained.

"Why not?" Jody asked as she sipped her coffee.

"Nobody there likes me," Scott complained.

"Now, Scott, you know that isn't true," Jody said as she flipped through the morning paper. "Everybody likes you just fine."

"But why do we have to go so early? School doesn't start for another forty-five minutes."

"I know, but I have a shipment of furniture due in at eight, and I have to be there for the movers to unload it. It's some more of those nice pieces from New York that your Uncle Doug had sent down."

"That's all right," Scott said. He mumbled something under his breath, and Jody thought she heard something about knocking a block off.

"What was that?" she asked absently.

"Nothing," he murmured.

Jody started to question him further but looked at her watch and made a face. She gulped down her own breakfast and loaded her plate into the dishwasher, telling Scott to do the same when he was through, and rushed upstairs to finish putting on her makeup. She wondered why Scott, who had always liked school before, was suddenly complaining about having to go. She hoped he hadn't decided he didn't like his teacher this year. She was new on the faculty but had come highly recommended from a district in San Antonio, and Jody had liked her the one time they had met. "Scott! Come brush your teeth before we leave," she called down the stairs.

"Aw, Mom, just this once—"

"Brush 'em," Jody said, pointing to the bathroom. She hurried Scott to the car, and they drove to the elementary school. "Have a good day, Scott," she said as he got out of the car.

"Love you, Mom," he said. He had outgrown a good-bye kiss last year but wasn't above telling her he loved her—quietly, of course.

Even though she was in a hurry, Jody watched as Scott ran up the steps to his school, his backpack bouncing on his back. She loved that child so much! As Scott greeted a friend, Jody told herself that his reluctance to go to school this morning was normal for his age and that she didn't need to be worrying about him.

Doug was waiting for her at the store. "Where were you? I thought you'd forgotten," he said as Jody jumped out of the car.

"Scott was dragging his heels this morning," Jody said. "Where's the truck?"

"They called me from San Marcos nearly an hour ago, so they should be here any minute."

"And you're out here waiting like an eager little kid," Jody teased. "Come on in and I'll put on a pot of coffee."

As Jody set up the coffeemaker, Doug asked, "Was Scott difficult this morning?"

"Oh, no, nothing like that," Jody said quickly. "Just normal little-boy reluctance to go to school."

Doug grinned. "I can remember feeling like that." He paused a minute. "Is Scott doing all right? Really?"

Jody looked at Doug resentfully. "He's doing fine," she said. "Did you see the article in the journal about sandwich glass?"

Doug hadn't, and he wasn't particularly interested, but he took the magazine from Jody, only the slight firming of his lips indicating his displeasure at Jody's refusal to discuss Scott. He had asked about the child periodically this last month, ever since the incident in the ice cream parlor, but Jody had told him nothing except that Scott was fine, and her reticence made him so mad he wanted to scream. He loved that child, and Scott needed a man's influence in his life. Jody's desire to take on the entire responsibility for Scott wasn't good for her or the child, but he knew that if he pressed her about it he would destroy the good working relationship they had built over the last three months, and he wasn't willing to do that.

Jody poured Doug a cup of coffee and glanced at him as she handed it to him. She knew that her refusal to talk about Scott with him had angered him, but she still didn't want Doug any more deeply involved in their lives. She and Doug had a fine business relationship, and she wanted to leave it at that. She was afraid that, if they started disagreeing about Scott, their working relationship would deteriorate. There had been a certain amount of tension and strain last month for a few days after their argument over Scott, and Jody didn't want that tension to become permanent.

The van arrived as Jody was finishing her coffee. They rushed around to the back, and Doug opened the garage-style doors to the workroom. "This is better than Christmas," he said to Jody.

They watched as the movers unloaded piece after piece of fine old furniture. "How does your friend find all this stuff?" Jody marveled. "Larry brought back some nice things from up there, but not like this!"

"Rob and his wife are antique freaks," Doug said. "They make every auction in upstate New York and have furnished two houses with the most exquisite things you ever saw. He told me when he called me last week that he and Sandra feel like they've died and gone to heaven—we're paying them a commission to do what they love most!"

"Yes, but are we paying them enough?" Jody asked as treasure after treasure came down the ramp.

"Probably not, but we don't have to tell them that," Doug said.

"That would look beautiful in your bedroom," Jody said as a big brass bed was carried down the ramp.

"How do you know?" Doug teased, winking when Jody blushed.

She had seen the light on in the big bedroom at the corner of the house and had assumed that that was the room Doug had chosen. "Blue flowered wallpaper and the bathroom next door?" Jody asked. "The former renters fixed that room up beautifully."

Doug wandered over and examined the bed. "You're right, this would look nice in there. What's the deal for owners?"

"Cost, of course," Jody said as the telephone rang. "How else could either one of us afford anything?"

Jody ran for the telephone. "Ford's Antiques," she said brightly.

"May I speak to Mrs. Jody Ford, please?" a deep voice asked.

"Speaking."

"Mrs. Ford, this is Lloyd Greer. I'm the principal at your son's elementary school."

"Is Scott all right?" Jody demanded. "Has he been hurt?"

"No, ma'am, your son's not hurt. But he did get into a fight with another child this morning. The fight seems to be your son's doing, and I'm calling you to get permission to discipline the boy."

"What kind of discipline do you have in mind?" Jody asked sharply.

"I'd like to administer a mild paddling," Mr. Greer said.

"Don't you dare lay a hand or anything else on that child!" Jody snapped. "I'll be right there." She slammed down the telephone and ran for the door.

"Jody, what's wrong?" Doug demanded as he ran after her.

"Scott's in trouble at school," she said. "The damned principal wants to paddle him."

99

Doug watched Jody as she jumped into her car. Like a mother hen protecting her chick, he thought as he turned back to the store. But he was afraid that Scott needed more than just Jody's love and protection in his life right now, even if Jody couldn't see that. He picked up the telephone and called Mario's sister. "Beatrice? This is Doug Ford. Jody and I both need to be away for an hour or so this morning. Can you come in and cover the store for us? Thanks."

Jody trembled as she hurried up to the school. She rushed to the office and stopped at the counter. "I'm Scott Ford's mother," she said. "I need to talk to Mr. Greer."

"I believe Mr. Greer's expecting you," the secretary replied graciously. "Come on back."

Jody followed the woman back to a small, bright office decorated with Snoopy cutouts. A huge man sat behind the desk, and Scott sat in one of the small chairs against the wall. His shirt was torn and his face was dirty. "Scott, are you all right?" she demanded.

"Yes," he mumbled.

"The other child looked a whole lot worse," Mr. Greer observed mildly. "Scott left a bruise on that boy's face. Mrs. Ford, I talked with both children, and the fight was clearly Scott's fault. Now, I think that the most effective discipline would be paddling him —it might make him think the next time he starts to pick a fight. But I need your permission to do that."

"No way," Jody said. "Come up with something else."

"I take it you're refusing?" Mr. Greer asked.

"Yes, sir, I most certainly am. I don't think it's your place to spank my child," Jody said.

"Scott, would you step outside and let your mother and I talk privately?" Mr. Greer asked.

Scott left and Jody shut the door behind him.

"Mrs. Ford, I can't help but regret your attitude toward this," the principal said. "The fight was Scott's fault, and he needs to be punished so that it doesn't happen again. I happen to think that a paddling's the best way."

"Fighting violence with more violence?" Jody countered.

"I hardly think a spanking is violence," Mr. Greer said. "And as unpleasant as it is to have to discipline a child in that way, there isn't much else at this age that makes much of an impression. When they're older we can suspend them, of course, but at this age that's a reward, not a punishment. And we need to maintain discipline here on the campus. We can't have Scott—or any other child, for that matter—thinking they can hit their fellow students and get away with it."

"I understand what you're saying, but spanking is not the discipline for Scott," Jody said.

"He needs firm discipline, Mrs. Ford, firmer than he's been getting, or you and I wouldn't even be having this conversation."

Jody's face burned with anger and embarrassment. "Perhaps you could use your imagination and come up with a more effective discipline than spanking," she snapped. "I'm taking Scott home for the rest of the day. I'll question him myself, and if the fight was truly his fault, I'll discipline him. Good-bye, Mr. Greer."

Jody marched out of Mr. Greer's office. "Scott, come with me," she said sharply.

Scott looked up at her with that all-too-familiar sullen expression. "Where are we going?"

"Home. You and I are going to have a little talk."

She and Scott said nothing to one another on the

101

way home. Jody pulled into her driveway and groaned when she saw Doug waiting on the front porch. "Who's at the store?" she demanded.

"I got Beatrice to come in for a little while," Doug said.

Jody sighed with exasperation. "Please go back, Doug. Scott and I need to talk."

"I know. That's why I came," Doug said.

"Please, Doug, go back to the store," Jody said. "This is my concern, not yours."

"It is my concern if you're having problems with my brother's son," Doug said. "Now, do we go inside to talk, or do we discuss it out here on the front porch?"

"I wish you'd butt out," Jody murmured as she unlocked the door. Doug and Scott followed her in, and they all sat down in the living room.

Scott looked at Doug resentfully. "Mom's right, you know," he said to Doug. "This really isn't any of your business."

"It is my business, Scott, if you're misbehaving and taking advantage of your mother," Doug said. "Moms are wonderful, but sometimes they don't come down on you as hard as they ought to. My mom used to be the same way."

"Thanks a bunch," Jody murmured dryly.

Scott looked at both of them mutinously. "I'm not taking advantage of Mom," he said.

"I disagree," Doug said. "You know she isn't going to spank you or let the principal do it, so you act up at school. That's taking advantage."

"Scott, I want to know what happened this morning," Jody said. "From the beginning."

"Tony Villanueva said I was an ugly gringo yesterday on the way home from school," Scott said.

Jody looked at her son incredulously. Tony Villanueva was in the first grade and was three inches shorter and probably fifteen or twenty pounds lighter than Scott. "And?" Jody prompted.

"I went up to him this morning and hit him in the mouth," Scott said. "He shouldn't have called me an ugly gringo."

"You hit him for *that?*" Jody asked in horror.

"I didn't want him to call me an ugly gringo again," Scott explained.

"You don't hit a little kid like Tony because he called you a name," Jody said. "That's terrible!"

"No wonder his principal was angry," Doug said. "Scott, I told you last month that you don't hit people just because you feel like it."

"You told me not to hit girls," Scott said.

"You also don't hit kids that are smaller than you are," Doug said. "Where's your sense of decency?"

Scott looked at them both sullenly. "So I'm supposed to let him call me an ugly gringo," he said. "That's not fair!"

"For crying out loud, Scott, you don't hit a little kid like that!" Jody snapped. "Call him something back if you must, but don't just start hitting him!" She turned anguished eyes on Doug. "It *was* his fault," she said.

"So what are you going to do?" Doug asked.

Jody looked at Scott, indecision written all over her face. With any other child, a spanking would be called for at this point, but with Scott, who had already experienced so much violence in his life? "You're spending the rest of the day in your room," she said firmly. "Meals included."

Scott brightened visibly.

"And the overnight camping trip with the Bohannons is off," she added. "I'll call Suzanne this evening."

"Mom!" Scott wailed.

"Maybe next time you'll think before you hit a little kid. Now get up the stairs like your mother told you," Doug said.

Scott glared at them both resentfully. He slid off the couch and ran up the stairs, and Jody could hear him start to cry as he shut the door.

"I hated taking the camping trip away from him, but he's got to learn," she said tiredly.

"Are you going to renege at the last minute and let him go?" Doug asked quietly.

"No, I am not going to renege on my punishment," Jody said bitterly. "Thanks for the vote of confidence."

"I didn't mean to criticize," Doug said. "But at that age I could have persuaded my mom to change her mind."

"Scott can't," Jody said. "Remember, I have to be just that much harder on him. I'm his only parent."

"That's good to hear," Doug said. "Do you have any other discipline problems with him?"

"No. That's the strange part about this whole thing," Jody said. "He behaves pretty well for me and for other adults, and for the most part he gets along well with his peers too. But he's got this thing about hitting, and I can't seem to get through to him that you don't do that."

"Jody, what you're saying makes it clear to me that Scott needs professional help," Doug said.

"No, he doesn't!" Jody said quickly.

"Jody, please, hear me out," Doug said. "If he were an all-around problem child, if he weren't disciplined and were just wild, it would be one thing. But I've been around Scott enough to see that you do discipline him, that he isn't allowed to run wild, and he's still hitting other children. That tells me that the child has a problem in that area that you aren't equipped to handle on your own."

"Scott may have been influenced by what he saw his father do, but he isn't crazy," Jody said.

"Jody, I never said he was," Doug said. "I said that he might have a psychological problem of some kind that he needs to work through."

"Dammit, Doug, he doesn't need a fancy doctor!" Jody snapped. "I'm doing just fine with him!"

"Sure, and that's why you had to go over to the school this morning," Doug replied.

"Every boy gets in a fight sooner or later," Jody said defensively. "I bet you were in a few, weren't you?"

"A few, maybe, but I never slugged a girl or beat up on a kid that was half my size," Doug said. "I fought equals or kids who were bigger than me. Larry's the one who used to fight little kids."

"Scott's nothing like Larry," Jody said. "He's just like me, everyone says so."

"He may look like you, but he's Larry Ford's son too, even if you'd rather not remember that fact at times," Doug said. "He could be very much like Larry, you don't know."

"If he's like Larry, it's because he learned from Larry how to behave."

Doug stood up and put his hands in his pockets. "If that's the case, then it's just that much more important for Scott to have a man's influence in his life," he said. "He needs to learn how men are supposed to act. He needs to spend some time with me, Jody."

"He's around Hunter a lot," Jody said. "And I'll ask Hunter if he can be with him more."

"He's not around Hunter very much at all," Doug argued. "And between his family and his congregation, Hunter barely has time to turn around. I'm sure

105

he'd be willing to spend more time with Scott, but the man won't be able to. And with the new baby, he'll be that much busier. It's not fair to ask Hunter to take on Scott too." He sat down beside her. "Jody, the only responsibility I have in this world is the store. I don't even have a girl friend. I have a lot of time I could spend with Scott, and I'm more than willing to do so. He needs a man to use as a role model."

"No, he doesn't," Jody said bitterly. "He's already had one hell of a role model, remember? And I'm still trying to get him over that."

"You could get him over it more quickly if you replaced the negative influence with a positive one, Jody. He's had a negative influence replaced by no influence at all, and that's not healthy. I know you don't think much of me, but I could be a pretty good role model for him, I think."

Jody shook her head. "No, thanks, Doug."

Doug took Jody's hand. "Think about it before you give me a flat-out no." He squeezed her hand before he released it. "You know, before, when people said that childrearing was the biggest responsibility that you could take on in this life, I thought they were exaggerating. You and Scott have made a believer out of me!"

Jody couldn't keep from laughing a little. "Makes you glad you stayed single, huh?"

Doug shrugged. "I'll take care of the store today. See you in the morning."

"Thanks," Jody said.

Doug was deep in thought as he drove back to the store. No, he wasn't particularly glad that he had stayed single and hadn't had any children—if he had, he might be better able to help Jody with hers. Frustration welled up in him as he thought of his resentful, confused nephew. He desperately wanted to help the boy, but without Jody's cooperation he wouldn't be able to do that. And she wouldn't cooperate because she still didn't trust him. Doug sighed. With Jody, it was always one step forward and two steps back.

Jody loaded the dishes into the dishwasher and wiped the counters in her kitchen. She had spent most of the day thinking, worried about her son yet not knowing what to do about him. Was Doug right? Did he need a man's influence in his life? And if he did, was Doug the right man for him to be around? Jody knew that Scott didn't particularly like Doug, and she wasn't sure that Scott's being around him more was going to change that much. And she still wasn't sure that Doug would be that much better for Scott to be around than Larry had been.

She tiptoed upstairs and peeked into Scott's room. His dark head was bent over a comic book, so Jody left him alone and went downstairs to call Marilyn and then the woman who babysat for her sometimes. Normally, if she were only going to be gone for a few minutes, she would leave Scott alone, but she and the Templetons might be talking for a while this evening.

The babysitter arrived and Jody went across the street. She and Hunter made small talk while Marilyn put Rachel to bed, and the three of them sat down in the living room with cups of herbal tea.

"Thanks for letting me come over," Jody said as she sipped her tea.

"Tell me, am I your friend or your minister tonight?" Hunter teased.

"A little of both, and I want Marilyn to listen too, since Scott's her second cousin. Scott got into a fight

107

at school today. He beat up on Tony Villanueva pretty badly."

Marilyn winced. "That little bitty guy?"

"Yeah. I wouldn't let Mr. Greer paddle him, but I did confine him to his room for the day and took away his camping trip with the Bohannons, and you know how much he was looking forward to that. Anyway, Doug and I talked, and Doug thinks that Scott needs a man's influence in his life."

"What do you think, Jody?" Hunter asked.

"I don't particularly want Doug any more involved with us than he is already," Jody said. "I'm not sure he'd be any better for Scott than Larry was."

"Oh, Jody, don't feel like that," Marilyn said. "I don't think Doug's anything like Larry. And I ought to know—he's spent enough time over here under my feet!"

Jody and Hunter laughed. "Why is he over here so much?" Jody asked.

"He's lonely," Hunter said gently. "You've shut him out of your life, and most of the people he knew before are long gone."

Jody's conscience stabbed her as she thought of her continual refusal to have anything to do with Doug. She had never thought about it before, but Doug would have to be a very lonely man. "But do you honestly think he's different? Sometimes his mannerisms are so much like Larry's, he gives me cold chills!"

"Mannerisms yes, but his personality is totally different," Hunter said. "Once you get to know him, he's very warm and outgoing. I never felt like I knew Larry, not really."

"But do you think he would be a good man for Scott to be around?" Jody asked.

"Oh, he'd be excellent," Marilyn assured Jody. "He

108

doesn't drink or swear, he's warm and friendly, and he would be out of my kitchen!"

Hunter and Jody laughed. "Seriously, though, I think it would be good for both Doug and Scott," Marilyn continued.

"Jody, I'd do more with Scott, but I just can't," Hunter added. "Go ahead and let Doug be with him. It will do Scott a world of good, and I think you'd be doing Doug a favor too."

"Well, if you really think so," Jody said.

Hunter and Marilyn spent ten more minutes reassuring her. She wished them good night and walked over to Doug's house. She knocked on the door, wondering what kind of welcome she would get.

Doug opened the door, clad in his running shorts and a T-shirt that had seen better days. "Were you just leaving to run? I'll talk to you tomorrow at the store," Jody said.

"No, I wasn't leaving—the clothes just happened to be clean," Doug said. "Come on in."

Jody followed him into the living room. "Where's Goldie?"

"Out in the back," he said. They both sat down on the couch Doug had purchased just last week. "Can I help you with something?"

"Yes, you can," Jody said. "I thought about what you said all day today, and I just talked to Hunter and Marilyn. You're right, Doug. Scott needs a man in his life, and you're the obvious choice, if you're really willing to spend some time with him. Do you still want to do that?"

"Of course I do," Doug said. "Jody, I love my brother's son, and I want to be with him. If I can, I want to help him get over the damage Larry did."

"Thank you," Jody said.

He leaned forward. "Have you thought any more about seeking help for him?"

"Not really," she replied. "I think that being with you will be all Scott needs to turn him around. Besides, I hate to admit it, but I really couldn't afford to pay a psychiatrist right now."

Doug started to offer to pay for it himself, but he remembered Jody's fierce pride and independence and said nothing. "All right, let's see if spending some time with me will help. Now, could you give me a rundown on Scott's likes, dislikes, and interests? Places we could take him?"

"We?"

"Yes, we. I'm not facing that child alone at first," Doug said. "He doesn't think too much of me right now, remember? You need to be along at least the first few times we go out."

"I was only teasing," Jody said. "I expected to go along the first few times." *And I wouldn't mind going along on some of the others,* she added silently.

"So what does Scott like?"

"French cuisine, season tickets to the symphony, Ernest Hemingway—"

"No, Jody, I asked what *Scott* likes, not Scott's mom." Doug laughed.

Jody grinned. "Well, I tried. Seriously, he loves space westerns, video games, comic books, and amusement parks. He likes football and basketball but hates baseball. He swims like a fish and likes to go fishing, but he doesn't sit very still, so don't expect to catch anything if you take him. He used to love to ride his pony, but he hasn't been on a horse since we lost the ranch. He was heartbroken when we sold the pony, but we couldn't afford to pay for a stall at the stable."

"Hunting?" Doug asked.

"He was just old enough to go when Larry and I separated," Jody said.

"Maybe we can go deer hunting later in the fall," Doug said. "Can you take a few minutes and tell me a little about him? About when he was little? I don't feel like I know him very well."

Jody nodded and, prompted by Doug, launched into Scott's biography. She told him how Scott's first years had been pretty serene, better than most kids, she thought, since she had been home with him. She described how later, when Larry had changed, Scott had changed too and had begun to avoid his father and turn to her more and more. As Jody talked, Doug's admiration for her grew. Jody had done the best job she knew how with the boy—it wasn't her fault that the child had problems now.

Jody finished her tale and looked into Doug's eyes. Somehow, as they had talked, they had moved closer to each other, and her hand was tightly clasped in his. It felt good to be this close to him, she realized, to feel the warmth of his body and the strength of his leg against hers. And he was looking at her with admiration and with the same kind of desire she had seen before when he had kissed her so passionately.

Doug stared into Jody's eyes, doing nothing to fight the mutual attraction that was flaring between them again. There was something very special that happened every time they were alone together. It was passion, yet it was more than just a physical attraction tonight—it was admiration and respect, it was a deepening friendship with the beautiful woman who sat next to him. Doug couldn't put his finger on what it was that they shared, but he knew that it was stronger than anything he had ever felt for another woman.

Jody basked in the caring she saw on Doug's face.

111

She was hungry, so hungry for what she saw in Doug's eyes—she needed his admiration and his approval. She needed his help with Scott, and tonight she needed his kisses and his arms around her.

"Doug," she whispered as she held out her arms to him.

"Oh, Jody," he whispered as he gathered her to him.

She opened her lips and met his embrace eagerly and ardently, opening herself to Doug like a desert flower to rain. He held her tenderly, tempering his passion with caution at first, but as desire overtook him he forgot to be gentle, pulling her close to his hard body as he bore her down on the couch. He followed her down, covering her body with his as he blanketed her face with tender kisses. Jody wrapped her arms around Doug and pulled him closer to her, reveling in the warmth of his solidly masculine body. They shared long, leisurely kisses, each one bringing Jody delight. Doug peppered her face with quick warm kisses, leaving no space untouched as he gave way to the desire and tenderness he had felt for her for so long.

She strained against him, thrusting herself as close to him as she could. Her small breasts were crushed against his chest, and her hands touched and kneaded his muscular back. Doug gasped with pleasure as she kicked off her shoe and daringly ran her toe up the side of his bare leg, her own legs soft and smooth against his hard, hair-covered ones. Tenderly, he stroked her soft midriff and strayed lower, rubbing sensuous circles on her quivering stomach through her shorts.

"Oh, Doug I—" Jody gasped.

"Do you want me to stop now?" he asked as his lips trailed down her slender neck.

"No, not yet, oh, please not yet," Jody whispered. He started to unbutton her blouse, but Jody put her hand over his. "Turn out the light first."

"I want to see you," he protested.

"Please," Jody said, blushing furiously.

Doug reached up and with an impatient motion snapped off the lamp. His hands made quick work of Jody's blouse and the front closure of her bra, baring her breasts to his touch, if not to his gaze. Eagerly he found the tender tips in the muted light from the streetlight outside, and Jody quivered with pleasure as he tasted and touched her nipple. It swelled and stiffened, revealing the state of her arousal. Doug smiled in the darkness, delighted with Jody's passionate response to him. His lips found her other nipple and tormented it until it too was hard to the touch.

Jody reveled in the delight that Doug was bringing to her. She let herself drift mindlessly for a few minutes, just savoring his passionate touch. He was so pleasing to her. But could she please him in the same way? Could she give him the same degree of pleasure he brought to her? Her fumbling fingers slid under his shirt and stroked his smooth back, and she longed to feel his chest against hers. But as Doug continued to touch and caress her, the feelings of inadequacy that had hampered her for so long returned to haunt her, and before long Doug could feel her pulling away from him in her mind if not with her body.

"Jody, what's wrong?" he whispered against her breast.

"I—uh, we've got to stop this," Jody said miserably. She tried to get up, but Doug's weight held her down. "Let me up, Doug, please?"

"Now why should I do that?" Doug asked in the darkness. "I have you where I've wanted you for ages."

Jody stiffened, and Doug immediately knew that he had said the wrong thing. He moved away from her quickly and she jackknifed into a sitting position, fumbling for her bra in the dark. She hooked it and buttoned her shirt before she turned on the light.

"I'm sorry," she said miserably. "I didn't mean to lead you on like that."

"I wouldn't have forced you to do anything you didn't want to do," Doug said quietly.

"Are you sure?"

"Dammit, woman, I'm not the local rapist!" he snapped. "I've never in my life had to force a woman, and I'm not going to start this evening. But there for a while you wanted me as much as I wanted you. So what happened?"

"I—I just didn't want to become your lover," Jody stammered. "I don't want to become intimate with a man I don't trust completely." *I don't want to make a fool of myself with a man who will make fun of me afterward,* she added silently.

"So we're back to the trust routine again," Doug said angrily. "When are you going to get it through your head that I'm not going to hit you?"

"I wasn't worried about that," Jody said. "Honestly."

"Then what is it?" Doug asked.

"I just don't want to!" Jody snapped.

Doug started to press her but stopped when he saw the miserable expression on her face. She wasn't afraid of him tonight, he realized. There was something else bothering her, something she found too painful to share with him. "All right," he said quietly. "Not tonight." He turned Jody around to face him. "But you're going to learn to trust me, I promise you

114

that. Sooner or later, you're going to trust me with whatever's holding you back. And on that day, we're going to make love. Do you understand?"

"Yes, I understand," Jody whispered.

CHAPTER SEVEN

"Mom! Are you ready yet?" Scott called eagerly up the stairs. "It's nearly time to go!"

"Relax, Scott, Doug's not due here for another fifteen minutes," Jody said as she twisted her hair into its familiar knot and started to pin it up. But she frowned at the businesslike image she made and dropped her hair, letting it flow smoothly down her back. She pulled on a pair of new jeans and a cotton sweater with long sleeves that she pushed up on her arms. Later, when the late October air got a little colder, she could push the sleeves down.

Jody heard Scott open the front door and step out onto the porch. She smiled as she saw him in her mind's eye, sitting on the porch swing waiting for Doug to walk over. Lately he had been doing that a lot, waiting on the porch swing, eager to go off with Doug. Jody marveled at the change in Scott since Doug had started spending some time with him.

Not that it had been easy at first. Jody laughed out loud when she thought about that first evening that she, Doug, and Scott had spent together. They had driven down to San Antonio for hamburgers and a movie, and Scott had said maybe three words to either of them the whole evening. But he had thanked Doug politely, and the next time they went out Scott had thawed out some. Doug had displayed incredible tact, going slowly with Scott and letting Scott increase their emotional closeness at his own pace. Jody knew that Doug was winning the battle the evening that Scott had asked her permission to go to Doug's and ask Uncle Doug a question about girls. At least it looked like Scott was accepting Doug as an important influence in his life.

And there had been no more hitting incidents since Tony Villanueva. Scott had returned to school the next day, suitably chastened by losing the camping trip, and Jody had talked again with the principal, assuring Mr. Greer that Scott had been punished for his offense. Since then, she had received no more telephone calls from the school, and Scott had not complained about school again. Doug was wrong, she told herself as she put on the finishing touches to her makeup. Scott didn't need counseling. Doug's influence had been enough for him.

Jody stepped back and looked at herself in the mirror, wondering if Doug would find her attractive tonight. Her face would still burn when she thought of their passionate embraces that she had cut short a few weeks ago. If she had not called a halt, she and Doug would have made love. And she had wanted to so badly that night! She would have loved for Doug to take her to the big brass bed he had bought and make love to her until morning. But if she had done that, she would have been at her most vulnerable with him, and she still didn't trust him enough to do that. He might say the same things about her that Larry had.

"Mom, Uncle Doug's here!" Scott called. "Hi, Uncle Doug!"

"Coming," Jody called as she smiled at Scott's youthful enthusiasm. She picked up her shoulder bag and switched out all the lights upstairs.

117

As she ran down the stairs, Doug thought that she looked like a girl herself tonight, with her lithe, youthful figure and her hair flowing freely around her smiling face. She was so beautiful, he thought, as he had so many times before. He wanted to reach out and touch her. He wanted her to trust him, to confide in him, to tell him her innermost secrets and share with him whatever it was that had made her unwilling to become his lover. Because she did want him. He could tell it sometimes when she looked into his eyes or when he caught her staring at him in the store. He could see longing and desire, the same longing and desire that he felt for her.

Doug reached out and took Jody's hand. "Your mom looks pretty tonight, doesn't she?" he asked Scott.

Scott grinned. "You know why?" He motioned Doug close and whispered in his ear.

Doug's eyes danced. "She pulled out a gray hair?" he whispered loudly.

"Yeah, right there in front." Scott giggled.

"It was just one," Jody replied.

Doug ran his fingers through his fair hair. "I'd be in bad shape if I started doing that," he teased. Jody had never really noticed before, but Doug's blond hair did have quite a bit of gray in it.

Jody patted Scott's head. "That's all right, Scott, if you take after your granddaddy White, you're going to be bald by the time you're Uncle Doug's age."

"Then I guess I better take after the Fords," Scott said. Doug noticed that Scott said "the Fords," not "Daddy," and he winced a little inside.

They piled into Doug's car and drove out to Landa Park, parking as close as they could. Although it was barely six in the evening, the park was already jammed with revelers and they had to park a couple of blocks away. People from all over south Texas drove to New Braunfels every year for Wurstfest, the ten-day festival that featured the many sausages that were made in New Braunfels and the surrounding German communities. Jody's mouth began to water as she smelled the delicious blend of sausages, German potatoes, and rich old-fashioned pastries. A variety of local beers were sold to help wash down the sausage, and by the end of the evening the crowd would be quite mellow.

Doug paid for tickets, and the three of them headed for the food pavilion. "Don't get too far away," Jody warned Scott, who had a tendency to wander off in a crowd.

Scott looked at Doug hopefully. "Uncle Doug, I sure am hungry," he said.

"No kidding!" Doug laughed. "What would you like to eat first?"

Scott chose the knockwurst, and Doug braved that booth and brought them each a sausage on a stick.

"Mmm, this is delicious," Jody said as she bit into hers. "It doesn't even need mustard or horseradish."

"I like them with catsup," Doug volunteered, laughing when Jody shuddered.

They finished those sausages and decided on the bratwurst next. Jody loved the delicate potato pancakes that volunteers were frying on the spot, so an indulgent Doug bought her a double order.

"I think I've died and gone to heaven," she said as she ate the last morsel and licked the butter off her lips.

"Here, let me get that," Doug said as Jody started to wipe her lips. Before she could stop him, he quickly kissed away the offending crumb.

Jody blushed and glanced around. Scott's back was

turned, and she didn't notice anyone else around who knew her.

"No, I don't think anyone caught us in our moment of decadence," Doug teased. "Would you like a beer?"

Jody said yes, so Doug bought them each a beer and a Coke for Scott. They wandered around the pavilion, laughing at all the silly German souvenirs being sold in the booths. Doug bought Scott a T-shirt with "Wurstfest" across it, and he decided that Jody needed a button that said "Kiss me, I'm German."

Doug put the button on her and kissed her cheek. "Are you?"

"Am I what?" Jody asked.

"German."

"No, I think we were one of the few families in New Braunfels that weren't. But I guess you aren't either, are you?"

"You vant to bet?" Doug teased, mimicking a German accent. "Our great-grandfather changed Friedrich to Ford. He thought it sounded more English."

"Well, I have to agree with him on that," Jody said. "Larry never told me."

"Well, hello there, are you enjoying Wurstfest?" Hunter asked. Marilyn was holding his hand and Rachel was riding on his shoulders.

"Well, hello yourselves," Doug said. "Yes, we're having a great time."

"You're not working tonight?" Jody asked Marilyn. Marilyn usually picked up some overtime patrolling at Wurstfest.

Marilyn made a face. "I've been confined to the office until after the baby's born. It's really exciting in there answering the telephone."

Jody glanced down at Marilyn's expanding figure.

"You'd look a little silly in your uniform, wouldn't you?"

"Jody, I'm gaining weight so fast this time, I can't believe it," Marilyn moaned. "I look at food and I gain."

"Well, don't watch this woman eat, or you'll go into a permanent depression," Doug teased. "I've never seen a little bitty woman eat like she does and stay so skinny."

"Sorry about that," Jody said ruefully, glancing down at her figure. So Doug did find her too thin, she thought. For some reason the knowledge hurt her more than it should have. She had been right not to become his lover, since her body would have disappointed him.

"Enjoy it, Jody," Hunter said.

"In fact, let's go enjoy it some more tonight," Doug suggested as he took Jody's hand. "See you in the morning." He glanced around at the crowd, most of whom had food in one hand and a beer in the other. "By the way, Hunter, what are you preaching on in the morning? Alcoholism or gluttony?"

"I thought I would preach on both and step on everybody's toes." Hunter laughed.

The Templetons wandered away and Doug treated Jody and Scott to some mouthwatering apple strudel. Doug was buying them soft drinks when Ryan Bohannon ran up and grabbed Scott from the back.

"Gotcha!" he said as he hooked his arms and legs around Scott.

Scott whirled his little friend around. "Ride, Ryan, ride," he said as both boys laughed delightedly.

"It's good to see them together, isn't it?" Suzanne asked as she and Jack Bohannon wandered up.

"Yes, it is." Jody watched as Ryan jumped off Scott's back.

"Have you had any more problems with Scott?" Suzanne asked.

"No. Doug's spent a lot of time with him lately, and Scott's eating it up. I think he just needed a little masculine attention." Jody had told Suzanne about Scott's fight at school, but she had not told her about Scott learning violence from his father.

"Well, children do go through stages," Suzanne said. "Ryan got into a couple of scuffles last year. Of course, as little as he is, he got whipped pretty badly, and he learned very quickly that he needed to find another way to solve his problems."

"Hey, Mrs. Ford, can Scott spend the night with me tonight?" Ryan asked.

"Well, uh, Scott doesn't have any clothes at your house," Jody said, glancing over at Suzanne.

"Jody, I don't mind if he comes tonight. He left a set of clothes at our place last month that I never returned to you," Suzanne said.

"Besides, we still owe you for the weekend Ryan spent with you last spring," Jack said.

"That's fine, then," Jody said.

"I'm sure Jody will enjoy the break," Doug said. And he would enjoy a little time alone with Jody!

"Gee, thanks, Mom!" Scott said. He hugged her quickly.

"You behave for Mrs. Bohannon," Jody warned her child. "I'll see you tomorrow."

Scott wandered off with the Bohannons. Doug took Jody's hand in his and squeezed it. "Those two are inseparable," he said idly.

"They're a handful together," Jody admitted. "I was practically waiting out on the front porch for Jack and Suzanne last spring!"

They strolled around the pavilion, eating a few pastries and listening to the polka band that was playing in Wurst Hall. "Would you like to go in and dance a little?" Doug asked.

"Why not?" Jody asked lightheartedly. "I used to love to polka."

Doug paid for admittance, and they found a table at the back of the room. They waited only until the dance was finished, then Doug took Jody by the hand and led her out on the dance floor. The oompah band went into a lively polka, and he took her into his arms, whirling her out into the dancers. Their movements were stiff only for a moment before Jody caught Doug's rhythm, and they moved together gracefully in the old-fashioned hop-one-two-three pattern of the polka. Jody flew around the floor, feeling like a young girl again.

Doug looked down into her happy, flushed face and smiled at the charming picture she made. "It's like we've been dancing together forever," he said as the band hit their final note and went into a slow, dreamy ballad.

"I know," Jody said as she moved closer for the slow dance. He put his arm around her and held her close as they shuffled around the crowded dance floor. Jody could feel Doug's heart thudding against her chest, and her own pounded in response, as much from excitement as anything else. She felt that magic attraction for him again and wished that things had been different with her and she could have become his lover.

Doug sighed when the music was over. "Come on, let's go sit down for a minute," he said. If he held her much longer, he thought, he was going to go crazy with wanting her. He took Jody's hand and they started back to the table.

"I swear, Gladys, can you believe that Jody Ford? Her husband barely in the grave, and she's out here hanging all over his brother! That woman's shameless."

Jody froze, and Doug looked around for the source of the voice. He spotted a couple of old ladies a few tables away, both wearing hearing aids.

"I thought she was crazy when she left Larry," the second old lady said. "But I guess she didn't want him anymore when he lost the ranch. That's probably the only reason she married him."

"Come on, let's sit down," Doug said. He half-pulled Jody to their table. "Do you want me to go set those ladies straight?"

Jody shook her head. "No, why spoil their only pastime? They're welcome to say and think what they like."

"But it's not fair for them to run you down that way," Doug objected.

"There are a whole lot of things that aren't fair in this life, Doug," Jody said softly.

They danced a few more times, but the magic was gone from the evening. Doug put his arm around Jody as they walked to the car. "I'm sorry those two old biddies spoiled it for you," he said.

"They only said what the whole town's thought ever since Larry and I separated," Jody said. "I really didn't care at the time, but now sometimes it bothers me when somebody says something like what we overheard, or they hint around, trying to find out what really happened. Why can't people stay out of what isn't their business?"

"It's like you said—other people's business is some folks' major pastime." He helped her into the car, then got in himself.

"Jody, have you ever thought of telling people the

124

truth?" he asked quietly. "Admitting that Larry abused you?"

"Dear God, no," Jody said passionately.

"Why not?" he asked. "It would make all the difference in the world in people's attitude toward you."

"Oh, Doug, their attitudes don't bother me all that much," Jody said. "Besides, Larry and I are old news by now."

"Their attitudes do bother you," Doug argued quietly. "Look how those two old ladies spoiled it for you this evening."

"But I could never tell people about Larry!" Jody protested. "Could you admit a thing like that?"

"I don't see why not," Doug said mildly.

"Try it sometime and see how you feel," Jody said. "Doug, it's not only a very painful thing when a husband hits you, but it's also extremely embarrassing. It's not the kind of thing you admit so all the world knows."

Doug pulled up in Jody's driveway and followed her into her house. "Jody, I'm sure they told you at the women's shelter that battered wives come from all social and economic backgrounds. It happens on the wrong side of the tracks and it happens in mansions. I know of a situation in San Diego where a doctor, of all people, was abusing his wife."

Jody sighed as she flopped down on the couch. "Yeah, I know that—at least, I know it in my head. But there is still that stigma attached to it. And what you're forgetting, Doug, is that a lot of people either wouldn't believe it or they would start to wonder what I had done to make him treat me that way. Look at the hard time you had believing it at first. Marilyn told me later that she had to show you that awful picture she took of me that night before you would believe her."

Doug cringed. "I guess you have a point. Why did she take it, anyway?"

"The picture? To use as evidence later, if we had to. But mostly to convince Larry that I meant business about him getting out of my life. Anyway, short of blowing the picture up and putting it on the wall in the store, people wouldn't believe that nice, sweet Larry Ford would do a thing like that. So I don't talk about it."

"No, you keep it bottled up inside you, where it festers," Doug said.

"Thanks a lot!" Jody said, rising off the couch.

"But Jody, isn't that true, at least to a certain extent?" Doug persisted. "You've obviously come a long way in getting over what happened to you, but you're still afraid to get close to another man. You know damn well that you and I have something very special together, but you make ridiculous conditions and shy away every time I try to get close to you. And it's not just me, is it? In all the time I've lived here, I've never seen a man come pick you up for a date. You've let what Larry did to you spoil any kind of relationship with a man that you might establish. But maybe if you talked about it, you could put some of it behind you and go on with your life. You need to talk about it, Jody."

"It hurts to talk about it!" Jody protested.

"That means you need to talk about it just that much more," Doug said quietly. "Jody, I care about you, and I'd like to get closer to you, and I think you'd like the same thing with me, but you're going to have to open up with me if we're ever going to do that."

Jody sat down again and leaned her head back on the sofa. "What do you want to know?" she asked softly.

126

"Anything and everything," Doug said. "Did you put up with years of abuse?"

"Oh, absolutely not," Jody assured Doug. "I couldn't have stood it, nor would I have put Scott through that."

"That's a relief," Doug murmured. "I had visions of you putting up with years and years of it."

"No, Larry only physically abused me three times," she admitted. "The first time he only slapped me."

"Hard?"

Jody thought a minute. "Yeah."

"What did you do?"

"Do? I was so stunned I didn't do anything," Jody said. "I knew that Larry was under a tremendous strain, and he had been yelling at us both a lot, but for a man I had been married to for almost ten years to actually hit me—you can't imagine what a shock that was. He stormed out of the house and came back a few hours later with a bouquet of flowers, apologizing all over the place and swearing that it wouldn't happen again."

"Had he been drinking?" Doug asked quietly.

"The first time no, but he had the last two times," Jody admitted.

"What did you do the second time he hit you?" Doug asked quietly.

"I tried to get him to seek help," Jody said. "I even threatened to leave him if he didn't. But he said we really couldn't afford it, and of course swore that it wouldn't ever happen again, and like a fool I thought it really wouldn't. I wised up after the third time. I realized that Larry had a problem, and that I could either get him out of my life or I could go back and let him kill me—if not physically then mentally. I didn't have a choice, Doug, not really."

"No, you didn't," Doug said. "So why didn't you cut your losses completely and divorce him?"

"Because in a way I still loved him," Jody admitted. "We had spent almost ten happy years together, remember? There were a lot of good times in those years, before Larry lost the ranch. We took some really wonderful trips together, we spent an enormous amount of time together looking for antique furniture for the house, we worked the ranch—we had made a whole life together. And even after it got bad and we lost the ranch, we still shared some good times. Larry wasn't impossible all the time."

"That's good to know," Doug said. "I'm glad it wasn't all bad."

"It wasn't, Doug, or I certainly wouldn't have stuck around," Jody said. "But in a way, it makes what happened to our marriage just that much sadder, and that's why I couldn't bring myself to end it."

"What would you have done if Larry had come back to New Braunfels?" Doug asked.

"Oh, I could never have gone back to him," Jody said. "He hurt me too badly, both physically and mentally, that last time. I could never have forgiven him for that." She stopped and wiped a tear from her eye. "He told me the last time I saw him that leaving me was going to break his heart. I told him he had already broken mine."

Doug's eyes filled with tears as he thought of both Larry's and Jody's pain. "What a waste," he said, his voice thick.

"Wasn't it, though?" Jody said. "But I'm over it."

"Are you really?" Doug asked quietly. "Are you really over all of it?"

Jody thought a moment. "No, I guess I'll never be over some of the hurt. But I've put it behind me and gone on."

"Are you sure you've put all of it behind you?" Doug asked. "You're still afraid of intimacy with a man. At least, you're afraid of intimacy with me. Is that because Larry was cruel to you in bed?"

Jody's face flamed a brilliant shade of red. "No, he was never actually cruel or abusive in that way."

Doug sensed that there was more that Jody had left unsaid. "So what did he do to you to make you afraid of intimacy?"

"He ran me down all the time, especially after I lost all the weight," Jody said. "He told me that I looked like a boy and that he didn't want to make love to a stringbean like me. And he quit making love to me."

"Did he have somebody else?" Doug asked.

"I wondered at the time, but looking back, I don't think so," Jody said.

"I'm no psychologist, but I've read that a major crisis in some men's lives can cause them to become impotent," Doug said. "I don't know, but I'd hazard a guess that that's what happened to Larry, and he ran you down and made you think it was your fault to cover up for his own inadequacy."

"But he never treated me that way before I lost the weight," Jody protested.

"Well, when did you lose the weight?" Doug asked.

"About the time we lost the ranch," Jody said slowly. "About the time everything else started to go sour."

"Jody, I seriously doubt that your weight loss had anything to do with Larry's attitude," Doug said. "Because I can assure you that you're plenty attractive. At least you are to me."

"Sure, and that's why you said I was skinny tonight," Jody scoffed.

"Jody, I didn't mean that you were unattractive,"

Doug said, astonished at the interpretation she had put on his teasing.

"But that's what Larry always said, that I was skinny and that I couldn't turn him on anymore. I haven't wanted to make love to a man since, because he's bound to be disappointed in me."

"Oh, Jody, did you really believe all the things Larry said to you?" Doug asked gently. "How could you? Don't you have a mirror?"

"Yes, I do," Jody said quietly. "And every morning I look at a very skinny woman in it."

Doug stood up and took Jody by the hand. "I want you to show me this mirror," he said. "Because I want to see the woman you see in it."

"Doug, what are you doing?" Jody asked as he led her up the stairs.

"Where's the mirror?" Doug asked.

"In the front bathroom," Jody said.

Doug led her into the big old-fashioned bathroom and stood her in front of the full-length mirror. "Now, look at this woman," he said tenderly. "Let's start at the top. She's got a glowing fall of soft, dark hair that a man could bury himself in. She has the face of an angel, and a smile that can melt an iceberg. She's got high, firm little breasts that a man could touch and kiss all night. She's got a waist I can span with my fingers." Doug made a loop with his fingers and thumbs around her tiny waist.

Jody could feel herself blushing. "Doug, please—"

"She's got slender but very feminine hips, a very nice little bottom, and long, beautiful legs that I would love to feel tangled up with mine," Doug said. He turned her around and stared down into her eyes. "Oh, Jody, if you only knew just how beautiful you are," he whispered. "If you only knew how much I want to make love to you."

"Do you really?" Jody asked breathlessly.

"Oh, dear God, *yes.*" Doug bent his head and kissed her lips, a wealth of love and tenderness in his touch. "I want to make love to you so badly I can taste it."

Jody's eyes clouded. "I've never made love to anybody but Larry," she said. "I—I'm—"

Doug put his finger against her lips. "The only things I need from you," he said, "are your tenderness and your caring. Can you give those things to me?"

"Oh, yes, Doug," she replied as she stood on her toes to kiss him.

He held her for long minutes, letting her kiss him and feel her own sensuality and strength. Her tender kisses inflamed him, but he banked the flames, determined to do nothing that would frighten her. He sensed that she needed to go slowly tonight, and he vowed to do whatever was necessary to restore the self-confidence that his brother had destroyed in her.

Jody broke off their kiss and stared up into Doug's eyes. "That was nice," she said.

"And what's coming will be nicer," he assured her. "But first, one of us needs to think about some protection."

"I'm on the pill for cramps," Jody said.

"Good," Doug said as he picked her up and carried her from the bathroom. "Which one is your room?"

"Right here." Jody pointed, and Doug carried her into a large room with a huge wrought-iron bed. He put her down on the edge of the bed and switched on the bedside lamp, bathing the room in a soft, muted glow.

"Turn out the light, Doug," Jody protested.

"No way," Doug said. "Jody, I meant what I said— you're a beautiful, appealing woman, and I want to

131

see you when I make love to you. It will add that much more to my pleasure."

"Shall I undress for you?" Jody asked shyly.

"Would you be more comfortable if I went first?" Doug asked.

Jody nodded, and Doug stood and slowly removed his clothing, never breaking eye contact with Jody until the last piece of his clothing was gone. "Now look at me," he commanded her huskily.

Jody stared at Doug's body. She had seen him nearly naked before, but removing the last barrier made him that much more masculine and appealing. Her eyes feasted on his lean, strong body, on the thick hair on his chest and legs, on the slim flatness of his stomach, on the strength of his masculinity that told her just how much he wanted her. Jody blushed, but at the same time she smiled, stood, and slowly removed her clothing, as he had done.

Doug stared at Jody's fragile femininity, taking in her small, high breasts, her tiny waist, and the gentle flare of her hips. Before, even in her swimsuit, she had looked larger than she really was, and Doug realized that she had learned to dress to hide her thinness. But she was far from unappealing as she stood hesitantly before him. He had never wanted a woman so badly before. He would cradle her tiny body next to his and bury himself forever in her warmth.

"Oh, Jody, you're beautiful," Doug said quietly as he reached for her. "You're so incredibly beautiful."

"So are you," she said as she ran her hands down Doug's sides and onto his hips. Unsure of herself at first, she explored his body with her fingertips, touching him tentatively.

Doug laid her down on the bed and followed her

down. "Go ahead and touch me," he said. "Explore me. Find out about me. I like it."

Jody nodded and sat up. She touched Doug everywhere, shyly at first, and then with confidence. She left no place on him unexplored as she moved her hands over his body, feeling the hard warmth of his chest and shoulders, his stomach. She ran her fingers around his navel and found out that he was ticklish there. Her hands and eyes drifted lower, finding his hips and the lean strength of his thighs. When she would have resisted touching him intimately, Doug took her hand and placed it against him, letting her feel the strength of his desire for her.

Jody's pulse pounded in her throat. He was on fire for her, there was no doubt about it. He was on fire for her, not for anyone else. For the first time in a long time, she was aware of her power as a woman. She made no objection when Doug pushed her down on the bed and sat up beside her. "Now I want to get to know you," he said. "I want to know all your secrets."

Doug's eyes feasted on her as they traveled up and down her body, taking in each and every curve and angle. Jody shivered from the desire she saw in his eyes. His hands followed his eyes, touching and exploring her body as she had done his. He found the tender tips of her breasts and caressed them to hard peaks of excitement. "Beautiful, just beautiful," Doug whispered as he bent to touch one with the tip of his tongue. "Does that feel good?"

"Oh, yes," Jody whispered as he caressed her other nipple with his warm, moist tongue. His hands ran down her body, drawing circles on her stomach before drifting down and stroking her slender hips and thighs.

Jody stiffened when Doug's hand moved to the

133

point of intimacy. "No secrets," he reminded her as he pushed her legs a little further apart. He found the warmth of her femininity and stroked it, his touch tender and slow. Jody relaxed and gave herself over to the pleasure he was bringing to her.

Doug touched her for long moments as he caressed her breasts with his lips and tongue. Jody could feel herself coming closer and closer to the point of exploding in his arms—she had never experienced this kind of unselfish giving on a man's part, and Doug's generosity was driving her wild. Higher and higher she soared, finally arching and moaning beneath him as waves of pleasure engulfed her. "Oh, Doug!" she cried as she shut her eyes and let herself experience the delight.

Doug's eyes were bemused as he looked down at her. "You surprised me," he said honestly.

"You surprised me too," Jody admitted. She opened her legs and put her arms around Doug. "Make love to me now," she said. "Let me give you the kind of pleasure you just gave me."

Doug moved over her and joined himself to her. Jody had thought her desire spent, that this would be all for Doug, and was amazed when she could feel the passion growing in her again. She soared with Doug this time, the two of them spiraling together as Doug took her higher and higher until they reached a shattering climax together, crying out softly to one another as they reached fulfillment in each other's arms.

Doug rolled onto his side, not moving away from his and Jody's intimate embrace. His eyes were moist with tears as he looked into hers. "I'm a sailor, Jody, and I've made love to women all over the world. But never—never—have I experienced what you just gave me."

Jody's eyes were wide. "Do you mean that? Did I really do that for you?"

"Yes," Doug said as he smoothed her hair from her face. "You really did that for me. I don't want you to doubt your femininity ever again."

"After this I won't be able to," Jody admitted. They kissed and caressed one another for a few minutes, and miraculously Doug made love to her again, tenderly bringing them both to the point of delight.

It was late when Doug finally turned off the light. Jody snuggled down next to his hard, warm body. She loved him, she thought sleepily. She must love him to have responded to him the way she had. Jody smiled to herself in the darkness. She was glad that she and Doug had fallen in love and that she had given herself to him. Now she could have love and warmth and caring in her life. She could have his passion and his affection, and she could have it from him without the ties and potential hurts of marriage.

Doug smiled to himself when Jody fell asleep minutes after he turned out the light. He cautiously raised himself and looked at her face on the pillow. She looked young, younger than she had since he had come back into her life, and so relaxed, so beautiful.

"You need me to make love to you every night, Jody," he whispered as he laid back down. And he would, every night, for the rest of their lives. Doug shut his eyes and put his arm around Jody's waist. He would ask her to marry him the first thing in the morning, he thought as sleep overtook him.

CHAPTER EIGHT

Jody sighed and snuggled closer to the sleeping man by her side, savoring Doug's hard, comfortable warmth. She was still sleepy, but her inner alarm was such that she woke up early whether she needed to or not. She yawned and turned over, intending to go back to sleep, but as she laid her arm across Doug's chest he stirred next to her.

"Is it time to get up yet?" he asked groggily.

Jody opened her eyes and peered at the alarm clock. "No, it's nowhere near that time," she said. "I don't get up for another hour and a half on Sunday." She thought briefly of Hunter and what he would think of her actions last night, but a tender kiss from Doug banished all thoughts but those of him from her mind.

"Good," Doug said as he ran his palm down the side of her face. He kissed her once again, this time more passionately, before releasing her and turning over. "We can go back to sleep."

Jody raised herself on her elbow and stared at him. "I can think of a better way to spend the next hour and a half," she whispered.

"Oh, by all means, go out and get us a paper."

"A paper!" She grinned wickedly as she kissed the back of Doug's neck. "We can read an old paper anytime." She left a trail of kisses down his spine.

"Whatever." He yawned.

Jody stared at him in consternation. Was he one of those people who wasn't good for anything without three cups of coffee? She ran her fingers around his waist and massaged his stomach lightly with her fingertips. Doug gasped quietly when she dipped her finger into his navel and drew a circle there.

He was faking. Jody's lips curled into a grin. He was no more asleep than she was. Her caresses became bolder and she stroked the hard muscles of his back and shoulders, peppering him with light, tender kisses at the same time. Then her hand moved around to find and torment the tip of one of his masculine nipples. It hardened into a small button, and Doug's breathing became faster and just a little unsteady. Glorying in the power of her femininity, Jody snuggled closer and pressed herself next to his back, letting him feel the feminine softness of her breasts and stomach. Her thighs lay next to his, and she moved her legs sensuously against Doug's, feeling his body tense with desire for her.

Still Jody said nothing. With fingers more bold than they had ever been before, she found and cradled his masculinity, her fingers playing delicately along its length. Her own breath came in shallow gasps as her level of desire grew.

"Are you trying to drop me a hint?" Doug asked suddenly as he turned over and pinned Jody against the mattress. "Are you trying to tell me something?"

"Me?" Jody asked, the picture of innocence. "I'm just trying to remember how your body feels so that I can accurately carve my marble statue."

"You carve me the way I look right now, and your statue would be arrested for indecency," Doug said as he bent his head to kiss her. His lips met hers for

137

long gentle moments, his body a comfortable weight over hers.

"I think you'd make a wonderful statue right now —a little risqué, maybe, but just what we need in the town square," she teased. "The old ladies around here need a treat!"

"I can think of one lady around here who needs a treat," Doug said as he feathered soft kisses down her face and onto her neck. "How about if I spray whipped cream topping on you and take it off?"

Jody laughed. "You'd be horrified if I called your bluff on that one," she said.

"Try me on mustard—the expensive kind."

Jody rolled over on top of Doug. "Seems to me you're getting too big for your britches, mister," she said as she nipped his neck lightly. "You better learn who's boss around here."

Doug cupped her breasts in his hands. "Feel good, boss?" he asked.

"You have an hour and a half to stop that," she teased.

Doug pulled her down so that he could reach her breast with his lips. "You're so pretty here," he said as her nipple hardened. His hands spanned her tiny waist. "You're pretty everywhere, Jody—at the store, at the movies, at the hamburger stand—"

Jody started laughing. "And here I thought I was going to get complimented," she said.

Doug laughed with her; then his expression became serious as he cupped her face between his palms. "But you are beautiful," he said. "Everything about you is beautiful. Your face, your spirit, your body—everything."

Tears sparkled in Jody's eyes. "I love you, Doug Ford," she said as she boldly joined their bodies together.

138

"And I love you, Jody Ford," he said as his hands cupped her bottom and held her as she made love to him.

Jody raised herself so that her arms were free, and she moved over Doug in a lithe, sensuous symphony of motion. The vision she made above him, with her hair spilling around her body, was as pleasurable to Doug as the joining of their bodies, and he feasted on the sight of her as she set the pace of their lovemaking. Her body found incredible ways to twist and turn above him as she would bring him almost to the brink only to slow down, leaving Doug at a point of intense pleasure. But Doug was not just an idle participant in this act of love—his hands stroked the tender skin of Jody's stomach and waist and rose higher to caress her breasts. *Sweet, oh, how sweet,* she thought as she and Doug rose together in a spiral of passion.

Doug reveled in the lovemaking of the woman who had just told him that she loved him. She was giving herself to him, giving to him with an unselfishness that took his breath away. Her movements were completely natural as she took him to the edge of delight over and over. When she sensed that the time of teasing was over, that mutual pleasure was about to overtake them both, she increased the pace, toppling them both off the passionate mountaintop they had climbed to free-fall through a burst of pleasure. Tremors rocked Jody's body as wave after wave radiated from her, and Doug arched beneath her to capture all of her warmth. Then Jody collapsed on top of him in a comfortable tangle of arms and legs.

When they eventually shifted to lie side by side, Doug raised himself on one elbow and stared down into her face. "Did you mean what you said about loving me?" he asked softly. "Did you mean it, or were you just saying it to be nice?"

"Of course I mean it," Jody said. "I love you, Doug. I would have to, to be able to make love to you the way I do."

"That's good, because I do love you," Doug said. "I love you like I've never loved a woman in my life."

"I know there have been a lot of women, Doug, but have you ever loved any of them at all?" Jody asked, more curious than worried.

Doug thought a moment. "There have been times that I thought I was in love, but I don't think I was, not really. This is the first time I've ever loved a woman enough to want to spend my life with her."

Jody stiffened. "That—that's nice," she said as she slid out of bed.

"Jody? Are you all right?" Doug asked as he followed her down the hall to the bathroom. "What's wrong?" he asked.

"Uh, nothing," Jody replied. Surely he hadn't meant that he wanted to marry her. He had just used a figure of speech. "Would you like to take a shower with me?"

"Sure thing," Doug said. He climbed into the claw-footed bathtub after her and drew the shower curtain around them.

Jody squealed when a blast of cold water hit her from the suspended shower. "Hey, run it at the bottom until it gets warm," she said.

Doug turned the water back to the bathtub. "Have you ever thought of getting the plumbing modernized?" he said as cold water splashed down the drain.

"Never! Do you know a modern plumber who would let me keep this bathtub?"

"You *like* this old tub?" Doug asked. Mercifully, the

water had begun to run warm. He adjusted the temperature before she turned the shower head back on.

"Of course," Jody said as she rubbed soap on a washcloth. "It might not be the best shower in the world, but it's great for a bubble bath!"

Doug and Jody soaped one another and rinsed under the shower, then he helped her shampoo her long hair. They dried each other with thick towels and Doug sat on the edge of the bathtub and watched while Jody dried her hair, the hand dryer blowing her hair around her head like a halo. She had wrapped a towel around her waist but had left her breasts free, and Doug could feel desire start to grow within him again as her nipples poked out impudently from the long fall of hair. He knew that, no matter how long they were married, she would always excite him this way.

"Would you like a little breakfast?" Jody asked as she put on underwear.

"Just coffee and toast." Doug picked up his underwear and made a face at it. "Guess it will have to do," he said as he pulled them on.

Jody pulled a robe on over her underwear. She made coffee and toasted several pieces of bread for each of them. "You should have borrowed my razor," she said as Doug kissed her cheek, his early-morning stubble scratching her face.

"It'll keep for another hour," he said as he rubbed his face. "But that won't be a problem for very long. We'll be married before too much longer, and I can shave before I kiss you."

"Doug—" Her hands trembled as she tried to pour a cup of coffee, and she splashed hot coffee on her hand. "Damn!" she said as she stuck her hand under the cold water.

Doug dried her hand and sat her down at the table.

141

"What's the matter with you?" he demanded. "This is the second time you've acted like this when I've implied that our relationship will be permanent. I do want to marry you, Jody—surely after last night and this morning you know that."

"No, you didn't say that you wanted marriage," she said quietly.

"Then let me rectify the situation. Jody, will you marry me?"

Jody could not disguise the horror that she felt. "No," she whispered.

"*What?*"

"Oh, Doug, of course I can't marry you!" Jody said. "Where did you get the idea that I ever wanted to get married again?"

"Well, forgive me," Doug said sarcastically. "I guess it was a line, wasn't it?"

"What was a line?" Jody demanded.

"The part about loving me. Is that part of your usual patter in bed?"

"No, it isn't part of the usual patter!" Jody snapped. "There isn't any usual patter!"

"Then why don't you want to marry me if you meant what you said about loving me?" Doug demanded.

"Why does marriage automatically have to follow love?" Jody asked. "Yes, Doug, I love you—deeply. I'm surprised you even question that after last night. I just don't want to get married again."

"Why not?" Doug asked, baffled.

"Why do you think?" Jody countered. "I've been married once, Doug. It's not an experience I care to repeat."

Doug flopped down in the chair across from Jody. "And why don't you care to repeat it?" His eyes flashed dangerously, and Jody felt a tremor of the old fear taking hold of her.

"Don't look at me that way, Doug. You're scaring me."

"Why shouldn't I look at you this way, Jody? I'm mighty angry right now."

"Because that's the way Larry used to look at me," she responded quietly.

Doug uttered a harsh oath. "So that's what this is all about," he said. "I thought you said you had put that all behind you. I thought that after last night—hell, Jody, you said it was all over for you. But it's not, is it? You're still scared of me."

"Scared of *you*, no. But I *am* afraid to marry you. I'd be afraid to marry anyone. I have no intention of ever giving another man that kind of control over my life."

"That's ridiculous and you know it," Doug said. "What kind of control would I have over you?"

"I'd have to share a house with you. I'd have to be with you all the time, I wouldn't have any freedom or a place to call my own."

"And you'd be there where I could hit you," Doug said bitterly. "That's what the problem is, isn't it? You don't trust me enough to live in the same house with me. You don't even love me enough to trust me not to hurt you."

"I gave a man that kind of love and trust once, and look what it got me," Jody replied. "I guess you're right, Doug, I don't trust you. I wouldn't trust any man on the face of this earth, but especially not you."

"And why especially not me?" he demanded.

"Because, as much as I love you, you're Larry's brother," Jody said quietly. "How do I know you're not like him?"

Doug struggled not to slap the table with his hand.

143

"Because I'm not, that's why!" he yelled. "Dammit, look at me! I'm not Larry, I'm Doug! I'm so sick and tired of you making the comparison!"

"I can't help but make the comparison!" Jody exclaimed, her eyes filling with tears. "Yes, Doug, I look at you. And I hear you too. You have his voice, his eyes, you look at me in anger the same way he did—you even clench your fist when you're nervous or upset, just like he used to do!" Jody pointed down at his fist.

Doug looked down in wonder at his hand. He slowly unclenched it and held his fingers out to her. "I'm not like Larry, Jody," he said, his voice filled with determination.

"I don't know that!" Jody said, her voice breaking on a sob.

Tears ran down her face as Doug rose and slammed out of the house. Why had he spoiled things by asking her to marry him? They could have had a lovely relationship. They could have loved and shared, given a wealth of affection and caring to one another. But that wasn't enough for him—he wanted her to do the one thing that she couldn't bring herself to do.

Jody tried to eat a piece of toast, but it stuck in her throat. As the tears rolled down her cheeks, she gave up trying to fight them and had a good hard cry. When her tears finally subsided, she dried her eyes and drank her coffee, and she swore when she looked at the clock. If she didn't hurry, she would be late for church.

"Marilyn, are you and Rachel ready to go?" Hunter called up the stairs.

"Daddy!" Rachel called as she ran for the steps. She

hurried down them as fast as her short legs could carry her. "Church, Daddy. Go."

"I hope you still feel that way when you're fifteen," Hunter said as he picked up his daughter.

Marilyn came down the stairs in the new maternity dress she had bought the day before. "Does this look all right?" she asked.

"Beautiful. But I like you better without it," Hunter teased.

"Hush, not in front of Rachel," Marilyn said, but she placed a not-too-wifely kiss on Hunter's lips anyway. "Now, let's get out of here before we're late," she said.

Hunter opened the front door and froze when he saw Doug jerk open Jody's front door and slam it behind him. Marilyn bumped into Hunter and stared over his shoulder as Doug marched across the street and slammed his own door. "Isn't that the shirt Doug had on last night?" Marilyn asked slowly.

"I don't know, but that was definitely his 'Kiss me' button," Hunter said. "And that's the angriest I've ever seen him."

"What do you think happened?" Marilyn asked.

"Marilyn, don't be naïve," Hunter said. "You know what happened."

"Of course I know what happened last night," Marilyn said dryly. "It was this morning that I was wondering about."

"Do you want to go over there and make sure she's all right?" Hunter asked.

"You don't think he—"

"Of course I don't think he hit her," Hunter said quickly. "But I bet they had one heck of an argument over something."

"Let's see how she looks in church, and maybe this afternoon we can go over and talk to her," Marilyn suggested. "Oh, dear, you're not preaching on that, are you? That's all she probably needs to hear this morning."

"No, I'm preaching on the sins of the tongue," Hunter said as he glanced up and down the street. "Speaking of which, I sure hope nobody else saw him this morning."

Marilyn said a hearty amen to that.

Jody picked halfheartedly at the chicken salad she had made for lunch. She wasn't at all hungry, but she hadn't been able to eat breakfast and figured she better eat a little if she didn't want to lose any more weight. Marilyn would notice immediately and would start to worry about her, and Jody didn't want that to happen. As it was, she had sat in the back of the church this morning, hoping that her perceptive cousin didn't notice her bloodshot eyes. Many in the congregation had eyes just as bloodshot as hers, thanks to Wurstfest, and she hoped it was assumed that she owed hers to Wurstfest as well and not to the crying she had done after Doug had left.

Jody swallowed a few more bites of her lunch but gave up and put it in the refrigerator. She started to go over the store's books but stopped when Doug's bold signature on an invoice brought tears to her eyes. Damn! Why had he spoiled everything this morning?

Jody wiped her eyes and was flipping through the newspaper when the telephone rang. "Jody? Would you like to walk over for a piece of Mom's chocolate cake?" Marilyn asked. "She brought us one this morning that's too big for us to finish."

"Um, I think I'll skip it," Jody said. "I wouldn't be much company this afternoon."

"I thought you might need to talk. You looked up-

146

set this morning in church, and I thought you might have something on your mind," Marilyn said quietly.

Jody's face flamed. "You saw him leave, didn't you?"

"Yes, we did. Come on over, Jody. We've always been able to talk about anything, you know that," Marilyn coaxed.

Jody thought of all the times they had shared their problems. "All right."

Marilyn met Jody at the door. "Come on in and eat your cake first," she said. "Hunter's trying to persuade Rachel she wants to take a nap."

Jody managed to eat the entire piece of cake that Marilyn gave her. She blushed again when Hunter entered the kitchen, and she reminded herself that he had been in the navy and had seen and heard of things a lot worse than what she had done last night.

"Is there any more coffee, Marilyn?" he asked as he straddled a kitchen chair.

Marilyn poured Jody and Hunter some coffee.

"Doug looked pretty upset when he left your house this morning," Hunter observed. "He looked so angry that Marilyn wanted me to go over and make sure he hadn't slugged you."

"Thanks, Marilyn," Jody said. "He didn't, but he was mad enough to."

Marilyn sat down at the kitchen table. "What did you argue about, or is it too personal to tell us?"

"He wants to get married," Jody said. "He became very angry when I told him no."

"Why don't you want to marry him?" Hunter asked. "Do you love him?"

"Yes," Jody said quietly. "Do you think I would make love to a man I didn't love?"

"Of course not," Hunter assured her. "But if you

147

love him, isn't marriage a natural progression from that?"

"Why does it have to be?" Jody asked. "Why couldn't we share love and caring outside marriage?"

"In front of Scott?" Marilyn asked.

"No, of course not," Jody said. "We would be discreet."

"But Jody, that kind of thing is just a hollow facade of what you and Doug could share if you were married," Hunter said.

"Marriage is out, Hunter," she said, "with Doug or any other man. I'm never giving a man that kind of power over me again. I'm never giving anyone the chance to hurt me the way Larry did."

Jody's expression was troubled as she faced her two friends. "I know that what I'm saying goes against everything the two of you believe in, and I'm sorry I'm hurting you. But there's no way that I will ever let a man get that close to me. I may love him, but I'll never marry again."

"Don't worry about us, Jody," Marilyn said.

"But Jody, I can't help but worry about you," Hunter said quietly. "You apologized for going against everything we believe in. But you're also going against everything you believe in. We've been neighbors now for years, and I've watched you live, Jody. You're a religious and moral woman, and what you're proposing to do at this point goes against everything you've ever believed in."

"So what?" Jody snapped bitterly. "Yes, I've been a paragon of morality all these years, and where has it gotten me? I was a good girl and a model wife, and what was my reward? I got abused."

"Oh, Jody, *please* don't feel that way," Marilyn said. "You have been rewarded for your decency, if only in the sense that you can look yourself in the eye when you get up in the morning."

"But I still don't want to get married," Jody argued stubbornly. "It's out of the question."

"Is it with any man, or is it just Doug that you don't want to marry?" Hunter asked.

"I wouldn't marry any man," Jody said. "Don't you understand how frightened I still am? I just can't give myself that completely to a man. If a lover gets violent or something, you can leave. You can't just leave a husband like that."

"Jody, do you still think that all men are like Larry?" Marilyn asked softly. "They aren't, honestly."

"But how do I know that?" Jody cried. "Besides, Doug is Larry's brother! Sometimes he reminds me so much of Larry that he scares me."

"Doug's not like Larry," Marilyn said. "He's a totally different man."

"Jody, I know Doug," Hunter said. "We were on the same ship for a year. I've seen him drunk, I've seen him in despair, and I've seen him scared out of his wits, but I've never once seen him violent."

"Yes, and I lived with Larry for ten years," Jody said. "I saw him drunk, and in despair, and frightened, and frustrated, and every other way that you can imagine. And I never dreamed in a million years that he would hit me—until the day he did. How do I know that Doug's not the same kind of walking time bomb?"

Hunter leaned his elbows on the table. "I honestly don't have an answer for your question. But none of us knows what we may or may not do in the future if life heads a certain way for us. If Larry, for example, hadn't lost the ranch, if his life had been what he wanted it to be, he probably would never have hit

149

you. Who knows how it might affect me if something happened to Marilyn and Rachel?"

"Look how it affected my first husband when we lost Bobby," Marilyn reminded Jody. "He left me, and the last I heard two years ago he had lost a third job because of his drinking."

"Yet Marilyn came out of her sorrow a stronger, more beautiful person," Hunter said. "What we're trying to say, Jody, is that none of us ever knows what the future holds. But I honestly believe with all my heart that Doug's nothing like his brother. I think you could live very happily with him."

"But I don't *know* that," Jody protested. "I just don't know that for sure."

"Jody, have you considered Doug's feelings in all this?" Hunter asked her.

"I know I hurt him this morning, and I'm sorry," Jody said honestly. "I realize that he asked me to marry him in good faith, but don't you understand? After what happened before, I have to put my own welfare first."

Hunter and Marilyn talked to Jody for a few more minutes, but Jody was adamant that she would not marry Doug. She dreaded facing him in the store on Monday, knowing they would have to talk. She would try to bring him around to her way of thinking and persuade him that an affair was the right thing for them. But Jody was honest with herself—she really didn't expect Doug to go along with the idea of an affair. Still, she had to at least try to get him to change his mind, because an affair was all she could offer him.

Hunter was thoughtful for most of the afternoon, and after evening worship he shed his coat and tie

150

and rolled up his sleeves. "Marilyn, I'm going over to Doug's for a little while," he said.

"Aren't you under ministerial confidence?" Marilyn asked.

"Jody didn't tell us anything that she didn't tell him," Hunter reasoned. "I just want to make sure he's all right."

"That's a good idea."

Doug looked up from the paper when he heard the knock on the front door. *Oh, please, Scott, not tonight,* he thought as Goldie barked and ran for the door. He had consumed several beers, and although he was far from intoxicated, he hated for Scott to smell the beer on his breath.

"Hunter!" Doug said as he belched loudly. He looked sheepish as he moved aside so Hunter could come in.

"Drowning your sorrows?" Hunter asked lightly.

"No, it would take a whole bottle of Scotch to do that, and I'd just be hung over in the morning," Doug said bitterly.

They moved into the living room and sat down across from one another.

"We talked to Jody this afternoon," Hunter said. "She admitted that she'd hurt you."

"Big of her," Doug said acidly. "For the first damn time in my life I love a woman and want to marry her, but she doesn't want that. Oh, no, *she* wants to have an affair." Doug heard the despair in his voice and cringed at the idea of showing his weakness in front of Hunter.

"And you feel like you've been kicked in the gut, don't you?" Hunter asked.

Doug nodded. "How do you know?"

"Marilyn made me feel the same way once when she told me she didn't want to have my children."

151

Hunter shifted in his chair. "In fact, the situation was very similar. Marilyn had been deeply hurt when she lost her son, and she wasn't about to risk that kind of pain again. Jody feels much the same way. She was terribly hurt by Larry, and right now she isn't willing to let herself get into a situation where that kind of thing could happen to her a second time."

"Marilyn obviously changed her mind," Doug said slowly. "What did you do?"

"I gave her time and a whole lot of love," Hunter said. "And it didn't really take her that long to change her mind. But I took it slow and easy with her. I let her make the decision to risk loving a child again. I didn't try to push her."

"What do you think I ought to do—go ahead and have the affair she wants?" Doug asked.

"Oh, heavens, no," Hunter said quickly. "I think that's the last thing a deeply religious woman like Jody needs to cope with. But I would definitely continue to see her, if I were you, as often as possible, and I'd plan on giving her a lot of time and patience to work through her feelings."

"And what about me and my feelings?" Doug asked. "Don't they count for something?"

"You're going to have to put them on the back burner for the time being," Hunter replied honestly. "You start pushing her for marriage, and she's going to back away more frightened of you than ever."

"Do you think she'll ever change her mind, or is she going to leave us in limbo forever?" Doug asked.

Hunter sighed. "I don't know, Doug. I do know that she isn't going to be willing to get married until she's sure she can trust you, and that may take a long time. Marilyn and I didn't know until today just how wary she is of another commitment or how bitter she still is over what happened."

"Just how bitter is she, Hunter?"

"When I told her that an affair would go against her moral code, she said so what—her moral code hadn't gotten her anywhere in the past," Hunter admitted. "I never thought in all my life I'd hear her say a thing like that."

"That's pretty bad," Doug admitted. "Well, I guess it's back to the twice-a-week-with-Scott routine."

"Give her time and be patient with her," Hunter pleaded. "Learning to trust is a hard thing for most of us, and it's going to be even harder for her."

"I love her so much I ache for her, Hunter," Doug said quietly. "I'll give her all the time and patience she needs. I don't really have any choice, do I?"

CHAPTER NINE

Jody unlocked the door of Ford's Antiques and turned on the lights before going to her office and starting a pot of coffee. She had been relieved when Doug's car wasn't in his usual parking place out back, and she hoped that he would wait until close to opening time to come in. She knew that they had to talk, but she needed more time to think about what she could say to him. She knew that she had hurt him badly yesterday when she had refused to marry him, but surely when he thought about it he would be willing to see her point of view. How could he expect her to enter into the same relationship that had caused her such pain in the past?

Jody took the jewelry out of the safe and laid it out in the counter, and when the coffee was done she sat down in her office and drank a cup, relaxing a bit as the minutes ticked by and Doug did not come in. There was no way they would have time to talk about their argument before the store opened, and Jody knew that Doug wouldn't want a come-and-go discussion in between customers. Besides, she had an appointment at one o'clock in San Antonio to look at some estate furniture and jewelry, so she would be out of the store for much of the day. But they would have to talk before the day was over, and Jody desperately hoped she could bring Doug around to her way of thinking. She loved him and longed to have his love in her life, but she just couldn't marry him.

Doug checked his watch and swore as he pulled into his parking place behind the store. He had wanted to talk to Jody this morning, but Goldie had gotten loose and it had taken him nearly a half-hour to find her. He had to find out if Jody was still as opposed to marrying him as she had been yesterday. He hoped, of course, that she would reconsider her adamant refusal to become his wife, but if she was as bitter as Hunter said she was, he doubted that she would.

Jody looked up when Doug came in. "Coffee or Coke?" she asked. "The store opens in five minutes."

"Coffee—don't get up," Doug said. He poured himself a cup and sat down in an old wing chair. "Jody, we have to talk."

"Yes, we do," Jody said, trying not to blush as she looked at the virile man who sat across from her. Memories of their lovemaking flooded her mind, and it was all she could do not to throw herself into his arms. She lowered her eyes, hoping Doug didn't see the telltale blush on her face. "But not right now—we have a store to run."

"I'll take you out to dinner and we can talk then," Doug said. "Call Scott's babysitter and tell her to fix him supper."

"That's not fair to Scott," Jody said. "We can talk here after work."

"I'd rather relax over dinner," Doug protested.

"I'd rather not talk in a public place where anybody in town can overhear us," Jody said stubbornly.

"Suit yourself, hardhead," Doug said as he rose and stormed into the workroom, slamming the door behind him.

Jody minded the store until eleven, and after tell-

155

ing Doug she was leaving, she drove into San Antonio and stopped at one of the large suburban malls to buy Scott an overcoat. She met Joan Davis, the woman who was selling her late mother's antiques, and Joan treated Jody to lunch at a charming outdoor restaurant overlooking Salado Creek. Although both the restaurant and the woman were charming, Jody's mind kept straying to the discussion that faced her back in New Braunfels. What could she say to Doug to convince him that an affair was best for them?

Jody followed Joan to a large stone home in Olmos Park. Joan's mother had lived there until her death just three weeks ago, and the family had taken what furniture and personal items they wanted. Jody temporarily forgot about her problems with Doug as she wandered through room after room filled with treasures—old brass and iron beds, an ornate oak dining-room table and matching breakfront, an old-fashioned pump organ that would still play—furniture even nicer than that which they had been getting from New York. Fairly trembling with excitement, Jody called Doug and told him to arrange short-term financing at the bank. They had to have this furniture, whether they had the cash for it or not.

Doug called her back a short time later and said that he had the financing arranged. Jody selected a number of pieces, all in such good shape that Doug would have to do no more than dust and polish them. She and Joan came to a quick agreement on the price, and Jody arranged for a moving van to pick up the furniture the following Wednesday, before the house was opened for a public estate sale on Friday.

She wrote Joan a check as a down payment and started back toward New Braunfels, the late-afternoon sun bouncing off her car and making her squint behind her sunglasses. She drove a little more slowly than she needed to, postponing the discussion with Doug for as long as she could.

Doug was waiting for her when she got back to the store. He had closed up and was sitting in her office, his feet propped up on a footstool, drinking a cup of coffee. "So it was good enough to borrow money for, was it?" Doug asked as he started to get up.

"I'll get it myself," Jody said. She poured herself a cup of coffee and eased off her pumps. "These things were supposed to be comfortable," she complained as she sat down across from Doug. "Yes, the antiques were that good. Unbelievable, in fact. And so were the prices. There's an oak dining room set that will bring in a pretty penny. And there's a fabulous old pump organ that I'm going to call Hunter about. He was looking for one for Marilyn's Christmas."

"Hunter came to see me last night," Doug said. "We talked for quite a while."

"That's interesting," Jody said levelly. "Did you get any of Aunt Maggie's chocolate cake?"

"No, Jody, we talked about you."

"I figured that," Jody said. "As it happens, I talked to Hunter and Marilyn about you too. They saw you leave my place yesterday morning, and they wanted to make sure I was all right." She took a deep breath. "Doug, I'm sorry I hurt you yesterday. I never meant to do that."

"I know," he said quietly, "but you have to realize that you have the power to hurt me deeply, now that I love you so much."

"Then you can realize that you have the power to hurt me too," Jody countered.

"I don't want to hurt you, I want to marry you! Can't you understand?" Doug pleaded. "Jody, please say you've reconsidered. Please tell me you'll marry me."

"Oh, Doug, I can't do that," Jody said, her voice trembling. "I love you very, very much, and I want you to be a part of my life, but I just can't marry you."

"Why not?" he asked. "If we love each other, I really don't see why you can't."

"It's like I tried to tell you yesterday, Doug. I'm never going to put myself in that kind of vulnerable position again," she explained. "I never want to live in the kind of intimacy where I'll be there for a man to turn on when he's angry or frustrated. I want to keep a little distance."

"Dammit, Jody, I don't *want* to keep my distance. I want to live with you and wake up every morning with you by my side."

"I'm sorry, Doug, but I just can't give you that," Jody said. "Anything else, but not that."

"So what do you suggest we do?" Doug asked dryly. "Have an affair?"

Jody got up and stood before Doug. "That's exactly what I'm suggesting," she said. "We could have the love and the sharing and the commitment, but without the headaches and hassles of being married to one another. We can go places and do things, yet each of us can maintain our independence. It's a great idea for us, Doug."

"The whole thing stinks," he said flatly.

"Why?" Jody demanded.

"For one thing, you have a nine-year-old son who sees quite well and who's very impressionable right now," Doug replied. "I don't think you want him to grow up with the idea that it's all right to have an ongoing relationship that isn't honored by wedding vows."

"I never dreamed you were that uptight," Jody jeered. "That sounds like something out of the Dark

Ages. I thought you were more contemporary than that."

Doug didn't try to hide his irritation. "I've had my share of affairs, Jody, and have nothing against whatever two consenting adults choose to do. But I've never dragged a child into it."

"I didn't plan to make love to you out on the living-room rug," Jody said. "We could be discreet."

"He's not stupid," Doug argued. "He would certainly see and hear enough to figure out what's going on. I'm sorry, Jody, but an affair is out of the question."

"Damn you, you're trying to pressure me into marrying you!" Jody cried. "That's not fair. That's blackmail."

"Pressuring you is the last thing I'm trying to do," Doug said angrily.

"That's sure what this seems like," Jody said hotly. "I don't want to get married, so you retaliate by refusing to have an affair with me."

"No, Jody, that isn't the way it is at all!" Doug said. "I'm not trying to pressure you, but I'm not about to have an affair with you."

"Why not?" Jody demanded.

"Oh, Jody, you're the last woman in New Braunfels who has any business having an affair," Doug said. "You're an honest, moral, and religious woman—you hold dear the values you were taught in church. Look, plenty of people who aren't anywhere as devout as you feel guilty over an affair. You're just too deeply religious to handle it—it goes against your moral code."

"Good old Jody, too fine and upstanding to have an affair," Jody mimicked bitterly.

"I'm sorry if that bothers you, but yes, Jody, you are too fine and upstanding to have a long-term affair,"

Doug said. "It would crush your spirit, not to mention your reputation."

"My spirit would be fine, and my reputation's already in tatters in this town."

"No, your spirit wouldn't be fine, and you're reputation's in good shape compared to what it would be if you and I were to have this affair you think you want," Doug said. "Do you want the rest of the neighborhood to see me leave your place the way Hunter did this morning? Hunter and Marilyn are terrific people and they won't judge us, but a whole lot of people in this town would."

"I don't care," Jody said bravely.

"Well, you better care," Doug said. "We run a business in this town, remember?" He cupped Jody's face between his palms. "It's because I love you that I'm saying no," he said softly.

"No, it's not," Jody said as she pulled away from him. "You just want to get your own way. And that's rotten, Doug. Don't you realize that I'm not just trying to be perverse? I'm frightened, genuinely frightened of getting married again."

"And I've told you that I won't hurt you like Larry did," Doug said. "I mean it, Jody. I'm not settling for an affair."

"And I'm not giving in to emotional blackmail," Jody said. "I can't give you marriage, but I can give you an affair. Please, Doug, don't punish both of us by saying no."

"Dammit, Jody, you're the one who's punishing us, not me!" Doug said, tears shimmering in his eyes. "We could have such a wonderful marriage."

"Yes, and we could have a wonderful relationship without it if you weren't so hardheaded about it!" Jody cried, her own eyes filling with tears. "I mean it, Doug. I won't marry you. It's an affair or nothing."

"No, thanks," Doug said harshly. "If I'd wanted an affair, that's what I would have asked you for." He sniffed, determined not to cry in front of Jody. "Remind me never to fall in love again."

Jody watched in silence as Doug left, two tears running down her cheeks. She had so hoped that he would be willing to have an affair with her! But she should have known that he wouldn't. Doug was basically an honest, forthright person, and he wouldn't want to be party to the deception that would be necessary in New Braunfels in order to have an affair with her. Still, he could have tried harder to understand her point of view. They could have reached some kind of understanding.

Doug wrapped his coat tighter around him and watched as the movers unloaded an old roll-top desk.

"Is it cold enough for you?" one of the movers asked as the wind whipped around them.

"Yes, for a first norther this one is a doozy," Doug said as he stared up at the leaden gray clouds. It would mean cold camping for him and Scott, but at least the deer would be running.

"Hey, do you really think you can get anybody to buy this?" the mover asked as he carried off an old brass coatrack.

"Don't worry—somebody will think it's the most wonderful thing he's ever seen," Doug assured the mover. Irritated by the man's constant chatter, he stepped into the building and poured himself a cup of coffee. He watched from the door of the store as they carried down an old spool bed that was badly in need of refinishing, and glanced around to see Hunter coming through the front door.

"Hi Hunter. What can I do for you?" he asked.

"I'm finally here to see the organ Jody's been holding for me for the last month," Hunter said. "I told her a couple of times to go ahead and put it out, but she insisted that I have first refusal."

"You better be glad she held it," Doug said. "The rest of that furniture's long gone."

Hunter followed Doug back to the storeroom where Doug uncovered the organ and pulled the seat up. "Here, try it," he said.

Hunter pumped the pedals and hit a few keys. "I guess it sounds all right," he said as he tried a few of the stops. "How would I know?"

"I heard Jody playing a one-fingered tune on it one afternoon," Doug said. "It sounds fine."

Hunter looked at the organ wistfully. "I wish I could get it for Marilyn," he said. "But money's awfully tight right now, with another little one on the way."

"Jody wanted you to have it at cost," Doug said, crossing his fingers behind his back and knocking fifty dollars off what they had paid for it.

Hunter's eyes widened. "Is that all? I can afford that!"

"Good. We can deliver it the week of Christmas," Doug said.

Hunter made a small down payment and met Jody coming in the door. "I'm getting Marilyn the organ. Oh, Jody, thanks for holding it!" Hunter said as he hugged her and kissed her cheek, his eyes sparkling. "She's wanted one all her life."

Jody smiled. "I'm glad you're happy with it, Hunter."

Hunter fairly danced out the door.

"I knocked fifty dollars off our cost," Doug said quietly. "If that's not all right, I can make it up out of my own pocket. He's been a real friend to us," he added defensively.

162

"You don't have to justify your kindness to me—I would have done the same thing," Jody said shortly.

Doug followed her into the office. "Is Scott all packed?" he asked.

"Not quite. I'll have him ready by eight or so." Doug had a deer lease just a few miles out in the country, and it would take him and Scott less than an hour to get there.

"Be sure to pack him some warm clothes," Doug said. "It's going to be cold camping."

"All right." Jody looked over at Doug, wondering if the tension between them would ever dissipate. "Why don't you go on home and get your packing done? I'll finish up here."

"I'll do that."

Doug shook his head as he got into his car. It had been weeks since Jody had told him that she wouldn't marry him, and it still hurt him just as badly as it had the first day. He had gone home that night and cried, really cried, for the first time since he had been a child. In a way, he could understand her bitterness and her reluctance, but why couldn't she let herself learn to trust him? That was what hurt him so badly.

Doug had made no attempt to hide his feelings of hurt and bitterness, nor had Jody made any attempt to hide hers, and their relationship had become very strained. They were carefully polite in front of customers and short with one another when they were alone. Doug had continued to see Scott, but Jody had declined to join them on any of their outings. Doug wondered if Scott could sense a change in his and Jody's relationship and wondered what he could say to the boy if he asked any questions.

Jody finished up at the store and drove home slowly in the gathering dusk. She wished there was

163

something she could do to ease the strain between her and Doug. They had gotten to the point where they could barely be civil to one another, and Jody wished that they could go back to the relationship they had shared before their argument. But she wasn't about to tell Doug that she would marry him, and she couldn't see him relenting, either.

Jody picked Scott up at his babysitter's. "Mom, is Uncle Doug ready yet?" he asked as he bounced up and down in the front seat.

"I imagine so," Jody said. "He said he would pick you up about eight."

"That's super!" Scott said. "Are you coming too?"

"Heavens, no," Jody said, hoping her laugh sounded casual. "Moms don't go hunting."

"Ryan's mom goes, and I heard you tell Uncle Hunter that you and my father used to go sometimes."

"That was a long time ago, Scott. Besides, you and Uncle Doug need some time alone together."

"But you never go anywhere with Uncle Doug and me anymore," Scott observed. "You used to go all the time. What happened? Did you and Uncle Doug have a fight or something?"

Didn't we, though, Jody thought. "No, Scott, we didn't have a fight. Everything's the same as it ever was with your Uncle Doug and me," Jody reassured him.

"It doesn't seem like it," Scott complained.

Jody was just packing the last of Scott's sweaters when Doug knocked on the door. "All ready, sport?" he asked as Scott bounced around the entry.

"Here's his duffel bag, all packed," Jody said. Scott had insisted on using one of Doug's old duffel bags instead of a suitcase. "I put in some long johns for him to sleep in. Is that warm enough?"

164

"I'm sure that will be fine," Doug assured her. Their fingers brushed together as Doug took the duffel bag from Jody, and she jerked her hand back as though it were scalded.

Jody turned to Scott. "Scott, you and Uncle Doug are going to be using real guns that could kill you if they aren't used properly. You do everything he tells you to, all right?"

"I promise, Mom," Scott assured her.

Jody bent down and planted a motherly kiss on his forehead. "Be careful," she said quietly. "I love you like the dickens."

"I love you too, Mom," Scott said as he kissed her cheek quickly.

Doug watched mother and son, and love swelled in his heart for them both. Damn, he wanted to take care of them, but Jody was too bitter or frightened— he wasn't quite sure which—to let him do that. How could she turn him away when he loved her so much?

Jody turned to Doug. "Take care of him," she said.

Doug nodded. "We'll be back late Sunday afternoon. Think the shop will survive without me?"

"If I get desperate I'll send up a flare," Jody said. "Have a good time."

She watched as Doug drove away into the night. She hadn't missed the way Scott had tucked his hand into Doug's as they walked to the car. He would make a wonderful father for Scott, she thought before she could stop herself. Firmly pushing that idea from her mind, she curled up on the couch and buried her nose in the latest paperback novel about the lives of the rich and famous, reading the evening away.

165

"That's right, Scott, look down the barrel of the gun," Doug said quietly as Scott squinted into the scope of the rifle. "Can you see the deer?"

Scott nodded slightly.

"Aim the crossbars directly at the animal's heart, and squeeze the trigger, don't pull it," Doug coached.

Scott aimed at the small buck, but the animal pricked up its ears and bounded away before he could pull the trigger. "He ran off," the boy said disappointedly.

"There'll be another one along later," Doug said encouragingly. Scott had proven to be a good camper, and Doug hoped that the child would have a deer to bring back tomorrow.

"But what about you? You should have taken a shot at it, not me," Scott said.

"Like I said, Scott, there's always tomorrow," Doug said. "Say, it's getting up in the morning. Why don't we go back to camp and I'll make us scrambled eggs and bacon?" Doug and Scott had gotten up before daybreak and had spent most of the morning in the deer blind.

"That sounds good. I'm hungry," Scott admitted.

After they put away an entire skillet of eggs, Scott laid down on his sleeping bag to rest for "just a minute." He was out like a light in no time, and Doug got out the paperback he had brought along. He had made it through two grisly murders and three steamy love scenes by the time Scott awakened.

"Have a nice nap?" Doug teased.

Scott yawned. "Yeah, I did," he said. "When can we go out to the blind again?"

"Late this afternoon," Doug said, explaining that the deer rested in the middle of the day and grazed early in the morning and late in the afternoon.

Scott had armed himself with a stack of comic books, but he began to get restless a little while later.

"Come on, wiggler, let's get in some target practice," Doug finally said. The deer blind was almost a mile away, and what the heck if the shots did scare off the deer? This trip was for Scott, anyway.

Doug set a coffee can on a rock thirty feet away. "Let's see how many times you can hit it," he called to Scott.

Scott hit the can three times out of four. "That's great, Scott," he said. "Let's make it a little harder." He moved the can farther away.

Scott was only able to hit the target about forty percent of the time at that distance. He in turn was suitably awed when Doug hit the can six times in a row. "Wow, did you shoot guns in the navy?"

"Sort of," Doug said. "At one time I was a gunner. I shot one of those big guns that are mounted on deck."

"That's neat!" Scott said. Doug fixed them a late lunch while Scott plied him with questions about life in the navy.

They spent the late afternoon and early evening in the deer blind but didn't even see a fawn. "Maybe there will be some tomorrow," Doug said as a disappointed Scott climbed down from the deer blind.

"I hope so," Scott said. "But if there aren't any, that's all right too."

Doug ruffled Scott's hair. "Good sport," he said approvingly.

Doug lit a lantern and hung it on the tent, then made smoked sausages and canned sauerkraut for dinner. The wind whistled through the trees that surrounded them, but in front of the fire it was warm.

"I hope you like sauerkraut," Doug said as he handed Scott his plate. "I'm sorry it's canned."

"I didn't know it came any other way," Scott said.

Doug shook his head and laughed. "I guess you never got to eat any of your grandmother Ford's homemade sauerkraut, did you? She died the year before you were born."

"Oh, that's right—Mom said something once about grandmother Ford's sauerkraut."

"Your father never mentioned it?" Doug asked.

"Naw, my father never talked much to me," Scott admitted.

"Did he ever tell you that the family's real name was Friedrich, or that we came over from Germany in 1870?"

Scott appeared interested, so Doug told him about his ancestors, the hardworking German family who had founded the ranch that was in the family for so many years before it had gone under with Larry. Scott asked a few questions and was willing to talk about the early Friedrichs, although he was careful not to mention his father specifically. When Doug had about exhausted that subject, he casually brought up the topic of school, asking Scott how things were going.

"Things are going super," he said. "Mrs. Wilson's nice, only she grades math papers pretty hard. And she's always standing at the door before school flirting with Mr. Evans across the hall."

"Oh, really?" Doug asked, his eyes twinkling.

"Yeah, and Angie Navarro took the library book that I wanted, and I would have hit her too, except that I found another copy of the book."

Doug raised his eyes from his plate. "You would have hit her, Scott?" he asked. "Just for taking a library book?"

"Well, sure," he said. "She took the book that I wanted, and that way I could get the book back."

"Scott, don't you realize that you're not supposed to hit people when they get in your way a little?" Doug asked gently. "That's not the way to deal with your frustration."

"I don't see why not," Scott said.

"Because it doesn't work," Doug said. "It just gets you in trouble, like it did when you hit Tony Villanueva."

"But Uncle Doug, what am I supposed to do?" Scott asked. "I mean, am I supposed to let people do whatever they feel like doing to me?"

"No, of course not. But did you ever think that it might be better to just ask for what you want, rather than hitting to get your way?"

Scott shrugged. "I do ask sometimes. I asked Angie, and she said no, that she wanted the book. But I had picked it out first and laid it on the table."

"Scott, I can understand why you would have been upset with Angie for taking your book, but if you hadn't found another one like it, don't you think it would be better for you to say something to the teacher?"

"No. Angie's the teacher's pet. The only way I could have gotten the book back would have been to hit her," Scott explained with his twisted reasoning.

"But what about Angie? What about her feelings? Don't you think it would hurt her when you hit her?" Doug persisted.

"She should have thought about that when she took the book in the first place," Scott said. Bored with the conversation, Scott changed the topic to what he wanted for Christmas.

Much later that night, Doug lay in his sleeping bag and stared into the sleeping face of his nephew. At times, talking to Scott was like talking to a brick wall. He simply couldn't see that hitting others just to get

169

his way or to relieve his frustration with them was wrong. In Scott's mind, the end justified the means, however harsh the measures were. Doug tried to remember if Larry had ever hit others just to get his way. Yes, he could remember a few occasions when Larry was Scott's age that Larry had displayed the same attitude Scott was showing. But Larry had grown out of that, and Doug had thought no more of it until now.

But what if there were a link? What if Larry's behavior as a child was related in some way to his violent treatment of Jody later? If it was, then Scott ran the risk of having the same kind of violent tendencies that had broken Larry's marriage and hurt his wife. Doug shuddered at the thought of the same thing happening to Scott. Jody was wrong to think that his companionship was all Scott needed to straighten out. Scott needed professional help, and he needed it soon, while he was still young and impressionable. Doug somehow had to convince Jody of that before it was too late for Scott. He sighed in the darkness and closed his eyes. He was going to have to talk to Jody, though he didn't think she was going to be receptive to what he had to say.

CHAPTER TEN

Jody looked up from the newspaper when she heard Doug's car pull up in the driveway. She opened the front door as Scott jumped out of the car.

"Mom, Uncle Doug shot a deer!" he said excitedly as he hugged her.

"Good for Uncle Doug," Jody said as she kissed Scott's cheek. "I gather you had a good time."

"Yeah, we had a great time," Scott said. "I had one in the scope yesterday, but it wandered off before I could shoot it."

"That's all right, maybe you'll have another chance next time," she said. "Congratulations, Doug," she added as she wandered closer to the deer that was tied onto Doug's fender. "That's a pretty nice set of antlers for this part of the country." She inspected the rack closely. "Are you going to have it mounted?"

"I might," Doug said. "Do you know a good taxidermist?"

Jody told him the name of one that she knew of as Scott unloaded his duffel bag.

"If you'll come over around nine or ten, you can have several packages of meat," Doug said. "I'm going to butcher it myself while it's still fresh."

Jody wrinkled her nose. "Not before nine or ten, huh?" She had seen animals butchered before and had helped with a couple, and she could think of a lot of things that were more appealing.

"Do you even want the meat?" Doug asked. "I'd hate to waste it."

"Sure, I want the meat!" Jody said. "I love it. All nicely wrapped up in clean freezer paper."

"I'll have you some by nine or ten," Doug promised. He put his hand on Scott's shoulder. "Scott actually spotted this one before I did, so it's partly his deer."

"I just couldn't have hit it that far away," Scott explained.

Jody fixed her and Scott hamburgers for supper. Scott, tired out by his hunting trip, was soon bathed and asleep in his bedroom, leaving Jody alone with her thoughts. Although she had seen a lot of Doug since their argument, it was always at the store and never in his home or hers. She had lain awake more nights than one, reliving the glorious night she had spent in Doug's arms, and she wondered if he remembered it the way she did.

Jody waited until nearly ten before she walked across the street. The door was open and she made her way into Doug's kitchen, where Doug was packing a number of neatly wrapped packages of meat into a grocery sack. The kitchen was clean and Doug was freshly showered, his hair still damp. Jody had to fight the urge to put her arms around him and kiss him senseless.

"Did you get finished already?" Jody asked.

"I've done everything except take a little of it in to be made into sausage," Doug said. "I think it's going to be delicious. If you soak it in milk, you can take out most of the wild taste."

"Wine works too," Jody said. "Thanks for the meat."

"Jody, would you like a cup of coffee?" Doug asked. "I need to talk to you for a few minutes."

"Do you have decaffeinated?"

Doug nodded and made them each a cup of instant coffee from a pot of hot water he had on the stove. They sat down at the table and Jody sipped her coffee, hoping that Doug was going to tell her that he had changed his mind about the affair.

"What did you want to talk about?" she finally asked.

"Scott," Doug said.

"Did he misbehave on the trip?" Jody asked.

"No, he was quite well behaved," Doug said. "But Jody, Scott and I talked for a long time after supper last night, and some of the things he said to me have me worried about him."

"Go on," Jody said quietly.

"We were talking about school, and when Scott said he almost hit a little girl last week, we got to talking about hitting. Have you ever talked to him about that?"

"Of course I have," Jody replied. "You've even heard me—twice, as I recall. You know I discipline him, Doug."

"I know that you discipline him," Doug said quickly. "But have you ever talked to him about it when you weren't angry?"

Jody thought a minute. "No, I guess I haven't. Why? What did he tell you?"

"Well, Scott's under the impression that it's all right to hit someone if they do something to you, or if it gets you something you want. The only reason he didn't hit the girl last week was because he found a second copy of the library book that he wanted. If he hadn't, you'd have been back up to the school."

173

"Scott doesn't think that!" Jody protested. "He hasn't been brought up that way."

"You haven't brought him up that way, but Scott did see violence at a young and impressionable age. There's no telling what it left him thinking."

"But he hasn't hit anyone for over two months," Jody said.

"Maybe nobody's made him mad enough yet," Doug suggested. "Jody, I wish you would reconsider and take Scott to a professional—someone who's trained in dealing with disturbed youngsters."

"Dammit, Doug, that's ridiculous!" Jody snapped. "He hasn't hit anybody, has he? Not since you started spending some time with him. You were all he needed, Doug. He doesn't need a shrink."

"Just because he hasn't hit anyone in the last two months doesn't mean that it won't happen again. I'm telling you, the boy sees nothing wrong with hitting someone when he thinks they've done something to him, or when he's frustrated in some way. He thinks they have it coming. That's a dangerous attitude to have, Jody, because society doesn't put up with it. Besides, Larry used to feel that way too, and look how he turned out."

"Stop comparing Scott to Larry!"

"Why shouldn't I compare Scott to Larry? You compare me to Larry, don't you?"

Jody recoiled as though he had struck her. "My son is not like his father, nor does he need to see a psychiatrist," she said. "Perhaps he does feel as you say. If he does, it's because of the example that was set for him, and you and I can rectify that. I'll see you in the morning."

Jody's shoulders were rigid with anger as she walked back across the street. She was tired of Doug's insinuations about Scott. The child was all right. He didn't need a psychiatrist. He hadn't hit anyone for over two months. There was nothing wrong with the boy, nothing at all.

"Well, I tried," Doug muttered under his breath as he watched Jody carry her meat across the street. He had done what he could, and Jody had rejected his advice, just as he had suspected she would. He just couldn't understand her at times. She wouldn't marry him because she thought he was like his violent brother, yet she refused to see the violence in her own son. Doug sat down in his easy chair and shook his head, wondering what kind of behavior it would take on Scott's part to convince his mother that he really did have a problem.

Doug continued to see Scott regularly, as he had been doing, hoping that he was wrong about his nephew but knowing that he wasn't. They spent a quiet Thanksgiving with Hunter and Marilyn, and Doug watched ruefully as Scott played patiently with Rachel on the floor. Scott wasn't a bad child, Doug thought, he was just confused. Doug decided that he would try to see Scott more often, but the minute Thanksgiving was over the Christmas rush started at the store, and he and Jody found themselves swamped at work. There was no way Doug could see any more of the child, in spite of his good intentions.

"What do you think of this?" Jody asked as she showed Mrs. Borrer a blue porcelain vase.

The elderly woman touched the vase with a veined hand. "It's lovely," she said. "But are you sure it's really antique? Georgina likes things that are quite old, you know." Mrs. Borrer's daughter-in-law had an extensive collection of glassware, most of which was over a hundred years old.

175

"I can vouch for it," Jody said. She turned it over and pointed to a signature and a date. "See?"

"Not with these old eyes, but you can bet Georgina will be able to!" Mrs. Borrer laughed. "You know, I love my daughter-in-law, but she can be a bit of a snob. Insists on only the best."

"Maybe that's why she married your son," Jody said. "Shall I wrap this for you?"

Jody boxed the vase and wrapped it in bright Christmas paper. "Is there anyone else on your list?"

"No, my granddaughters all want clothes with a fancy label on them." Mrs. Borrer sighed. "I just give Georgina the money and let her buy them the things they want. They love what she gets them, so I guess it's all right."

Doug poked his head in the door. "Jody, are you— oh, hi, Mrs. Borrer, how are you?" he asked. He wiped his grimy hand on a handkerchief and offered her his hand.

"I'm just fine, Doug," she said. "Are you looking forward to Christmas?"

"Oh, I guess," he said.

"Spending it with Jody and Scott, I bet," she said.

Jody and Doug glanced at one another. "I—we—"

"Jody and I haven't made our plans this far ahead," Doug said smoothly. "But whatever we do, we'll think of you that day. Will you be with your son and his family?"

Mrs. Borrer chatted happily with Doug while Jody rang up the sale. Doug held the door for her and wished her a Merry Christmas, even though it was only the first week of December and a bit early.

Jody looked up from the counter when Doug walked by. "Have you made plans yet for Christmas?" she asked quietly.

176

"Not really," Doug said nonchalantly as the telephone rang. "You get that. We can talk later."

Jody shot him a dirty look and picked up the telephone. "Ford's Antiques."

"Is this Jody Ford?" a terse voice snapped.

"Yes."

"This is Lloyd Greer, your son's principal. Scott's been in another fight. I'd like to see you right away."

Jody banged the telephone down and ran to the back. "Doug, I have to go over to the school," she said. "Scott's in trouble again."

"I'm coming with you."

"You can't come, you're covered with varnish," Jody said. "I can handle it," she added tightly.

Why, Scott, why? she cried inwardly as she drove toward the school. She had taught him right from wrong. She hadn't brought him up to be mean to others. Why did he act like this toward other children? What was she, his mother, doing wrong?

Jody hurried into the school. "I'm supposed to see the principal," she said to the secretary.

"Yes, ma'am," she said as she opened the counter and Jody entered Mr. Greer's office. She gasped when she saw Ryan Bohannon sitting there beside Suzanne. He was crying and had scratches on his face and the beginnings of a black eye. Suzanne looked furious, and Scott sat in the corner looking sullen.

"Scott, how could you?" Jody demanded. "Ryan's your best friend!"

"He took my Gobot away from me," Scott said belligerently. "The one you gave me for my birthday. I told him he couldn't play with it, but he took it anyway."

"Didn't you ask him to give it back?" Jody asked.

"He said he would give it back later," Scott said. "He had no right to take away my Gobot."

"I would have given it back," Ryan cried. "Mom, my eye hurts."

"I'm sure it does," Suzanne said gently. She looked up at Jody and Scott angrily. "Scott knew that Ryan couldn't defend himself," she said coldly.

Jody looked at Ryan and her own son and her temper erupted. "Damn you, Scott, how could you do that to your own best friend! Don't you give a damn about him? You really hurt him!" She jerked Scott up and made him stand in front of Ryan. "Take a good look at him, Scott. Is that the way you treat people that you love?"

"I'm not so bad!" Scott yelled back. "Daddy loved you and he hit you, didn't he?"

The three adults in the room were equally stunned. Jody released Scott and sat down before her trembling legs gave way. "Scott, we talked about that at the shelter. We said that what Daddy did was wrong. Don't you remember?"

"But you said that Daddy wasn't a bad man," Scott said as he started to cry. "You said that he loved you in spite of what he did." The child's shoulders started to shake. "I love Ryan, really. I didn't want to hurt him."

Jody's eyes swam with tears as she reached out for her son. "Scott, it's wrong to hit people we love." She looked helplessly at Suzanne and Mr. Greer.

"Jody, we had no idea," Suzanne whispered in horror. "Is that where you were for the two months you were gone?"

"I was letting my broken nose heal and getting my teeth capped," Jody admitted painfully as Scott sobbed in her arms.

"Oh, God," Suzanne said quietly. "Mr. Greer, I'm going to take Ryan on home and patch him up a little.

Call me later, Jody. I don't want the boys to stop being friends."

Jody swallowed back more tears as Suzanne shut the door behind them. "She's a bigger woman than I would be under the circumstances," she told Mr. Greer quietly.

"Yes, Mrs. Bohannon is a wonderful woman," he said.

Scott lifted his head. "I guess Ryan will never speak to me again," he said tearfully.

"I don't know, Scott," Jody said, thinking that Ryan might not be as willing as his mother to resume the friendship.

"Scott, I have to talk to your mother alone for a little while," Mr. Greer said. "Will you sit down in one of the chairs outside the door?"

"What's going to happen to me?" he asked anxiously.

"Just let me talk to your mother," Mr. Greer urged.

He waited until Scott was out of the room. "I wish you had told me about this last fall," he said quietly. "The knowledge that Scott has been exposed to family violence sheds a completely different light on his behavior."

"That's not the kind of thing I'm willing to tell the world," Jody said tightly.

"But Mrs. Ford, don't you realize how severely children are affected by violence in the family? It takes years for them to get over it, if they ever do. It affects them socially, it affects their relationships with their peers—it even affects them years later when they're married. You should have said something the first time he got in trouble. We could have taken steps with him then to help him. We could have warned his teachers—"

"That's just the point. I didn't want his teachers to

know!" Jody said. "I didn't want them thinking that Scott came from a troubled home, and I don't want it to get out all over town."

"Our teachers know some things more shocking than your situation, and they're not out spreading it all over town," Mr. Greer said gently. "Mrs. Ford, we're here to help. And now that we know what the problem is, we can. But we can't do it alone. It's gone too far."

"What should I do?" Jody asked quietly. "His uncle is spending a lot of time with him. Won't that help?"

"Of course, if the uncle is a positive role model. But in my professional estimation, Scott needs more than either his uncle or the school can do for him." Mr. Greer jotted a name and a telephone number on a piece of paper. "George Blundell and I were roommates in college. He's one of the best child psychiatrists in Austin."

"A psychiatrist?" Jody asked in horror. "My child isn't crazy!"

"No, but right now he's terribly confused, Mrs. Ford. You heard him this morning. He honestly doesn't know whether what he did was right or wrong. I can't force you to take him, of course. But I'll tell you this: If he were my son, I'd have him up there fast."

Mr. Greer suggested that Scott would be better off spending the rest of the day in school, and Jody drove back to the store in a daze.

"What happened?" Doug demanded as she walked through the door.

"He beat Ryan Bohannon up," she said. Tears welled up in her eyes and she let them spill over. "Oh, Doug, he beat Ryan up over a Gobot! He gave Ryan a black eye over a ten-dollar toy!"

180

"Here, sit down and tell me about it," Doug said as he led her to her office. "What happened?"

Jody sank down in a chair. "Oh, the boys tied up over the Gobot and Ryan wouldn't give it back, so Scott started in on him. By the time the teacher got them separated, he had given Ryan quite a shiner."

Doug shook his head. "I knew it was only a matter of time, Jody," he said quietly. "Did you go in there and defend him again?"

"No. I lost my temper with Scott and started yelling at him, and he blurted out that he wasn't so bad, that Daddy used to hit me and he wasn't a bad person. So now Suzanne and Ryan know what happened, and I guess Mr. Greer will tell it all over the school. He was mad that I didn't tell him one of the other two times Scott hit someone."

"It's happened twice before?"

"Yes, he got in a fight once last spring, before you moved back. Anyway, Mr. Greer thinks I should have told him then."

"You should have," Doug agreed.

"Sure," Jody scoffed. "Scott's teacher last year was Jeannie Stewart, and she has the biggest mouth in New Braunfels. I hope his teacher this year doesn't."

"Jody, they're under professional confidence, the same as Hunter," Doug said. "Those teachers aren't going to gossip about you."

Jody leaned back and closed her eyes. "It's bad enough that they know," she said. "And Suzanne—how can I ever face her again?"

"Oh, Jody, don't feel that way," Doug said.

"Doug, what am I doing wrong?" she asked, anguish in her voice as she looked at him pleadingly. "I tried so hard to be a good wife to Larry, and he hit me, and I've tried so hard to be a good mother to Scott, and he hits everybody else! Why?"

181

Jody buried her head in her hands and sobbed. She felt Doug sit down beside her and take her into his arms, cradling her head on his shoulder. "Hush, Jody, it's not your fault," he soothed. "It's not your fault that Larry hit you, and you're a wonderful mother."

Jody raised tearful eyes to Doug. "Then why?"

He reached down and wiped the tears from her cheek. "I don't know why," he said gently. He got a handkerchief out of his pocket and wiped her face. "Now, you sit here for a minute and calm down, and I'll go out and get us some hamburgers for lunch," he said. "We can talk some more while we eat."

"I'm not hungry," she protested as Doug stood up.

"You need to eat a little," Doug said firmly. "I'll be right back."

Doug was back a short time later with hamburgers from the best drive-in in town. Jody sniffed appreciatively and got them each a Coke from the refrigerator.

"The burger does smell good," she said.

Doug handed her a burger and took a big bite out of the other one. "What did Suzanne say when she found out about Larry?" he asked.

"She said that she didn't want the boys to stop being friends," Jody said. "She was very kind."

"See? She doesn't hold Larry's behavior against you or Scott," Doug said.

"I know, but it's still embarrassing to me that she knows," Jody admitted.

"What else did the principal say?" Doug asked gently.

Jody swallowed. "He said that Scott needs professional help. He gave me the name of a child psychiatrist in Austin."

"Now do you believe me?"

"All right, I admit that you were right and that I

was wrong," Jody said a little sharply. "Does that satisfy you?"

Doug raised his eyebrow. "I didn't realize that this was a contest," he said mildly. "I thought we were talking about the welfare of your son."

"Doug, I'm sorry," Jody said quietly. "But it hurts to have to admit that there's something wrong with your child."

"Jody, there may not be anything seriously wrong with him at this stage," Doug said. "But he is confused right now."

"I saw that this afternoon," Jody admitted.

"And if you don't get him some help now, he could very well end up like Larry," Doug pressed on. "Think about it this way: Do you want him to end up as unhappy as Larry was at the end? Do you want him to make another innocent woman as unhappy as Larry made you?"

"Of course not," Jody mumbled.

"So take Scott to the doctor. There's no shame or stigma attached to it. Didn't you say you tried to get Larry to see one? It's no more shameful for Scott to go than it would have been for Larry."

"Oh, I know all that," Jody said. "At least, I know it in my head. Sometimes I don't know it in my heart." She took the paper out of her purse. "I guess I better call and make an appointment."

Doug smiled his approval as Jody dialed the number. She was surprised when the receptionist put her straight through to the doctor, who sounded very calm and competent over the telephone. Briefly, Jody explained the problem and gave Lloyd Greer as a reference, and Dr. Blundell suggested that she plan to bring Scott to Austin the following Wednesday, so the child would have time to get used to the idea of talking to a psychiatrist. He also arranged for Jody to

183

talk with him before Scott did so that she could fill him in completely on what had happened in the past. Jody winced when he told her his fee, and she was glad they weren't face-to-face so he could see her dismay. She thanked Dr. Blundell and hung up the telephone.

"Well, there goes the new water heater," she said dryly.

"Check your insurance," Doug said. "It might be covered."

"I doubt it, I carry the low-option coverage." Jody got out her policy and scanned it. "No, it won't pay a penny."

"Jody, let me help," Doug said. "That old water heater of yours is dangerous, and Scott needs the doctor."

"No, I'll pay for it," Jody said. "He's my responsibility. Besides, it may run into the thousands. You don't have that kind of money."

"You have less than I do," Doug argued. "Either you let me pick up part of the tab, or you let me get you a new water heater."

Jody argued, but Doug was adamant. She finally gave in and let him buy her the water heater, provided it proved to cost less than Scott's doctor bill.

"You are one hard-headed woman," Doug said when he had finally gotten her to agree to accept his help.

"You think I'm hard-headed, you ought to try to convince Scott of something," Jody said. "I'm not looking forward to talking to him tonight."

"Would you like some support?" Doug asked quietly. "Sometimes someone other than a parent can get a child to agree to things a parent can't."

"Sure, I can use all the support I can get," Jody admitted.

Scott was very quiet and subdued when Jody picked him up at school. Jody said nothing to him about her discussions with Doug or Mr. Greer and let him disappear into his room, as he usually did when something was troubling him. Jody half-listened to the news as she cooked supper for them and Doug. She had asked Doug at the last minute to come over and eat with them so that it wouldn't seem like he had come over just to talk to Scott about Dr. Blundell. *Oh, please, Scott,* she thought, *please agree to talk to the doctor. You don't want to end up like your father did.*

Doug knocked once before letting himself in. "How is he?" he asked. He wanted to take Jody into his arms and kiss her, but except for those few moments in her office this morning, he hadn't taken her into his arms since they had made love, and he wasn't sure how she would react. But he ached to comfort her, to reassure her that everything was going to be all right.

"He's been very quiet," she admitted. "I'm sure he was upset by what he did today. He cried this morning in Mr. Greer's office and said that he hadn't meant to hurt Ryan."

"You know, he might be ready to talk to someone," he said thoughtfully, "if he was that upset by what happened."

Doug set the table and watched Jody as she finished frying the chicken. He couldn't say that he had missed actually seeing Jody this last month, but he had missed their easy, loving companionship, and their one night together had only made him long for her that much more. He thought that she probably missed what they had shared as much as he did. But had she changed her mind about marriage? Maybe

185

he could talk to her this evening after Scott had gone to bed. Maybe if he approached it differently . . .

"Doug, could you go up and get Scott?" Jody asked. "Supper will be ready once this gravy thickens."

Scott opened his door warily, but Doug only smiled at him. "Come on down, your mom has dinner ready," he said.

Scott returned Doug's smile and followed him down the stairs. He retreated into silence, however, leaving Doug and Jody to do most of the talking during dinner. Scott finished quickly and asked to be excused.

"Scott, would you stick around a few more minutes?" Doug asked quietly. "There's something your mother and I need to talk to you about."

"I knew it—you're going to yell at me," Scott mumbled.

"No, Scott, if I was going to yell at you, I would have done it already," Jody said. "Why don't you catch the last few minutes of that game show you like while Doug and I finish eating?"

Jody and Doug finished dinner, and Jody left the plates on the table. They joined Scott in the living room just as the credits were rolling on the game show. Jody switched off the television and they both sat down. "Scott, we need to talk about what happened at school today," Jody said gently.

"Do we have to?" he asked. "I already said I was sorry that I hurt Ryan. I feel rotten about it."

"Scott, sometimes feeling rotten about something isn't enough," Doug said.

"I knew you were going to punish me," Scott grumbled.

"No, we're not going to do that," Jody said. "But we are worried about you. This is the fourth time in

186

less than a year that you've hit someone smaller than you."

"But I didn't mean to hurt any of them!" Scott protested. "It's just that they either took or broke things that were mine!" Tears welled up in his eyes. "Does that make me a bad person, Uncle Doug? 'Cause if it does, then my daddy was a bad person too."

"Do you think about your dad a lot, Scott?" Doug asked.

Scott nodded. "I think about him all the time. Sometimes I like what I remember about him and sometimes I hate him."

Doug and Jody both tried to hide their dismay. "You know, Scott, those are pretty big feelings for a boy your age to have to handle on your own," Doug said. "And your mom and I can't really help you with them. But there's a doctor in Austin who could."

"I don't want to talk to a doctor," Scott said quickly.

"But, Scott, he could help you," Jody said.

"I know you don't want to talk to a doctor, but I think you really need to," Doug said gently. "It's not going to be easy to tell a stranger all about your father and how you feel about him and what he did, but if you don't, you're going to keep on hitting people and getting into trouble, or hurting your friends like you did today."

"I'm not a bad person!" he protested.

"Scott, nobody's saying that you're a bad person," Jody soothed. "But you're confused, honey, or you wouldn't keep hitting others and hurting them."

"Scott, think a minute. Do you remember after the second time your father hit your mother? Didn't she ask him to talk to someone about what was happening?" Doug asked gently.

Scott nodded. "She asked him to go and see a psychiatrist. He wouldn't go."

"And he hit me again, and I took you and left him," Jody said. "And then he started drinking too much and crashed his car." She looked Scott straight in the eye. "If he had gone and talked to the psychiatrist when I asked him to, he might not have hit me that third time, and I might not have left him, and he might not have died."

"I'm gonna die if I don't go?" Scott asked in alarm.

"No, I didn't mean that," Jody said hastily. "I just meant that if you don't get help now, you're always going to be hitting people and getting into trouble."

"We're not trying to punish you or embarrass you," Doug assured him. "We're just trying to prevent you from the same sadness that your father went through."

"What's the doctor's name?" Scott asked suspiciously.

"George Blundell, and he's one of the best," Doug assured Scott. "How about it? Will you talk to him?"

"I don't want to, but I will," Scott said gruffly.

"That's good, Scott," Jody said.

"I think you'll be glad you went," Doug added.

Scott plied them with questions for the next half-hour about what to expect. They answered him as best they could but had to admit to him that they didn't know much more than he did about it. They reassured him that it wouldn't be an unpleasant experience and that the doctor would be very nice.

"It's getting late," Jody said finally. "Scott, let's get you ready for bed. Go take your bath, and I'll be up in a few minutes."

When Scott had climbed the stairs, Jody said, "Doug, thanks for coming. I don't know if I could have convinced him alone."

"I think you could have, but I'm glad I could help," he said. "Here, let me give you a hand in the kitchen."

Jody protested, but Doug insisted that it was the least he could do after such a delicious dinner. They shared a companionable silence as they worked, and Jody found herself wishing desperately that she and Doug could have continued their affair. There would have been many evenings like this one, with her and Doug and Scott spending time together. She loved Doug and she wanted his love and his companionship in her life. But enough to marry him? Jody shuddered inwardly. She didn't think she could go that far.

Jody put Scott to bed, her heart breaking inside as he prayed for God to make him a better boy. She found Doug waiting for her in the living room with two glasses of wine.

"I don't know about you, but I could use one about now," he said as he handed her one.

Jody sat down next to Doug on the couch. "Thank you. This is just what I need." She took a sip.

"Jody, we haven't talked, not really, for the last month."

"I know," she murmured.

"I shouldn't have gotten mad like I did," he said softly. "I should have talked to you more about it."

"I wish you had," Jody admitted. "I thought about trying to talk to you, but I couldn't bring myself to do it."

"Can we talk now?" Doug asked.

"I guess so."

"Have you thought any more about marrying me?" he asked. "I know now that I didn't go about things the right way last month, but I was really hurt."

189

"I know that, Doug," Jody said quietly. She reached out and stroked his hand. "I hated hurting you."

"Thank you for that," he said. "Have you thought any more about what I asked you?"

"Every day," Jody said honestly. "Have you thought any more about what I want?"

"Some," Doug admitted. "But what about you—do you still not want to marry me?"

Jody looked at Doug, anguish in her eyes. "I love you very much, and I hate making you unhappy. But the thought of getting married, of making that kind of intimate and binding commitment makes me want to throw up. Literally. I'm that afraid of it."

"Oh," Doug said flatly.

"What about you?" Jody asked. "How do you feel about having a love affair without getting married?"

"I still don't want to," Doug said honestly. "I don't think it's the right thing for us."

Jody's face fell. "I guess that's that."

"There has to be a way we can work this out!" Doug cried in frustration. He took Jody by the shoulders and pulled her close to him. "There has to be a way for us," he murmured as his lips met hers.

There has to be a way, Jody thought over and over as she and Doug kissed one another eagerly. They were like people dying of thirst as they clung to one another, their mouths and their bodies molded together in anguished passion. Jody could feel desire rising in her as Doug pressed his hard, firm chest against hers. Their hearts pounded together in a frenzied rhythm, frustration and need mixed together in their fevered embrace. There had to be a way for them to share the beautiful feelings that they had for one another, to experience the caring and giving that they had found before.

Doug groaned as he pushed Jody away. "We have to stop this," he gasped. "Scott's upstairs."

"Oh, Doug, I—"

Doug silenced Jody with a hard, sweet kiss. "I'll see you tomorrow," he said. "Do you want me to go to Austin with you next Wednesday? We can get Beatrice to stay with the store."

"Yes, that would be nice," Jody whispered. She watched Doug pull the door shut behind him, a troubled expression on her face. There had to be a way for them to be together—but if she wouldn't marry him, and he refused to have an affair, what was left?

Doug toweled himself dry and drank the last of his beer. He climbed into his bed with the evening newspaper, but his mind kept straying to Jody and what she had told him this evening. She loved him and she didn't want to hurt him, but the thought of marriage made her physically ill. And after the way Larry had violated her trust, Doug could understand why she felt the way she did.

But an affair? With Jody? Doug settled back against the pillows and thought about it. The logistics wouldn't be easy, and they'd have to be very, very discreet, but they could do that. San Antonio was only a half-hour away, and it had plenty of places they could be together anonymously. Doug found the thought of a motel room a little distasteful, yet they couldn't very well carry on at his house or hers. But they could work out the practical problems of being together.

Could Jody really handle an affair? She thought she could, even if Doug had his doubts. Maybe she was right—maybe she could handle it. And maybe settling for half a loaf would be better than not having anything at all. Doug sighed as he turned out the light. He could feel himself weakening toward an affair with Jody. He loved her like he had loved no other woman, and he missed the closeness they had shared for a few precious hours. She sincerely wanted to be close to him and to share at least some of their life, and if the thought of marriage frightened her that badly, then all she could offer him was an affair. If that was all that she could offer him at this point, maybe he ought to go ahead and take her up on it. But he wasn't going to stop hoping that someday she would become his wife.

CHAPTER ELEVEN

Scott stopped his pacing and peered out the living room window. "Mom, Uncle Doug's on his way over," he called up the stairs.

"Yes, Scott, I saw him leave his house," Jody said as she pinned up her hair with trembling fingers. She knew she was being ridiculous, but she was dreading the drive to Austin and her upcoming interview with Dr. Blundell. And then she and Doug would have to wait while Scott talked with him.

Jody fingered the dark circle under one of her eyes. She hadn't slept much last night, and she had heard Scott still tossing and turning after she had gone to bed. She wished she could have been more of a help to her son, but she couldn't when she was as nervous about the upcoming session as he was.

Jody came down the stairs as Scott let Doug in. "Do you want to eat breakfast in town or wait until we get to Austin?"

"Let's wait," Scott said. "I'm not very hungry."

Scott went out and got into Doug's car. As Jody locked the door behind her, Doug ran a gentle hand down the side of her face. "You look tired," he said. "Have trouble sleeping?"

Jody nodded.

"Are you nervous?"

"Wouldn't you be, if it was your child?" Jody countered.

"What do you mean, 'my child'? I'm as strung up as you are, and he isn't even mine!"

Jody squeezed Doug's hand. "Thanks for caring."

They didn't say much on the drive to Austin. Jody stared out at the bleak December landscape. It was cold and overcast, much the same as it had been on the day they had buried Larry. She checked the date on her watch and realized with a start that Larry had died a year ago today. It was hard to believe that an entire year had gone by. Jody still felt sick when she thought of the senseless waste his death and the last few years of his life had been.

Jody glanced back at Scott, who was reading a comic book he had brought along. Yes, it was worth whatever this doctor was going to cost her if his treatment could keep the same thing from happening to her son. She had talked with Suzanne Bohannon just two nights ago, and Suzanne was more than willing to forgive Scott and forget the incident. But Ryan was afraid to play with Scott, and Jody could understand that. Scott had cried again when Jody had told him that Ryan wouldn't play with him, and Jody hoped that Ryan might soon be able to forgive Scott and get over his fear. And she hoped that Dr. Blundell could help Scott with his problem before the child alienated all his friends.

Doug glanced over at Jody, wondering if she remembered that today was the anniversary of Larry's death. He hoped that she hadn't—she had enough on her mind today without remembering that. He longed to take her hand and assure her that everything was going to be all right for her and her child. The longing to hold her, to comfort her and caress her and bring her passion to life had grown within

Doug to the point that he was almost ready to accept the affair Jody had offered him. It wasn't what he wanted from her, but he wanted anything in the way of caring and affection that she could offer him, whether or not it was the way he wanted things. He needed Jody in his life, and he knew he would accept her terms. They would have the affair.

Doug stopped at a diner on the outskirts of Austin. They ordered pancakes for breakfast, with coffee for Doug and Jody and milk for Scott, but only Doug was able to finish his meal. Jody could feel a knot growing in her midsection as Doug pulled into the parking lot of a large medical building. She and Scott followed Doug inside, and as the elevator carried them to the top floor she whispered a short prayer for her son.

Dr. Blundell's waiting room was decorated in cheerful stripes, and an inviting stack of comic books and children's books was sprawled on a big table in the middle of the room. For the smaller children there was a play area in the corner of the room with tables and chairs and a hobby horse, as well as a play kitchen. The receptionist gave Jody some forms to fill out, and she had barely had time to complete them when a tall, redheaded man in western clothes opened the door of the inner office. "Mrs. Ford? Scott? I'm Dr. Blundell."

Neither Jody nor Scott could hide their apprehension. They both shook hands with the doctor, and Jody had to admire the way he put them both at ease with his warm, caring manner. "Now, Scott, I'd like you to wait out here for a little while so that I can talk to your mother," he said. "And then you and I are going to talk. How's that?"

"That's fine, sir. I'll wait here with Uncle Doug."

Doug rose and extended his hand. "I'm Doug Ford, Scott's dad's brother," Doug said quickly.

"Doug and Scott have become quite close in the last several months," Jody said. "He helped me convince Scott to come and talk to you today."

Jody followed the doctor past a cheerfully decorated little room with two rocking chairs to a more sophisticated office. "I find that the parents prefer a little more sedate setting," he said as Jody settled herself into a comfortable wing chair.

"But the other room would certainly put children at ease," Jody observed.

Dr. Blundell sat down in the other wing chair across from hers. "Mrs. Ford, before I can talk to Scott, I need to find out from you everything that has happened to him in the last few years that might have any bearing on his behavior. Let's start from the beginning, with what Scott experienced when his father still lived with you. How old was he when he first saw his father hit you?"

Jody spent the next hour and a half answering Dr. Blundell's thorough questions. He wanted to know exactly what had brought on Larry's violence and what her response to that violence had been, as well as Scott's reaction to it. Jody's face burned as she recalled the details of those last months with Larry and described the way he had yelled at them both all the time after he had lost the ranch. The man's caring and sympathetic attitude made it a little easier to describe what Larry had done to her and what Scott had seen, but it was still a painfully embarrassing experience for her. Dr. Blundell nodded his approval when she described her flight to the women's shelter and commended her for not staying around for more abuse, telling her that many women took years of cruelty before they made the break, and some never did.

Dr. Blundell then wanted to know everything that

had happened to Scott since she had left Larry. When had he started to behave inappropriately? Jody described Scott's confrontation with Doug, when he thought that Doug meant her harm, and described Scott's behavior for the last year. Dr. Blundell questioned her closely on her relationship with Doug as well as Scott's, and she felt comfortable enough with the doctor to admit that she and Doug were close, but that they were in disagreement over the idea of getting married. Finally, when it seemed like Dr. Blundell knew more about her and Scott than they did, he told her that he was ready to talk to Scott. They went together to the waiting room and found Scott and Doug immersed in a game of checkers.

"Scott, Dr. Blundell's ready to talk to you," Jody said as she sat down beside Scott on the couch. "I'll finish your game of checkers for you." She squeezed Scott's hand reassuringly. "He's really nice. Don't be afraid to tell him anything."

Jody watched as Scott left with the doctor.

"Your move," Doug said quietly.

Jody looked down at the checkerboard. She moved one of her checkers three times and pretty well cleaned Doug out.

"I knew I should have insisted that Scott finish this himself," he said wryly. He loaded the rest of the checkers into the box. "You look like that session took a lot out of you. Why don't you come down with me to the coffee shop for a cup of coffee? Scott's going to be in there awhile."

"Thanks, I could use one," Jody admitted. "He wore me out with his questions."

Doug and Jody found a small coffee shop on the ground floor, and Doug persuaded Jody to order a sweetroll along with her coffee. "I don't know, but I

197

can imagine that talking with Dr. Blundell was pretty exhausting emotionally," Doug said.

"Yes," she agreed. "He wanted to know everything. I think he knows more now than I do!"

"More than me and the Templetons?" Doug asked.

Jody nodded. "He knows how to ask questions," she said. "He even knows all about you."

"Me?" Doug asked, surprised.

"Of course," Jody said. "He asked about all of Scott's violent episodes since Larry left, and I told him about the night Scott tried to defend me from you."

Doug's face turned red. "He must think I'm a real heel," he murmured.

"I doubt it, especially since I told him how much time you had spent with Scott lately," Jody said. "And remember, he's there to help Scott, not to make value judgments about you and me. Although he did want to know exactly what our relationship was."

"And you told him?" Doug asked.

"I said that we were close but that we disagreed on whether or not to get married," Jody said mildly. "I wonder what he's asking Scott?"

Doug started to tell Jody that he had changed his mind about an affair with her, but he could sense that now was not the time. Her mind was still upstairs with her son, and he thought she had enough to deal with right now. They dawdled over a second cup of coffee each, then returned to the office, where Jody tried and failed to get interested in a magazine article. She and Doug both stood up quickly when the door to the inner office opened.

Scott came out, a smile on his face. "You were right, Mom," he said as he squeezed her hand, "he's nice."

"Mrs. Ford, can I see you for a moment?" Dr. Blundell asked. "And would you like Mr. Ford to be included?"

Jody looked up at Doug's tense face. "Of course," she said. "Mr. Ford has worried about Scott right along with me."

They returned to Dr. Blundell's office. "I'll want to go over my notes a bit before I put my analysis into writing, but at this point I feel that Scott has been disturbed by the violence he saw as a young child. He's basically not a mean young man, but he's unsure about dealing with anger and frustration, which, from what both you and your son have told me, was his father's problem as well. So that's the bad news."

Dr. Blundell cleared his throat. "Now for the good. Although Scott does have a problem, it doesn't seem to be that severe, and it shouldn't take all that long or be too hard to correct. I'd like to see him at least two more times, maybe three, then we'll see at that point how far he's come. Scott isn't going to need years of therapy, but a few months should really help."

Jody didn't even try to hide her relief. "Thank goodness!" she exclaimed. "Is there anything more that Doug and I can do for him?"

"No, nothing more than continuing to provide the love and support you've given him already," Dr. Blundell replied. "You know, Mrs. Ford, his problem would have been a lot worse if he hadn't had the love and caring you've shown him."

Tears rushed to Jody's eyes. "Thanks," she whispered.

She made an appointment for the next week, and they joined Scott in the waiting room. Since Scott was already counted absent at school for the whole day and Doug and Jody had arranged for Beatrice to take the shop until closing time, the three of them

199

decided to make a day of it. Doug treated them to lunch in a café, and afterward they looked around in one of the shopping malls.

After that, Doug asked if either of them had been to the Lyndon Johnson Memorial Library. Scott, to Jody's surprise, was fascinated by the displays and the memorabilia of a president who had died before he was born, and Jody and Doug found themselves reminiscing about the Johnson years in the White House. Jody laughed out loud at some of the letters on display that the president had received while he was in office, and Doug admitted that he was more interested in Johnson's early years in Congress.

It was late in the afternoon when they finally headed back toward New Braunfels, and Jody was appalled by the traffic on the Austin expressways. "I can't believe this!" she said as they drove, bumper to bumper, at ten miles an hour.

"Well, Jody, Austin's growing up," Doug said.

"I guess so. It does make you appreciate New Braunfels, doesn't it?"

They finally got outside the city, and Doug was able to drive faster. It was dark by the time they got back to New Braunfels, and Jody invited Doug to have supper with them, suddenly loath to end their pleasant day together.

"It's just roast beef sandwiches, but there's more than enough for you to join us."

"Why, thank you, I will," Doug said as he shed his coat and tie. *Thank you, Jody!* he thought. This would give him a chance to talk to her after Scott had gone to bed.

Scott and Doug set the table and made iced tea while Jody prepared thick spicy roast beef sandwiches. Scott chattered to them about the things they had done that afternoon, although both Jody and Doug noticed that he said very little about what he and Dr. Blundell had talked about. But neither of them was worried, after Dr. Blundell's assessment of Scott's emotional state. He could be helped, and he could be helped fairly easily, and that was what mattered.

"Thanks for dinner," Doug said as he wiped his mouth with his napkin. "It was delicious."

"It was leftovers," Scott teased.

"Scott, your mother's leftovers are better than my first-time-arounds, believe me," Doug said. "Your roast tastes like my mother's used to, Jody."

"That's no coincidence," Jody said. "I've used her recipe for years."

"Daddy loved it that way," Scott volunteered. He started toward the kitchen with his plate and missed the look that Jody and Doug exchanged.

"That's the first time he's brought Larry into a conversation since I left him," Jody said softly.

"Dr. Blundell must be helping already," Doug said.

They cleared the table, and Jody insisted that Scott get ready for bed. "You have school tomorrow," she said when Scott protested. She turned uncertainly to Doug. "Thanks again for today," she said.

"Running me home?" Doug teased.

"No, I didn't mean—"

Doug laughed. "Jody, I want to talk to you this evening after Scott's gone to bed. Should I come back in a few minutes?"

"Are we going to have another argument?" Jody asked warily.

"We shouldn't," Doug said easily. "I'll read a magazine until you have Scott in bed."

Had Doug changed his mind about the affair, or was he going to ask her to marry him again? Jody

201

wondered as she climbed the stairs. Or maybe he wanted to talk about the business. In any case, Doug's timing was lousy. She was tired and emotionally spent and would have loved nothing more than to crawl under the covers and sleep for a week.

Scott was already bathed and was waiting for her in his bed. "Mom, I'm glad I went today," he volunteered. "Dr. Blundell's okay."

"Yes, I thought he was," Jody said.

"He said that it was natural for me to remember Daddy and that I wasn't supposed to try to forget him."

"Oh, Scott, is that what you were trying to do?" Jody asked.

"Yeah," Scott said. "After he was so mean to you, I tried to forget all about him. But Dr. Blundell says that I shouldn't try to do that. He said that I should try to remember everything about my father, the good and the bad, and that I shouldn't try to lock it away inside."

"That's a good idea," Jody said as she wondered just how much "forgetting" she had tried to do herself. "It's late tonight, but tomorrow or the next day I have some pictures you might enjoy seeing. They're of you and Daddy when you were little."

"I'd like that," Scott assured her.

Jody kissed her son good night and joined Doug in the living room. "I hope you're not going to lay anything heavy on me," she said as she sank down on the couch. "I can't handle much more today."

Doug closed the doors to the room. "I don't want Scott to hear us," he said. He sat down beside Jody and took her hand. "Jody, I've been doing some thinking this week," he said quietly. "Before when we talked, I don't think I realized just how frightened you are of the commitment of marriage. Not until you said that the thought makes you physically ill."

"It really does, Doug."

Doug stroked the back of her hand. "Anyway, I've thought it over, and I'm willing to have that affair, if that's what you still want."

Jody was still a moment. Doug was now willing to have the affair that she wanted. She had gotten her wish, after all. So why wasn't she elated? Why did she feel little pinpricks of guilt at the thought?

Jody pushed the guilty feelings to the back of her mind and thought about the glorious night she and Doug had spent in one another's arms. "Oh, Doug, of course I'm still interested!" she said as she put her arms around his neck, her face wreathed in a smile. "I love you and I've missed you so much!"

"I've missed you too, Jody," he said as his arms went around her. He tilted her face and pressed his lips against hers, their breath mingling as Doug kissed Jody with all the love and passion he felt for her. Jody returned his ardor, boldly thrusting her tongue between his lips.

Doug opened himself to Jody, letting her savor his sweetness as he tasted hers. *Oh, Doug, it's going to be like this for us always,* Jody thought as her fingers teased the tender skin at his nape. *We're going to have this sweetness and this passion to share—it's going to be glorious!*

They kissed and touched for long moments, their hands rediscovering one another's delights, before Doug pulled away, his breathing ragged. "If we don't stop this, we're going to make love right here on the couch," he said. "And we can't do that." He looked down at his hand resting on Jody's breast.

"Why not?" Jody asked before her glance fell on the closed door that Scott could walk through at any

203

moment. "You're right," she said as she unwound her arms from Doug's neck. "Damn! I want you so badly."

"You think I don't want you?" Doug asked gruffly as he removed his hands from Jody and placed them in his lap.

"Gonna be one heck of an affair," Jody said as she grinned. "So how do we go about it? I must admit this is my first."

"If you and I were the only consideration, I'd carry you up those stairs and finish what we just started," Doug said. "But there's Scott to think about, and our reputations here in New Braunfels."

"Yeah," Jody said slowly. "I don't want the kids making cracks about us to Scott." She thought a moment. "I guess we can drive down to San Antonio."

"We're going to have to," Doug said. "What about Scott? Will his babysitters stay late?"

"That's no problem," Jody said. "And you can always come along on some of my buying trips. You're learning the business, so it would make sense that you would need to travel with me. In fact, I'm supposed to drive down to Corpus Christi this weekend to look at a houseful of furniture." She grinned sheepishly. "I was going to ask you to keep Scott, but I'd rather have you for myself. Would you like to come with me?"

"Sure, if Beatrice can cover for us," Doug said.

Jody called Beatrice, who was more than happy to cover for them and make a little extra money for Christmas.

"What about Scott?" Doug asked as Jody hung up the telephone.

"Um, I don't know," Jody said. "Maybe I can ask one of his friends' mothers if he can stay. I guess I could call Suzanne Bohannon and see if Ryan has changed his mind."

"How about Marilyn?" Doug asked. "I bet she would keep him gladly."

"I don't think so," Jody said quickly. "I know she's tired from the pregnancy, and she has a million things to do to get ready for the Christmas pageant at church. I'll ask someone else."

Doug looked at Jody curiously but said nothing. "Well, do ask her if you can't find someone else," he said. He moved over to Jody, once again closing the space between them. "Let me kiss you again," he said as he cupped the back of her head in his hand.

Jody gasped as their lips once again met with joy and passion. Love flowed between them as Doug stroked the smoothness of her back through the dress that she wore. Jody clung to him, touching his shoulders, his chest, his back, savoring the warmth and strength of Doug's body. She could feel her breasts start to swell with passion and grow hard against his chest. Doug could feel her response, and he longed to see and to touch them again. Slowly, he lowered his lips, tasting and touching as he trailed tender kisses along her face, her neck, down to the vee neckline of her dress. Boldly he unbuttoned the top two buttons and pushed her bra out of the way. "Just a taste," he whispered. "Just a taste to hold me."

Doug bathed her rosy nipple with his tongue, its moist, raspy surface stiffening her breast into a peak of pleasure. For long minutes he nibbled and suckled her until she was fairly whimpering with need and desire. "Oh, Jody, I've missed holding you and kissing you," Doug whispered as his lips claimed hers in a passionate salute, her sensitized breasts crushed against his chest. "I can hardly wait until the weekend."

"I know," Jody said. They kissed again, and Doug reluctantly moved away from Jody and helped her straighten her clothes.

"I'll see you in the morning," he said. "Do you want me to make reservations at a hotel on the bay?"

"I'd love that," Jody assured him. "Thank you for changing your mind."

"I had no choice—I love you too much," Doug replied softly.

Jody walked Doug to the door and watched as he walked across the street. Her lips still tingled from his kisses, and her breasts were heavy with passion for Doug. She started to follow him across the street, to beg him to carry her up his stairs and make love to her, but she glanced over at Hunter and Marilyn's house and stopped. Doug was right. They had their reputations to consider in this town, and she had no business leaving Scott alone in the house for that long at night.

Jody leaned against the doorpost and looked up at the full moon. She and Doug would have a marvelous relationship, she assured herself. There would be love, caring, and passion. There would also be tenderness and affection, and there wouldn't be any risk to her. She glanced again toward the parsonage but quickly pushed the pangs of guilt to the back of her mind. She wasn't doing anything wrong. Millions of people had affairs, she told herself, and lightning didn't strike them. Besides, even if what she was doing was wrong, it wasn't anybody else's business but hers.

Jody sighed as she hung up the telephone. Thank goodness Suzanne had been able to persuade Ryan to play with Scott again! It had taken Suzanne a couple of hours, but she had convinced Ryan to forgive Scott and let him spend the weekend with them. When Ryan refused at first to have Scott over, Jody had begun to worry that she and Doug would not be able to go away for the weekend after all. She had asked her regular babysitter if she could stay with him and had even called the mothers of a couple of Scott's other friends, but they all had plans for the weekend. She had promised Suzanne that she would take Ryan for a weekend in January so that Jack and Suzanne could go to a convention in Dallas, and she wasn't particularly looking forward to that, but it would be worth it for her and Doug to have this weekend together. Jody wasn't sure how they would be able to manage many entire weekends with one another, and she hated to have to cancel the first.

Jody had kissed Scott good night and was looking in her closet, trying to decide what clothes to take to Corpus Christi, when she heard someone at the front door. She answered the door, half-expecting Doug, and was surprised to find Marilyn standing there with a plate covered with tin foil. "Mother sent us too much cake again."

"Oh, Marilyn, you and Aunt Maggie spoil me," Jody said as she threw open the door. "I never have a chance to repay either one of you."

"That's all right, we love to watch you eat it," Marilyn said.

Jody carried the cake out to the kitchen. "Would you like a cup of hot tea?"

Marilyn nodded and Jody put the kettle on. They chatted a little about the Christmas program at church, but Jody noticed that Marilyn seemed rather quiet, as if she had something on her mind. "Is something bothering you, Marilyn?" she asked as she poured the tea.

"Were you able to find someone to keep Scott for

you this weekend?" she asked quietly. "Joan Albers said you had asked her, and that you sounded almost desperate."

"Uh, yes, Suzanne Bohannon's keeping him."

"Jody, you know that Hunter and I love having him over," Marilyn said. "Why didn't you ask me? We would have kept him gladly!"

"Oh, Marilyn, you're so busy right now, with the pageant and Christmas coming up," Jody said. "I hated to bother you."

"Scott's never a bother," Marilyn said stiffly. "We love having him."

"I'm sorry. I know you love him," Jody said guiltily. Marilyn had said more than once that Scott reminded her a little of the boy she had lost. "And I should have asked you."

"So why didn't you?" Marilyn asked.

Jody's face turned red. "I was embarrassed. Doug and I are going to Corpus Christi for the weekend to look at some furniture."

"And you're resuming your affair with him," Marilyn added.

"Yes, I am," Jody said quietly, her head held high. "I love Doug and I want to be with him."

"Then why not marry him?" Marilyn asked. "He wants to, you know."

"You know why not. Marilyn, you saw me that night! Do you think I could ever let myself in for that again?"

"Oh, Jody, it wouldn't be like that with Doug," Marilyn said. "Besides, I don't care how much people carry on in this world we live in, it just isn't right. It wasn't meant for people to share that kind of intimacy outside the bonds of marriage. This affair you want is a mistake."

"Don't preach to me, Marilyn," Jody said tightly.

"I'm sorry if you think I'm going against your moral code, but this relationship is between Doug and me. We're not hurting anybody else."

"I didn't say you were," Marilyn said quietly. "God knows, I know what you went through with Larry and I'm not judging you. But what you're planning goes against your *own* moral code, not mine or Hunter's or anybody else's—yours, Jody. When people act against their own beliefs, they usually end up miserable. That's why I think you're making a mistake."

"Please, Marilyn, try to understand," Jody pleaded. "I love Doug, and this is the only way that we can be together. I don't want to throw away what we have!"

Marilyn started to say more but shook her head. "Just remember that I love you, Jody, and that it's because I love you that I worry about you."

Jody put her arm around her cousin and hugged her. "I know, and thanks. Now, please don't worry about me!"

"All right, but do feel free to ask me to keep Scott for you," Marilyn said. "Any time, for any reason."

"You'll be the first number I call next time," Jody assured her.

After they finished the tea, she walked Marilyn to the door and watched her cross the street, much the way she had watched Doug just a few nights ago. She felt the pinpricks of conscience again, and tonight they were harder to push away. She was planning to act contrary to the moral code she had lived by for so long. Was Marilyn right—was she going to make herself miserable? Jody didn't know. But an affair certainly didn't have the potential to make her miserable, as another marriage did.

CHAPTER TWELVE

Jody folded her new rose-colored dress and laid it on top of the other clothes in her suitcase. She looked down ruefully at the dress. It was pretty enough, but it was an all-occasion dress. Jody wished she could have afforded a second dress, something sexy and provocative, to wear in the evening, but she couldn't. Besides, she was still too thin to carry off provocative. But she still wished she could have worn something that would knock Doug's eyes out when he saw her in it.

Jody started to shut the suitcase but remembered that she hadn't packed any pantyhose. She opened her dresser drawer and got out two new packages, then looked up and stared at her reflection in the mirror. Doug would still find her appealing, she was confident of that, but she wished that she could be truly beautiful for him. A man like Doug deserved to have a beautiful mistress on his arm. But he really wanted to have a wife on his arm, Jody thought before she could stop herself. She shoved the pantyhose into the suitcase and was pushing down on the lid when Scott came into the room. "Come here, Scott, and sit on this, will you?"

She held the suitcase so that Scott could sit on it. "Thanks, hon," she said as she snapped it shut. "Is your duffel packed to go to Ryan's?"

"Yeah," Scott said slowly as he hopped down. "Mom, why do I have to stay with Ryan this weekend? Why can't I go with you and Uncle Doug, the way I used to go with you and Daddy?"

"Because you'll have a lot more fun with Ryan than you will with us," Jody said, hoping she sounded casual.

"But I used to have a lot of fun on those trips!" Scott protested. "We would get to eat out and sleep in a motel. Besides, you're going to the coast."

"Scott, look out the window," Jody said. "It's forty degrees and raining. How much fun do you think you would have on the beach in this weather? You and Ryan can play together all weekend."

"Ryan still doesn't like me," Scott said. "Mom, why won't you take me?"

Because I don't want to have an affair in front of you, Jody thought. "Scott, this is just a business trip," she said. "We won't be out on the beach or doing any of the things you like to do. Look, we can always go next spring when the weather warms up." She planted a kiss on his nose. "Will that do?"

"I guess it will have to," Scott said. "I'm going over to tell Uncle Doug good-bye," he said as he got down off the bed.

"That's fine," Jody said absently as she loaded her cosmetics into her carryall bag. She shouldn't feel guilty for leaving Scott behind this weekend, she reassured herself. She needed to have a life of her own apart from him. She needed to have love in her life, to have adult companionship. But she couldn't help thinking that, if she and Doug were married, they could have taken Scott with them this weekend, and the three of them would have had a wonderful time.

"Jody? Is that you?" Doug called out as he heard the front door open.

"No, it's me, Uncle Doug," Scott called out. He took the steps two at a time and ran into Doug's room. "Need me to sit on that for you? I just sat on Mom's for her."

"Yes, that might be a help," Doug said, even though his suitcase was hardly bulging. Scott hopped up and sat until Doug had secured the fastenings. "Is your mother almost ready?" he asked.

"I think so. Her suitcase is packed," Scott said. "Say, why don't you ask her if I can come along?"

Just what we need, Doug thought ruefully. "Scott, have you already talked to your mother about this?" he asked.

"Yeah, and she said I'd have more fun at Ryan's," Scott replied. "But I won't. I'd have a lot more fun with the two of you!"

You might, but we wouldn't, Doug thought. "I think your mom's right this time," he said firmly. "This is just a dumb old buying trip. Why don't you wait until next spring when it's warm, and I'll take you back down there?"

"That's what Mom said. Aw, please, Uncle Doug, ask her. She never tells you no!"

"Damned if that isn't true," Doug murmured under his breath.

"Huh?"

"Oh, nothing, Scott. Look, you really wouldn't have much fun if we took you this time. The Bohannons will be a lot more fun for you than the trip would. All right?"

"Okay," Scott said. "But you have to bring me a T-shirt."

"You got it," Doug promised.

"Oh, no, I forgot to pack my new Frisbee!" Scott

212

said as he jumped off the bed and ran out of the room. Doug chuckled under his breath, but at the same time he felt a little sorry for Scott. If the situation had been different and they had been married, Doug would have welcomed Scott on the trip. He guessed that Scott had been badgering his mother to let him come and that this trip across the street had been a last-ditch effort to enlist Doug's help to change her mind. He could imagine that Jody was feeling a little uncomfortable right now about having to lie to Scott. In fact, he hoped that she was. The more unsatisfactory she found having an affair to be, the more likely she would be to change her mind about marrying him. And he sincerely hoped that someday she would change her mind about that.

Jody was ready by the time Doug walked across the street for her. He put her suitcase in his trunk, and they drove Scott to the Bohannons. Suzanne met Scott and Jody at the door. "I'm glad Scott could come for dinner," she said as Scott carried his duffel inside. "Ryan, Scott's here."

Ryan poked his head around the corner. "Hello, Scott," he said solemnly.

"Hi, Ryan," Scott replied, then followed Ryan out to the family room.

"Here's where we'll be staying," Jody said as she handed Suzanne a piece of paper with the name of their hotel written on it. "Have them ring my room if you need me."

"I hope you find a lot of nice things," Suzanne said. "Did Doug lend you his car?"

"Uh, no, he's coming with me," Jody said, hoping that Suzanne couldn't see her blush in the dim light on the front porch. "We both think it's time he learned to do some of the buying."

"That's good," Suzanne said, apparently thinking nothing of the two of them traveling together. "Have a safe trip."

"Thanks," Jody said.

"What do you want to do about supper?" Doug asked as Jody got back into the car.

Jody checked her watch. "It will be after ten by the time we get to Corpus," she said. "Is that too late to go out?"

"No, but I can think of other things I'd rather be doing about eleven," he teased, bringing a blush to her cheeks. "Why don't we get something simple somewhere down the road?"

Jody agreed, and Doug pulled away from the curb. They drove in companionable silence through the cold winter dusk, the light rain making the highway just slick enough to be dangerous. Jody let Doug concentrate on his driving and busied herself with a book that she read by the light of a small flashlight. When they reached Seguin Doug suggested stopping, but she suggested that they eat a little farther down the road when they were both hungrier.

They found a café open in Kenedy. It was a little dreary, but the hamburgers that the bored-looking waitress brought out were excellent.

"Mmm, Scott would love these burgers," Jody murmured as she swallowed a bite of hers.

Doug leaned toward Jody. "Did Scott give you a hard time about coming?" he asked.

"Oh, not about me coming, but about us not bringing him along," Jody admitted. "Why? Did he hound you too?"

"He asked me to go over and talk you into letting him come," Doug said.

"Poor kid," Jody said a little ruefully. "I had to promise him a trip to the coast in the spring."

"I promised him one too," Doug admitted. "I'll have to stop here for a hamburger for him." They looked at each other and laughed.

The rain stopped about halfway to Corpus Christi, and moonlight sparkled in the waters of the bay as Doug drove down Shoreline to their hotel.

"Oh, Doug, it's so beautiful here!" Jody exclaimed as the waves pounded the seawall. "Does our room have a view?"

"It better. I specifically requested one," Doug said. He pulled up to their hotel, and a bellhop helped Doug unload their luggage.

Jody noted with amusement and a little embarrassment that Doug had registered them as "Doug and Jody Ford" rather than "Mr. and Mrs."

"Don't forget to save your receipts—we can write off this whole trip as a business expense," Jody whispered.

Doug looked surprised. "We can, can't we? But how are we going to explain to the accountant that we shared a room?"

"I do the income tax myself," Jody said, blushing a little.

When they got to the room, Jody opened the drapes and stared out at the moonlight dancing over the water. The wind whipped the palm trees and made the little flags on the boats stand straight out. "Come here, Doug," she said softly.

Doug stood beside her and put his arm around her shoulders. "It's as beautiful as you are," he said as he drew her into his arms. "I love you, Jody."

"I love you too," she said as she wrapped her arms around him and held him tightly.

"Glad we came?" he asked softly.

"Very," she said. "Glad you changed your mind?"

"Very," Doug assured her as he tipped her face up

215

to receive his kiss. She met his lips eagerly, joyfully, so glad to be in Doug's arms again. The moonlight dappled their faces as they shared a lovely, passionate kiss with one another. This was where she belonged, Jody thought as her lips tasted and nibbled Doug's. She needed to be with this man, loving him and being loved by him.

They were both trembling by the time they finally broke apart. "I love you, Jody," Doug said quietly, his face solemn. "I love you so much. I just want you to know."

"And I love you, Doug," Jody whispered as she kissed his palm. "I don't know when I've loved a man more."

"Did . . . did you love Larry like this?" Doug asked quietly.

Jody's face fell. "Oh, Doug, please don't be jealous of what I shared with Larry! It was so long ago, and it ended so badly."

"I wasn't jealous of him," Doug explained. "I only hope that maybe sometime, in the early days, he knew a little of the joy that I know tonight."

Jody's eyes filled with tears. "You're a beautiful man, Doug Ford," she said as she pressed her face into his shirt front. "You have a beautiful, generous spirit."

"So do you, Jody," Doug said. He planted gentle kisses in her ear. "And I'd like to commence this affair with you, but I need a shower first."

Jody stepped away from him. "Don't take too long," she said.

Doug quickly stripped his clothing from his body, totally unselfconscious of his muscular nudity as he rummaged around in his shaving kit for his razor and toothbrush. Jody waited until he was in the shower before she took off the slacks and shirt she had traveled in and stepped into the steamy bathroom. "Can you reach everything?" she asked as she joined Doug in the shower.

"No, I have this spot right in the middle of my back that I can't get to," Doug said as he dipped his head and kissed Jody's nipple, grinning approvingly when it puckered. "Did you need a shower, too?"

"No, I needed to be with you," Jody said as she took the washcloth from Doug. "Besides, I have a thing about naked sailors in the shower." She soaped his back and his bottom and traced the outline of his tattoo with her finger. "Is it my imagination, or is this the same pattern as Hunter's?"

Doug grinned sheepishly. "They're very much alike. We'd each had one beer too many one evening in San Diego, right before we were shipped to Nam."

Jody kissed the tattoo. "I can't believe this thing turns me on."

"Want me to get a boat on my chest? Or a butterfly on my bottom?" Doug teased.

Jody stepped back and pretended to think about it. "The boat, no. Turn around." She stroked his bottom lovingly. "A butterfly, huh? Could you get a pink one?"

"Jody!" Doug said as she caressed his soapy bottom. "Hey, that tickles!"

"Does this?" she asked as she tormented the skin under his arms.

"Yes! Stop that!" Doug pleaded as her fingers found yet another ticklish spot just below his armpits.

"How about here?" Jody asked as she reached for his navel.

Doug grabbed both of her wrists in his own and drew her closer to him. "You have given me a permanent case of the tickles," he said. "And according to my doctor, there is only one cure."

217

"And what's that?" Jody breathed.

"A night of unparalleled passion," he answered as he drew her body next to his. He bent his head and captured her lips in a long, slow, drugging kiss, designed to draw her very soul from her.

Water poured over them as Jody met his demanding passion with demands of her own, giving of herself and yet drawing an equal surrender from Doug. She could feel the heat of his masculinity against her hips and unconsciously arched herself closer to his passionate warmth. She needed this man to make love to her tonight, to take her body and give her back her soul.

They kissed and clung together for long moments before they drifted slowly away from one another. Doug rinsed himself under the spray and lovingly soaped Jody's body, rinsing her too before turning off the water. They dried one another with thick towels.

"You're so beautiful," he said as he ran eager fingers down her body, lingering for a moment on her breasts before drifting lower. "More beautiful than I remember."

"I haven't gained any weight," Jody said.

Doug tipped Jody's face up. "You don't need to gain an ounce," he told her. "I love the way you look. Can't you tell?"

Jody peered down at his aroused body. "Yes, I can tell," she said, blushing.

Before she could utter a protest, Doug swept her into his arms and carried her to the bed, laying her down and following her quickly.

"Doug, make love to me," she whispered as he trailed tender kisses down her body.

"Not just yet," Doug said. "We've waited over a month, we can wait a little longer and make it perfect."

218

How could it be any more perfect? Jody wondered at first, but as Doug touched and kissed and caressed her body, she soon could see why he had wanted to postpone their union for just a while. He touched and caressed her all over, her breasts, her waist, her stomach, the heart of her femininity—nothing was neglected as Doug made her delight in her womanhood. He was not shy with her and would not let her be shy either as he touched and stroked and tormented her until she was aching with delight. And he encouraged her to touch him with the same need and passion with which he touched her. She kissed and caressed his male nipples, his navel, his slender waist. She stiffened for only a moment as she reached his masculinity, but her love for Doug overcame her natural shyness and she kissed him there too, teasing him until they both were almost at the peak of their arousal. Doug gently pushed Jody down and the two of them became one.

Their lovemaking before had been beautiful, but it paled in the passion that they shared tonight. The moonlight streaming in the windows bathed their bodies in a silvery glow, and Jody whispered her delight in each and every stroke and caress that they shared. Doug said her name over and over as they climbed toward fulfillment together, her breasts straining against him as her hips moved with his. Finally, when Jody thought she could no longer bear it, passion stormed within her, and with a hoarse voice she called out Doug's name as tremors of delight shook her. Doug stiffened as the ultimate overtook him too.

"That was beautiful," Jody whispered as she buried her face in his chest.

"Very," Doug said. He moved away from Jody just

long enough to pull up the covers. Jody snuggled up next to him, and sleep quickly claimed them both.

"What's the plan for today?" Doug asked as he and Jody sat in the hotel dining room enjoying a leisurely breakfast.

"We're supposed to be at this address by ten," Jody said, handing a scrap of paper to Doug. "It's another estate that's being liquidated. We take as long as we need there, and after that the day is ours."

Doug raised his eyebrows Groucho Marx style. "You mean we have the whole day to play around?"

Jody blushed. "Lower your voice, Doug," she whispered. "Somebody might hear you!"

"You mean you don't want them to know we're going to build a sand castle?" Doug teased. "Besides, it doesn't matter who hears us here. We're not in New Braunfels, you know."

"I know, but it still embarrasses me a little," Jody said.

Good! Doug thought, but he said nothing. He reached over and tenderly brushed the crumbs from Jody's lips. "I would have kissed them off, but you're too far away. Would you like to come closer?"

"I would, but we'd never get any furniture bought that way," Jody said.

They finished their breakfast and drove to the address on Jody's paper. The house was in an older, rather rundown neighborhood, and Doug looked around doubtfully. "Do you really think there's anything of value in there?" he asked, eyeing the shabby old house.

"You might be surprised," Jody said. "I frequently am."

A sleek Porsche pulled up a moment later, and a good-looking young man got out. "Hello, I'm Hal

220

Brien," he said as he shook hands with them. "I hope you like my grandmother's things."

"I hope so too," Jody said. "Did she pass away recently?"

"No, it's been almost a year," Hal said as he unlocked the door. "It's taking awhile to get her estate settled."

Jody and Doug followed Hal into the two-story house. Hal turned on a light in the entry and opened the doors to the living room. "Look around and see if there's anything you like in here. I'll turn on the lights in the rest of the house."

Jody sneezed from the dust and looked around the living room. The furniture was a mixture of antique and Oriental, skillfully selected to blend perfectly. She felt her excitement rising as she quickly appraised the resale value of the furniture and bric-a-brac that adorned the room. This room alone was as good a find as the furniture in San Antonio had been. Jody turned around and laughed when she saw Doug's astonished face. "Didn't I tell you that we're sometimes in for a pleasant surprise?"

"But the house is so shabby on the outside!" Doug marveled. He looked at the smug expression on Jody's face. "You knew there was some good stuff here, didn't you?"

Jody nodded. "I had a pretty good idea. I don't know the whole story, but one of my mother's old friends was this lady's best friend, and she called me the day she gave the family our name. She said to get down here as quickly as I could." Jody fingered a mahogany coffee table with an intricate inlaid pattern. "But I can't understand it—the family apparently doesn't want a thing in the house."

Hal poked his head into the room. "I've turned on the lights all over the house. We don't want anything, so you can buy anything you see." He sat down on the couch and took a magazine from his pocket.

"Come on, let's look around," Jody said.

They spent the remainder of the morning and part of the afternoon in the old house. The rest of the house was every bit as elegant as the living room, and Jody examined the furniture and the glassware carefully to be sure of its authenticity. As she went, she explained to Doug how she could tell if a piece was genuine or a reproduction. She found herself impressed with Doug's appreciation of the elegant furniture and bric-a-brac. Most men couldn't have cared less, but Doug really seemed to enjoy the beautiful pieces. A little more training and he could run the store himself, she thought.

"I can't believe that the family doesn't want any of this," Jody marveled as she opened a dresser drawer to check it. "They haven't even cleaned out her things."

"It isn't usually like this, is it?" Doug asked.

"Oh, no, most of the time the family has pretty well cleared things out, and all I see are the things that are left behind," Jody said. She opened a small jewelry box and found a beautiful cameo ring inside. "Oh, Doug, will you look at this? Isn't it beautiful?"

Doug looked down at the cameo ring. "Why don't you try it on?"

"No, I couldn't," Jody protested. She picked up the ring box and ran down the stairs. "Hal, we found this in the dresser drawer. Surely this was left here by mistake."

Hal looked down at the ring. "Yeah, I guess Aunt Edna missed that one when she took my grandmother's jewelry to sell. I'll have to take it myself." Hal sounded rather put out.

"But doesn't anybody want it?" Jody asked incredulously.

"Are you kidding?" Hal scoffed. "None of them would touch her things with a ten-foot pole."

"But why?" Jody blurted, though it was none of her business.

"Oh, I thought you knew," Hal said. "There was quite a bit of ill will generated when my grandmother left my grandfather and her children for another man. It's been forty years, and none of them ever forgave her. I never even met her—my mother wouldn't let me."

"That's a shame," Jody murmured.

Doug took the ring box from Jody. "Here, try it on," he said as he took the ring and placed it on her finger.

"Doug, I can't—"

"If they're going to sell it anyway, you might as well have it," Doug said. "How does it fit?"

"Perfectly."

"Merry Christmas," Doug said as he kissed her finger.

"But Doug, it's—"

Doug silenced her with a hard, sweet kiss. "Don't expect anything under the tree."

Jody smiled. "All right." She glanced down at the ring and noticed that Doug had put it on the third finger of her left hand. Had that been a coincidence, or had he put the ring there for a reason?

Jody and Doug ended up taking most of what was in the house. They offered Hal a conservative but fair price for the furniture and bric-a-brac, and Doug called their banker and floated another short-term loan. Jody's eyes sparkled as they got into Doug's car. "I'm sorry the family feels that way about their

223

grandmother, but what an opportunity for us! We should sell those things pretty quickly."

Doug pursed his lips. "Jody, how would you feel about expanding the store next year? As it is, we're not going to be able to display all of that at one time, and if that house in Brennan you're supposed to see next week has as many things as it's supposed to have, we won't have room to buy it all."

"I've thought about it," Jody said. "If we'd been getting along better, and I hadn't been so worried about Scott, I would have said something. Do you want to talk about it now?"

"No, I think we've done enough business for one day," Doug said. "But we should talk about it soon." He picked up her hand and kissed it. "The rest of the weekend's for us, love."

"Where are we going now?" Jody asked when Doug didn't take the street back to the hotel.

"I thought we could drive out to Padre Island," he said. "We can walk on the sand, if nothing else."

The beach was almost deserted, with only the occasional beachcomber interrupting the solitude. The sun was shining, but the wind was blowing and the air was cold and damp. Doug sucked in a lungful of the cold, salty breeze.

"Do you miss the ocean?" Jody asked as they strolled in the sand, their arms around one another.

"Oh, a little, I guess. But my life's been full in New Braunfels, especially since you and Scott let me be a part of your lives."

Jody thought guiltily of all the months she had held Doug at arm's length. "I'm sorry I didn't welcome you at first," she said quietly.

"You had reason," Doug admitted. "You don't know how many times I mentally kicked myself in the pants for chewing you out that night and scaring you to death." He looked down at her and smiled. "But that's all water under the bridge," he said as he bent his head. "You've let me into your life now, and that's all that matters." His tender kiss was full of love.

But he wanted to share even more with her, Jody thought as she returned his kiss. He wanted to be a complete partner in her and Scott's lives, and she had said no to that. Jody deliberately pushed away that thought as she wrapped her arms around Doug's neck and held him close. They shared love and caring and affection, and that was enough. They didn't need to get married too.

"If you don't get up, lazybones, you're not going to have time to get ready for dinner," Doug said as Jody snuggled up next to him.

"I'll have plenty of time," Jody assured him as she kissed his lips. They had returned from Padre Island and had planned to go shopping, but they had exchanged a few kisses, and one thing had led to another, and they had ended up spending the rest of the afternoon and early evening in bed, making tender, passionate love. "Kiss me again, Doug—I need that."

"Woman, you're insatiable," he teased as he covered her lips in a long, slow, affectionate kiss.

Jody broke off their kiss and looked at him expectantly. "You're going to have to wait until tonight," Doug admitted. "I'm thoroughly satiated."

"So am I, really," Jody said. "I just thought we might go for a record."

"Up!" Doug said as he swatted her behind.

"Tonight?" Jody asked as she got out of bed.

"And tomorrow morning too," Doug said. "We'll

try to get in enough loving to last us until we can get to San Antonio on a date."

"Uh, sure," Jody said as she took her underwear from the suitcase. She started to invite Doug to join her in the shower, but he had turned over and shut his eyes.

Jody adjusted the water temperature and stood under the spray as she washed her hair. She knew that it was ridiculous, but she felt a little guilty about her relationship with Doug. Although she certainly didn't feel guilty or ashamed when she was in his arms, she did feel badly when she realized that, for all the love they shared with one another, their relationship was essentially a clandestine one. They did not have the luxury of being openly loving and affectionate with one another, and their moments together would be limited to times when they could get away. Jody knew that Doug was a loving, affectionate man, and she wondered how long it would be before he began to chafe at the restrictions the nature of their affair placed on him. And how was she going to feel about it as the months passed? She already hated the sneaking around.

Jody was quiet as she got dressed. Doug chattered to her as he showered and as she dried her hair and plaited it into an artful arrangement. She carefully made up her face in glamorous shades and put on the rose-colored dress that she had just bought. Doug came up behind her and placed a kiss on her nape as she looked at herself in the mirror. "Beautiful, just beautiful," he told her.

"I wish I could have bought a different kind of dress," Jody admitted as she stared critically at the demure, though elegant, dress. "I would have bought something more provocative."

"Why didn't you, then?" Doug asked.

"Mostly because I didn't have the money for two dresses, and I had to buy something I could wear a lot," Jody admitted. "And I still don't have the figure to carry off something daring."

"You know, if you don't quit moaning about your figure, I'm going to bring you buttered biscuits every morning and get you so fat you'll have to roll out the door," Doug teased. "Seriously, Jody, the dress is beautiful, and you look beautiful in it." He hugged her from behind. "And I hope you'll wear it often, because every time I see you in it I'll think of this weekend together."

"Thanks, Doug," she said softly.

The restaurant on the top floor of the hotel overlooked the water, and Doug had requested a table near the window. "This is perfect," Jody said as she gazed out over the water.

"I wanted this whole weekend to be perfect for you," he said as the waiter appeared with a small box.

"Madame, this is for you," the waiter said as he handed the box to her.

Jody opened the box and found a perfect white orchid. "Oh, Doug, thank you," she said softly. She pinned the orchid to her dress.

"Congratulations to you both," the waiter said. "How many years have you been married?"

"Oh, we're not married," Jody blurted without thinking, blushing brightly when she realized what she had said.

"This is just a very special occasion for us," Doug said quickly.

The waiter recovered quickly from his mistake and apologized as he handed them each a menu. "See?" Jody said dryly. "If I'd had on something provocative, he wouldn't have made that mistake." She lowered her burning face and hoped that Doug couldn't see her chagrin in the dim light of the restaurant.

"It bothers you, doesn't it?" Doug asked quietly.

"What bothers me?"

"The affair."

"No, it doesn't bother me at all," Jody lied.

Doug stared at her across the table. "Jody, be honest with yourself," he said. "You blush and stammer and look embarrassed every time something reminds you that this is, in fact, an affair, and that you're not married to the man you're sleeping with."

"Well, what do you expect?" Jody asked. "I've never had an affair before. It's going to take me a little time to get adjusted to it."

"I've seen sixteen-year-olds who are more comfortable with the idea than you are," Doug said.

"I'm sorry I don't come up to your usual standards of sophistication," Jody said tightly.

"Jody, I didn't mean that," Doug said gently. "Believe me, you know everything you need to when you make love to me. But I still don't think an affair is right for you."

Jody looked at him in horror. "You're not backing out now, are you?"

"I couldn't if I tried," Doug admitted. "You're stuck with me. But I don't think you should be having an affair if it makes you this uncomfortable."

"I'll get used to it," Jody said stubbornly.

"But should you get used to it?" Doug argued. "Wouldn't you be better off if you married me?"

"Doug, we've been over this before," Jody said. "You know that I don't want to get married, and you know why. Can't you just leave it at that?"

"Can't you even think about marrying me?" Doug countered. "Won't you even consider it?"

"I can't," Jody insisted.

"Yes, you can," Doug said, "if you just would. Think about it, Jody. Please. For both our sakes."

Jody paused, then asked, "If I promise to think about it, will you promise not to bug me about it every week?"

"Every other week?" Doug asked.

"No, Doug, I mean it," Jody said. "I'll think about it, but you have to promise not to pressure me."

"Do you promise?"

"I promise. Do you?"

"I promise too," Doug said. "Now that we have that settled, may I have the honor of this dance?"

CHAPTER THIRTEEN

"Mom, are you ready to go to Aunt Marilyn's yet?" Scott called up the stairs.

"Yes, I'm ready," Jody said as she came downstairs. She looked lovingly at her son, who was bent over the new construction set she had given him for Christmas. She got her scalloped potatoes and fruit salad from the kitchen. "Here, carry this for me," she said as she handed the salad to Scott.

"Do you think Uncle Doug will like the shirt and tie I got him?" Scott asked.

"I'm sure he'll love them," Jody said absently.

"But how did you know his size?" Scott persisted.

Because she had peeked one night when he had it off. "I just guessed," she said to Scott. "Pull the door shut, will you?"

They crossed the street to Hunter and Marilyn's house, which was filled with relatives. Jody greeted her various aunts and uncles and cousins and caught up on all the latest gossip while she helped in the kitchen. She had offered to have the family dinner herself this year, since Marilyn was pregnant and tired, but Marilyn had insisted, saying that Hunter and her mother would help her. Marilyn's eyes were suspiciously moist when she came up to Jody and hugged her. "I know that organ cost you more than Hunter had to spend," she said. "Thanks."

Jody hugged her cousin back. "Be sure and thank Doug. I would have done the same thing, but he's the one who actually negotiated the deal."

"You're both such special people," Marilyn said. "Such beautiful people."

Jody's eyes grew a little misty. Marilyn was the beautiful person. Even though she knew that Doug and Jody were breaking the moral code that as a devout churchgoer Marilyn held so dear, she could still love them as she did. Marilyn had said nothing more to Jody about the affair, but Jody knew that she was hurting her by her actions. And Hunter—he hadn't said a word either, but sometimes his expression was a little sad when he looked at them. Jody hated hurting them, especially when they had stood beside her so many times in the past.

Jody carried a platter of turkey out to the dining room and almost ran into Doug coming toward the kitchen.

"Oops," she said, her eyes shining up into his. "Merry Christmas." She wished she had the freedom to reach up and kiss his cheek, but their affection for one another had to be kept a secret.

"Merry Christmas yourself," Doug said. "Let me help you with that."

Jody handed the platter to Doug. As his hand brushed hers, she remembered how his hands had felt stroking her body just two nights ago in the motel room in San Antonio, bringing her excruciating delight. They had spent four glorious hours together before they had had to drive back to New Braunfels, and the next day Jody had been vaguely depressed. She had gloried in their intimacy, but she hated having to get up and get dressed and drive thirty miles home. It made their love seem tawdry somehow.

231

And the way they felt about one another was anything but that.

Jody and the others helped Marilyn get the huge buffet laid out, and the family held hands in a circle as Hunter said grace. Marilyn had long ago given up seating everyone at the dining table; she served her twenty-odd guests buffet style, with folding tables scattered around the living room. Jody fixed herself a generous plate and sat down at a card table with Marilyn's mother, Maggie White.

"Aunt Maggie, did you bake another cake today?" she asked. "I always help Hunter and Marilyn eat the ones you send them."

"Mine's the German chocolate," Maggie said. "How is your store doing these days? Is your new partner working out?"

"She's going broke and her new partner's a slave-driver," Doug said as he sat down beside Jody. He extended his hand to Maggie. "Hello, I'm Doug Ford."

"Maggie White. I'm Marilyn's mother," Maggie said.

"Oh, so you're the one who bakes all those delicious cakes," Doug said. He pointed out the living-room window. "I live in the big red brick over there, and I love spice cakes."

Maggie laughed. "I'll bake Marilyn two cakes next time. Jody, do you ever bake anymore? You used to make the best cinnamon rolls I ever tasted."

"I don't have much time these days, with the store and D— Scott," she said. "Sunday's my only day off, unless I hire Beatrice to come in for me."

"You're working too hard, child," Maggie said. "And you're still so thin!" She turned to Doug. "I worry a lot about Jody now that her mother and father are gone. God rest their souls, I miss them, even though it's been six years. I know Jody does."

"Yes, I do," Jody said.

"Did you ever meet Jody's parents?" Maggie asked Doug. "There were never finer people than my brother-in-law and his wife. Jody's parents were the salt of the earth."

Maggie chattered on, but Jody's thoughts remained wth her parents. They would have been disappointed in her if they had lived, she realized with a start. They were deeply religious, and although they wouldn't have judged her or condemned her, they would have been hurt by the affair she was having, just as Marilyn was. Jody forced most of the guilt from her mind and returned to the conversation, but a certain discomfort remained.

Everyone pitched in to clean up, and before long they were all gathered in the living room around the Christmas tree. Scott and two of the nieces were appointed to be Santa Claus, and soon everyone was opening presents and the room was filled with delighted talk and laughter. For Jody there was a peach colored sweater from Hunter and Marilyn, a scarf from her Aunt Maggie, and a bottle of cologne from Scott. Jody had thought she had received the last of her presents when one of the nieces handed her a small box. "Here, Aunt Jody, this is for you."

Jody looked down at the small box. The tag was unsigned, but her name was written in Doug's handwriting. She glanced down at the ring on her finger and looked up at him with surprise. He was too far away to speak, but his eyes danced as she bent her head to open the box.

With trembling fingers Jody withdrew a cameo locket that was a perfect match to her ring. *He shouldn't have,* she thought, but the locket was beautiful. She stared across the room, wishing she had the right to kiss him and thank him in front of everybody. Instead, she thanked him across the room with her eyes and quietly, when nobody was looking, slipped the cameo around her neck.

"Thank you for the locket," Jody said later as she and Doug walked back across the street. "I love it."

"I thought you might," he said easily. "I love the gloves and the books too." Jody had found Doug an original set of Zane Grey westerns at an estate sale just last week.

"Have you read them?" Jody asked.

"Just one or two," Doug said.

"Uncle Doug, did you like the shirt I gave you?" Scott asked. "Did Mom get you the right size?"

"Yes, she did," Doug assured Scott.

"I guess she's just good at guessing those kinds of things," Scott said. "Can we go to the movies tomorrow night?"

"Night after next," Jody said. "Doug and I are going out by ourselves tomorrow night."

"Again?" Scott asked with disappointment. "All you ever do these days is go out by yourselves. You used to take me all the time."

"Now, Scott, you get to come along a lot of the time," Jody said.

"And you get to go out night after next," Doug reminded him. "Scott, your mom needs to spend time with other grownups."

"Yeah, I know," Scott said. "She says that she needs to talk to somebody over four-and-a-half feet tall."

Doug and Jody both laughed. Jody pushed open the front door. "Go up and get your bath, Scott, and I'll be up soon to kiss you good night."

"Mom, can't I stay up for a little while?" Scott wheedled.

"I have to work tomorrow, even if you don't have school," Jody said firmly. She pointed toward the stairs.

"Awright. 'Night, Uncle Doug."

Doug grabbed Jody's hand and led her to the darkened kitchen. "I can't make it through the day without at least one kiss from you," he said as he put his arms around her and pulled her close. Jody's arms curled around him as their lips met in a warm, passionate caress. Jody groaned and moved closer, her breasts pressed against his warm, muscular chest as she touched and stroked the back and shoulders of the man she loved so much. Doug's breathing became ragged as he ran his hands down her arms.

"I can hardly wait until tomorrow," he said as his lips trailed down her cheek.

"Mom, I'm getting a glass of milk—Mom, what are you and Uncle Doug doing in here in the dark?" Scott asked. Doug and Jody had jumped away from each other just in time and now stood a couple of feet apart in the light streaming in from the dining room.

"Your mother thought she heard a mouse," Doug said quickly. "I'm trying to find out where it's coming from."

"With the light off?" Scott asked.

"Of course," Jody answered shakily. "The light would scare it off."

"Oh. Well, can I have some milk?"

Jody turned on the light and was relieved to see that her lipstick wasn't smeared all over Doug's face. Scott got his milk to take back upstairs, and Jody walked Doug to the front door. "That was more effective than a cold shower," he said.

"My God, he almost caught us," Jody said.

"Yeah, and as bright as he is, he could probably put two and two together," Doug said.

"I don't think he knows all that much about sex yet," Jody said.

"Don't you count on it," Doug said. "I'll see you in the morning."

Jody climbed the stairs and took off her clothes, then got into a robe and went to kiss Scott good night. He was sitting in bed, reading one of the new books Doug had given him. "This is neat," he said. "Uncle Doug picks the best books."

"That's probably because he was a little boy once himself," Jody said thoughtfully.

"Where are you going tomorrow night?" Scott asked.

"Dinner and a movie," Jody replied with her stock answer.

"Then why can't I come?" Scott argued. "Why do you and Uncle Doug want to go off by yourselves all the time? You used to take me."

"We do take you, Scott," Jody said. "But it's like Uncle Doug said—sometimes adults like to be with other adults."

"But I didn't think you liked him all that much," Scott said. "When he first came, you didn't want to have anything to do with him."

"I thought he was like Daddy," Jody said honestly. "I realized later that I was wrong about him. He's a good person."

"Good enough to marry?"

"What makes you ask that?" Jody asked quickly.

"Oh, nothing. I just heard Aunt Maggie tell Aunt Marilyn that you and Uncle Doug would make a nice couple," Scott said.

"Aunt Maggie would like to see everybody married," Jody said.

236

"But would you and Uncle Doug make a nice couple?" Scott persisted.

"I don't know, Scott," Jody said impatiently. "Now get under the covers, and I'll see you in the morning."

Scott slid down into the bed. "I think you and Uncle Doug would make a terrific couple," he volunteered. " 'Night, Mom."

" 'Night, Scott," Jody murmured, wondering what Scott would say if he knew that Doug wanted to marry her and that she had turned him down.

Jody and Doug continued their affair through the dark, cold month of January and into February, and as time wore on Jody found the relationship more and more unsatisfactory. She loved the time she shared with Doug, but other aspects of the affair got old quickly. She got tired of her and Doug having to drive to San Antonio one or two evenings a week and get up and drive home afterward, especially when she was having to drive Scott to Austin once a week also, but she didn't feel that it was right to leave Scott with a babysitter all night long. Scott was doing well with Dr. Blundell, and he and Ryan had resumed their close friendship, but he still needed a lot of love and attention from her, and he needed the security of having his mother home at night. She and Doug had managed another buying trip, this one in the middle of the week, but they had only had one night to share, and that was after driving for most of the day and looking at furniture for much of the evening. Jody was tempted to try to arrange some private time together in New Braunfels, but Doug was adamant that they do nothing that would cause them or Scott any embarrassment.

And Jody's conscience bothered her. She tried to

rationalize what she and Doug were doing, telling herself that she was doing nothing that terrible, but deep down her actions bothered her. She was proud of her love for Doug, and it frustrated her to have to keep it under wraps for the most part. Jody knew that the secrecy bothered Doug too, even though he didn't complain about it. She knew that he would have preferred their relationship to be open, as a marriage would be. And she wondered what Scott would think when he realized what was going on. He wasn't a stupid child, and he had already complained bitterly on several occasions that she and Doug were leaving him out. Jody felt that she was being torn apart by the conflicting demands on her. She owed time to her son, and she owed time to the man she loved, and sometimes there wasn't enough time to do both of them justice.

So in spite of her earlier firm denials, Jody could feel her stance against getting married again weakening. She loved Doug deeply, and she was tired of the secretive nature of their relationship. She knew that Doug loved her at least as much as she loved him, and that he loved her son as he would have loved a child of his own. But was Doug like his violent brother? Did he have the potential for abusing her too?

Jody watched Doug as he carefully sanded down an old washstand. The lovely old piece was stained and scratched badly, but the underlying wood was of a very high quality. "It's going to be beautiful," she said as he wiped away some of the sawdust.

Doug looked up at her and smiled his lover's smile, the one he saved for when they were alone. "You're beautiful," he said.

"Oh, Doug, I love you," Jody said as she bent down

238

and kissed his lips, careful not to touch his dusty clothing.

"Don't touch me—I'm dirty and you look like a million bucks," Doug said. "I hope they have something we can use." Jody was driving to another estate sale in San Antonio.

"So do I," Jody said. "I'll see you in the morning."

Jody was on the outskirts of town when she reached into the console to make sure she had her San Antonio map. She picked up a small box that lay partially hidden there, and, curious, she pulled over. "He remembered Valentine's Day," she murmured as she unwrapped the small package and withdrew a single pearl on a gold chain. She laughed at the silly card Doug had left with it, but her eyes were misty as she fastened the necklace around her neck. This was the third fine piece of jewelry he had given her in the last two months, she thought as she pulled onto the highway that would take her to San Antonio. He would be a generous husband. Generous as well as loving.

Was she being fair to the both of them? she asked herself. Except for that one incident on the day of Larry's funeral, Doug had never done anything that indicated he might become violent. And Jody had to admit that he really hadn't done anything that day either, that it was mostly her frightened imagination that had made her react the way that she had. Doug had been angry with her a few times since, but his anger had not been the unreasonable kind that Larry had displayed. She really didn't think Doug would ever abuse her the way his brother had.

But how could she be sure? she asked herself. The answer was simple—she couldn't, not positively. But she had every reason to believe that the man she loved so much would be good to her, and to her surprise Jody found herself wanting to marry him after all. Jody guessed that Doug and Marilyn were right. She was the kind of woman who would want to be married to the man she loved.

The estate sale proved to be a disappointment, and Jody found herself in a San Antonio shopping mall a couple of hours later, thinking about how she could tell Doug she now wanted to marry him. She hated to just ring his doorbell and baldly announce that she had changed her mind, yet she wasn't the kind to hire a skywriter or something like that. She was mulling over her problem when she walked past a jewelry store with a big sign proclaiming that all wedding rings in stock were thirty-five percent off. Jody wandered in, and half an hour later she left with a small, gaily wrapped package that she would give Doug when she got home that night.

Doug peered out the window as Jody drove into her driveway. It was after dark, and he was beginning to get worried about her. She had promised that she would walk over for a few minutes after Scott had gone to bed and tell him about the estate sale, and since it would be an hour or more before she had Scott to bed, he had time for a shower and dinner.

Doug was just finishing his meal when she knocked on the door. She was dressed in jeans and her hair was damp from the shower, and Doug took her into his arms and kissed her thoroughly.

"I was getting worried about you," he said when they finally broke apart.

"I didn't mean to be this late," Jody said as she sat down on the couch.

Doug touched the pearl necklace with one finger. "Like it?"

"Love it," Jody said. She took the package out from

240

behind her back. "Happy Valentine's Day," she said as she handed it to Doug.

"You didn't have to get me anything," Doug said.

"Go ahead—open it," Jody said a little anxiously.

Doug opened the package and stared at the matching pair of Florentine wedding rings. "Are—are you telling me what I think you're telling me?"

"Yes, I am." Jody smiled at him.

"Jody, are you sure?" Doug asked anxiously. "I mean, you were so opposed to the idea before."

"That was before we started the affair," Jody said. "Oh, Doug, you and Marilyn were right. I don't like sneaking around and getting up and driving home afterward and having to keep the way I feel about you a secret. And I don't like splitting myself between you and Scott. I want the three of us to be a family."

"But what about marriage?" Doug asked. "Are you still afraid of it?"

"A little," Jody admitted. "But I'm willing to take the risk."

To Jody's amazement, tears formed in Doug's eyes and ran down his cheeks. "Oh, Jody, I don't think I've ever been this happy in my life!" Doug said as he tried to wipe the tears from his cheeks. "Thank you. I promise that you'll never regret it."

Jody opened her arms and held Doug tightly. *I hope I never regret it,* she thought as she kissed the tears from Doug's cheeks. *I hope to God that I never regret it.*

"Jody, I just wanted to tell you how happy I am for you," Mrs. Borrer said. Her veined hand trembled a little and her eyes were suspiciously moist. "I've been hoping for the longest time that you would find happiness again."

241

"Why, thank you, Mrs. Borrer," Jody said as she hugged the little lady.

"And what about you, Scott? Are you excited?" the woman asked.

"I think it's super," Scott replied with a smile.

The door of the vestibule blew open, and a brisk March breeze whipped in. "Here, let me get that," Doug said. He pushed the door shut, leaving Hunter shaking hands on the steps.

"And I want to congratulate you, too, Doug," Mrs. Borrer continued. "Jody's a fine woman, and I know you'll do your best to make each other happy."

"We certainly will, Mrs. Borrer," Doug said.

"Marriage is such a wonderful institution," Mrs. Borrer said. "John and I spent fifty-five happy years together with seldom a cross word between us."

Jody and Doug looked at one another, and Jody laughed uneasily. "Actually, we've already had a few cross words at times," she admitted.

Mrs. Borrer winked. "I said seldom, dear, not never." She asked when they planned to be married, and told them to be sure and send her an invitation.

"I think that small wedding you wanted is getting out of hand," Doug whispered into her ear.

"Do you mind?" Jody asked.

"No, the more witnesses I have, the harder time you'll have getting out of it later," Doug said.

Jody laughed and tried to hide the unease she felt, but Doug could sense that he had said the wrong thing again. In the two weeks since Jody had brought him the wedding rings, he had become increasingly sensitive to her feelings, and at times he could tell that she wasn't completely at ease with the thought of getting married. She tried to hide it, as she was doing now, but he knew that she wasn't entirely comfortable with her decision. Doug's insides twisted

242

with apprehension, as they always did when he sensed her unease. He hoped she wasn't going to try to back out of the wedding, yet at the same time he didn't want her to get married unless she was completely sure about it.

Marilyn came up to Jody with a peculiar expression on her face. "How much longer do you think Hunter will be?" she asked.

"He may be a little while. Mrs. Matthews has him buttonholed, and you know how she loves to talk."

"Oh, dear," Marilyn said. "We have to get out of here."

"Is it what I think it is?" Jody asked.

Marilyn nodded. "It started right after the offering."

"And you sat through the whole sermon?" Jody asked, incredulous.

"What could I do—stop the service?" Marilyn asked. "If I had walked out, Hunter would have been out the door behind me."

"Sometimes you're too dedicated for your own good," Jody grumbled.

Jody stepped out the door and whispered in Hunter's ear, and he left Mrs. Matthews standing there with her mouth open.

"How much time do we have?" he demanded as he took Marilyn's arm and started toward the door.

"We can make it to San Antonio, but I wouldn't stop for hamburgers," Marilyn admitted.

Jody got Rachel from the nursery and took her home. Rachel ate a big lunch and promptly fell asleep on a pallet that Jody fixed for her on the living-room rug. She sat on the couch and watched the sleeping child, who was so much like both her parents, and she felt the desire for another child stirring

243

in her. She had loved Scott's early years and wouldn't mind raising one or two more.

Doug sat down and took Jody by the hand. "Does she give you ideas?" he asked.

"Yes, she does. But what about you? Do you want to start a family at your age?"

"I didn't realize that forty was over the hill," Doug said dryly, making Jody blush. "Of course I want a child with you. Or maybe more than one. Hunter's somewhere in his middle forties by now, and he didn't let it stop him." He put his arm around Jody. "Besides, I won't be starting a family. I'll just be adding to it. I couldn't love Scott any more if he were my son."

"You're a precious man, Doug," Jody said. And he was, so why did she still have doubts about marrying him? Why did the thought still make her feel so uneasy?

Hunter called at about four with the news that Rachel had a little sister. Jody got a babysitter, and she and Doug drove to San Antonio that evening to see Marilyn and the baby. Marilyn had not needed medication and was sitting up in her bed eating a big supper. "How's Rachel?" she asked when Doug and Jody came in.

"She's been trying to say 'sister' ever since Hunter called," Jody said. "It's coming out 'sisee.' What's the little one's name?"

"Ruth," Hunter said.

"Have you seen her?" Marilyn asked. "She's beautiful."

Jody and Doug agreed, and they visited with the proud parents for a little while. On the way home, Doug volunteered that he planned to breed Goldie in the summer, providing that she didn't come into heat while they were away on their honeymoon.

Jody told herself that she was being ridiculous, but her feelings of unease about her upcoming wedding continued to grow. She would replay scenes with Doug, their arguments and their confrontations, and she would remind herself that he had never done anything that could vaguely be considered cruel or violent, to her or anyone else. But over Doug's face Larry's face would superimpose itself, and she would remember what Larry had done to her. She could tell herself all day that Doug was different, but down deep she continued to have her doubts.

Jody said nothing to Doug, hoping that he could not tell, but he could sense her feelings and they worried him more and more. He wanted to marry her, but he didn't want her to marry him if she had any doubts about him. His concern grew as the days passed, and late one evening he walked across the street and knocked on Hunter and Marilyn's door.

Hunter came to the door with Ruth sleeping on his shoulder. "Is it too late to talk to you for a minute?" Doug asked.

"Of course not. Come on in," Hunter replied.

Marilyn offered Doug a cup of tea, and he sat down with them at the kitchen table. "I'm worried about Jody," he admitted. "I don't think she's entirely comfortable with the idea of getting married. Or is it just my imagination?"

Hunter and Marilyn glanced at one another. "No, it isn't your imagination, Doug," Hunter said. "We can feel it too."

Doug looked at both of them helplessly. "What can I do? I want to marry her, but not if she's not sure. We could just keep on with the affair, I guess."

245

"I think that made her uncomfortable," Marilyn said softly.

"Doug, have you and Jody had any time together since you became engaged?" Hunter asked. "Have you spent much time just enjoying one another?"

"Very little," Doug admitted.

"Why don't you two get away for the weekend?" Hunter asked. "Spend a little time just being Doug and Jody. We can keep Scott for you, if you like."

"We couldn't impose on you like that, not with a new baby," Doug protested.

"Nonsense. Jody kept Rachel the whole time I was in the hospital," Marilyn said.

"Take her, Doug. It will do her a world of good," Hunter said.

"How can I get her to go?" Doug asked.

"Take her shopping for her wedding dress," Marilyn suggested.

"Do you think it will help?" Doug asked.

"It's bound to," Hunter said reassuringly.

Jody waved to Scott as they pulled out of the driveway. "Are you sure we have any business leaving Scott with Marilyn?" she asked anxiously. "She has enough to do right now."

"It was her idea," Doug said. "She said it was high time you picked out your wedding dress. The wedding's only two months away, and we haven't really made many arrangements yet."

"I've been so busy with the store, I haven't had time to turn around," Jody said evasively. She had been busy with the store, but she had also been dragging her feet as far as the arrangements went.

"At least we have Hunter and the church reserved," Doug said. "And once you get your dress picked out, we can call the florist."

"Maybe we ought to just elope," Jody teased.

"Don't tempt me!" Doug replied.

Jody laughed and they talked all the way in to San Antonio. They checked into their hotel on the Riverwalk and strolled a couple of blocks to one of the city's most fashionable department stores.

"You know, you're not even supposed to see me in the dress before the wedding," Jody teased as they went into the bridal boutique.

"That's all right, I've seen you in a lot less," Doug retorted, laughing when she blushed.

The bridal consultant was very helpful. She assured Jody that there was no reason that she couldn't wear off-white, as long as she didn't wear a veil with the dress. Jody tried on several styles that were all right, but they weren't the special dress that she wanted. The consultant was sorry, but that was all she had in Jody's size. She suggested another store a few blocks away.

"They sure didn't have many dresses," Jody said once they were out of the store.

"Maybe you'll have better luck at the next store," Doug said. "Do we have time to stop for ice cream?"

They had huge ice cream cones at a parlor on the Riverwalk. Afterward, they climbed the steps to get to street level and walked to the store that the bridal consultant had recommended. There was no consultant at the second store, but one of the salesgirls was very helpful when Jody explained what she was looking for. The girl, who confided that she was getting married herself in July, brought out several dresses on hangers and held them up for Jody and Doug to see.

Doug immediately pointed to an empire-style off-white dress with a lace bodice and sleeves. "Try that one on," he said.

247

Jody looked at the dress and nodded. A few minutes later, she, Doug, and the salesgirl were standing in front of the mirrors just outside the dressing rooms. "It's perfect," Jody said, staring at her reflection. The easy styling disguised her angularity, and the lace at the throat framed her face beautifully.

"There's a detachable train if you want it," the salesgirl said.

Jody shook her head. "No, it's perfect just like it is." She met Doug's eyes in the mirror. "Do you like it?"

Doug nodded wordlessly. Jody changed back into her street clothes, and the salesgirl carefully wrapped the dress in a plastic sheath before she put it into a big box. She offered to have it delivered to their hotel, but Doug volunteered to carry it.

Jody bought shoes to go with the dress, and Doug insisted on buying her a couple of sexy negligees. They carried their purchases back to the hotel like a couple of kids and fell into one another's arms.

"Happy?" Doug asked tenderly as he smiled down at Jody.

"Oh, yes." Jody could feel her doubts about Doug melting like a snowball in the July sunlight. She loved him with all her heart, and marrying him was the right thing to do. She threw her arms around Doug and kissed him passionately. "Make love to me, Doug," she said. "It's been too long since we've made love."

"It's only been a week," Doug teased. They had continued slipping away to San Antonio for a few hours of privacy, and it hadn't bothered Jody so much lately, now that she knew the situation was only temporary.

"That's way too long," Jody said as she started unbuttoning Doug's shirt.

248

"You really are insatiable," Doug teased. "Lift your arms."

Jody obediently raised her arms, and Doug pulled her sweater from her body. Jody's trembling fingers undid Doug's shirt, and she pushed it from him, baring his chest to her eager gaze. "I will never get enough of looking at you," she said as her fingers touched and stroked the warmth of his body.

Doug unhooked Jody's bra and pulled it away from her. "You're going to be beautiful when you're old," he said. "You have those kind of bones in your face. I noticed them the minute I met you, all those years ago."

Jody stopped what she was doing. "You noticed then? Why?"

Doug ran gentle fingers down Jody's face. "I was half in love with you when you married my brother," he said. "That's part of why I was so furious when I thought you had cheated on him. I thought you weren't the woman I had always imagined you were, and it disappointed me."

"You've felt that way about me all this time?" Jody asked, incredulous.

Doug nodded. "That's one of the reasons I never married, I think."

"I never even guessed," Jody admitted. She gave Doug a trembling smile. "I'm glad you waited for me."

"I am too," Doug said.

Gently, reverently, they removed one another's clothing, touching one another with gentle passion as they lay down together. Jody was astounded by Doug's confession and sought to assure him of her love for him. She held Doug lovingly, stroking his back, his shoulders, his chest. Her lips caressed his small masculine nipples the way he so loved for her

249

to do, until they were stiff with desire. Her lips trailed down his midsection, nibbling a little at his waist before she tormented his stomach and navel. Her loving touch drifted lower, kissing and caressing Doug intimately as he moaned with delight. When he protested, she shook her head and smiled at him.

Jody finally joined their bodies, taking him with her on a sudden ascent to delight. They cried out together as passion quickly overtook them, and Doug deftly rolled Jody over onto her back. "Now I want to love you," he whispered.

Doug separated his body from hers, but his hands and his lips speedily rekindled the flames of desire in her. Jody could feel the excitement starting to grow in her again, more slowly this time but with even more force than before. She gasped as Doug's lips kissed and suckled her swollen breasts in the way she loved so much. His hands stroked her waist and her stomach and sought and caressed the heart of her femininity, each loving touch bringing her closer and closer to reaching fulfillment again. Doug soon felt her stiffen next to him as tremors of pleasure wracked her body for the second time, this new moment of delight even more beautiful than the first.

"Oh, Doug, I love you," she said as she looked up at him with her heart in her eyes. Calm and relaxed, she realized that her uneasiness about him was gone.

"Jody, I love you so much I hurt with it," Doug said as he brushed the hair from her face. "I hope you know that."

Jody nodded. "I know that. I've never been more sure of anything in my life."

CHAPTER FOURTEEN

"Are you ready yet?" Doug asked as he looked up from the magazine he was reading. "The whole river's out there just waiting for us."

"Don't you think it might still be a little cold to go swimming?" Jody teased.

"In that green murk? Surely you jest," Doug said. "I meant the Riverwalk. I can hardly wait to go to Queenie's. They used to serve the best Irish coffee this side of the Atlantic."

"I'm sure they still do," Jody said. She smoothed on peach-colored lipstick and started to pin up her hair but caught the shake of Doug's head in the mirror and swept it to one side with a comb instead. "I never have understood why you don't like my hair up," she grumbled as she put her lipstick in her purse.

"Makes you look like an old-maid schoolteacher," Doug teased.

"Doug!" Jody protested.

"Well, it does," he said cheerfully. "And then it's so much trouble to get unpinned later." He threw his magazine down and ran his hand down the silky fall of hair. "Wear it down at the wedding, will you?"

"I was thinking about cutting it, now that I'm past thirty," Jody said thoughtfully.

Doug moaned theatrically behind her and clutched his stomach. "You can't do that!" he protested dramatically. "Then I'd have nothing to run my hands through when we make love!"

"All right, all right, the hair stays," Jody laughed. "Come on—we mustn't keep San Antonio waiting."

They strolled along the river hand in hand, laughing and acting silly. They had needed to get away, Jody mused, and become attuned to one another again. She had been ridiculous to worry about marrying Doug. They would be very happy together, if today was any indication of what their life together would be like.

They had dinner at a well-known seafood restaurant on the river. The evening was warm enough so that they could eat outside on the patio, and only a narrow sidewalk separated them from the water. Over dinner, they made the rest of their wedding plans, and Doug suggested that Jody spend Monday at home making the arrangements. Doug also suggested going to the coast for their honeymoon, but Jody laughingly reminded him that they still owed Scott a trip there, and they better make it the mountains unless they wanted him along!

They lingered over coffee, and Doug bought her a silk rose at a stand under the bridge. They walked down the river, stopping at a well-known nightspot and listening to the jazz musicians while they sipped their drinks.

"Do you still want to go to Queenie's?" Jody asked as they left the nightclub, the smoke and the jazz saxophone still lingering around them.

Doug checked his watch. "It's only a little after eleven," he said. "Are you tired?"

"No, I'd love to go," Jody said, not altogether truthfully. She was tired, and she had heard that the clientele in Queenie's wasn't the best in the world. But she hated to spoil Doug's evening.

They walked a couple more blocks to the small, dimly lit bar with a green canopy over the entrance. "I haven't been here in years," Doug admitted. "I hope the Irish coffee's still good."

Since the tables were all full, they sat down at the bar next to a young man in a motorcycle jacket. Jody started to ask Doug if they could leave, but the bartender stepped up and Doug ordered two Irish coffees. The man in the motorcycle jacket turned bleary eyes on Jody. "You're not a bad-looking broad," he said, burping. "Is that your old man?"

"Huh?" Jody asked, startled.

"I said, is that wimp you're with your old man?"

Jody stiffened.

"Yes, I'm her old man," Doug said levelly. "Jody, what do you think about—"

"He's too old for you, honey," the man said, grinning lewdly at her. "Too old and too wimpy. What say you and I hightail it out of here?"

"Ricky, that's enough," the bartender said, giving Doug and Jody a don't-mind-him glance.

Ricky settled back on the stool.

"Doug, I don't feel very comfortable in here," Jody whispered.

Doug started to say something, but the bartender put their drinks in front of them. "Let's drink these, and then we'll go," he said softly, eyeing Ricky as he picked up his drink.

"He's probably not worth nuthin' in the sack, honey," Ricky said.

"That's enough," Doug said firmly. "Come on, Jody, let's go."

Jody and Doug hopped off the stools, but Ricky jumped between them and the door. "I mean it, sweetie, dump him and come with me." He reached out and grabbed Jody's arm, his foul breath making her gag.

"Let go of her," Doug said as he grabbed Ricky's arm. Jody saw two large men start across the floor, but Ricky's other fist flew up and caught Doug in the eye.

Doug's fist shot out before Jody knew what had happened. He hit Ricky square in the jaw, and his other fist sent Ricky sprawling across a table filled with dismayed tourists. Doug started to hit him again, but one of the large men grabbed him from behind.

"Easy, fella," he said. "You're in the clear right now, but if you hit him again you won't be."

Jody stared in horror at Doug. His face was contorted with rage, and his fists were doubled up for another attack. *Oh, dear God, no,* she thought as the large man struggled to subdue Doug. He was capable of violence, after all. He had just laid Ricky out cold across the table. He could do that to her someday, if he had the right provocation.

"Oh, no!" she moaned as she put her hands in front of her face.

Vaguely, through the mists of rage, Doug heard Jody moan and whipped his head around. She was staring at him as though he were a monster. "Jody, wait, I—" he called out, but she was through the door and gone before he could even speak to her. "Please, let me go," he said to his burly captor. "She's scared to death. I have to go to her now."

"I think you better stay for a few minutes and answer this gentleman's questions," the guard said as a young policeman came through the door.

Jody ran through the inky darkness all the way back to the hotel, as though the hounds of hell were on her heels. Doug had just laid that drunk kid out cold, she kept thinking, he *was* a violent man. There was no way she could marry him now, now that she knew what he would do when he was angry. She suffered the strange glances of the people in the hotel lobby and asked the desk clerk to arrange for her to rent a car. She had to get back to New Braunfels tonight—she had to get away from the man who had just proven that he was every bit as violent as his brother had been.

Jody threw her clothes in her suitcase. She started to pack the wedding dress and the negligees, but she couldn't even bring herself to touch them, so she left them in the department store bags. She knew that she should wait for Doug, to at least let him drive her back, but she had no desire to be anywhere near him tonight.

But her conscience wouldn't let her leave him without a word. She picked up a piece of hotel stationery and a pen and scrawled a quick note that read, "Have gone back to New Braunfels. Please return wedding dress tomorrow before you go back." She left the note unsigned and put it in the middle of the bed.

Her rented car was ready by the time she got back to the lobby. She got to the outskirts of town before tears of hurt and disappointment started to fall. *Oh, why, Doug,* she wondered over and over. *Why do you have to be like Larry? Why do you have to be as violent as he was?* Jody tried to drive but finally gave up and pulled over to the side of the road, venting her grief as huge sobs shook her body.

Doug marched down the Riverwalk, his jacket slung over his shoulder. The policeman had been nice enough once he had found out what had happened, and the patrons had all spoken up in his de-

255

fense, but he had been detained for the better part of an hour, and he wondered what visions Jody had conjured up in her mind while he was away. He had seen the terror on her face when she had looked at him, but he was still aggravated with her for running away. What did she think he was going to do next? Hit her? As it was, this was only the second time in his life he'd been in a barfight, and it was embarrassing enough without having Jody act the way she had.

Doug opened the door of their hotel room and glanced around. "Jody? Are you here?" When silence greeted him, he opened the bathroom door and the closets, swearing out loud when he found her suitcases gone. "Dammit, how could she run out on me like this?" he snapped as he picked up her note and read it. *Take the dress back?* Doug sat down on the bed when he realized what that implied. She had changed her mind about marrying him.

Angrily, Doug gathered up his clothes and started stuffing them into his suitcase. "Dammit, Jody, you're not running out on me, not like this!" he murmured aloud as he shut the suitcase. "You love me and I love you, and you're not going to let one barfight change all that." Besides, what was he supposed to do? Let the drunk manhandle her?

Doug glanced at the neatly boxed wedding dress. He gathered it up along with her shoes and negligees, determined not to take any of it back. She would marry him—he loved her too much to let her go now.

Doug checked out and carefully put her new clothes in his car for the drive back to New Braunfels. He pulled into his driveway and started to go to talk to Jody, but it was after three and her house was dark. Doug shrugged and got her things out of the car. She was probably in no mood to talk to him tonight anyway, and he wasn't particularly in the best frame of mind to talk to her either. It could wait until tomorrow. He unlocked his front door and slammed it behind him, and only then did Jody sigh in relief and drift into an uneasy sleep, grateful that Doug did not intend to confront her tonight.

Jody stared at her half-eaten sandwich, glancing furtively out the window at Doug's house. He had come in from church just a few minutes ago, and she expected him to walk across the street any time now. In the cold light of day, she realized that she had overreacted last night. She should have at least stayed and told the police what had happened. But fear had overridden her common sense, and she had behaved like a frightened child. She owed Doug an apology for that.

But she was still frightened by Doug's behavior. If he had gotten mad enough to hit the punk and knock him out last night, he could very easily get mad enough to hit her and hurt her someday too. And there was no way she could marry him now, with that threat hanging over her head. Jody rued the moment they had decided to go to the bar. A part of her was bitterly hurt and disappointed by what she had discovered about Doug, but a part of her was relieved that this time she had found out before the wedding.

Jody saw Doug crossing the street, and she tossed her sandwich into the trash can. She met him at the door before he had a chance to knock.

"How do you feel today?" she asked, eyeing Doug's shiner.

"Not good, but I bet Ricky feels a whole lot worse," Doug replied. He glanced around. "Is Scott here?"

"No, I thought it best that we have this discussion in private," Jody said. "I'll talk to him later."

She and Doug sat down in the living room, facing one another. "I'm sorry I ran out on you," Jody said. "That was the coward's way out."

"I'm sorry if the incident upset you," Doug said levelly. "The police would have liked to question you."

"I'll call them this afternoon and give them a full statement," Jody said.

"That won't be necessary. The other patrons vindicated me," Doug said sardonically.

"I'm glad," Jody said quietly. "Are you going to press charges against Ricky?"

"I'm still thinking about it." Doug shifted in his chair. "May I bring the wedding dress over here?"

"No, I told you to take it back," Jody said nervously.

"Why?" Doug demanded.

"You know why," Jody said. "After what I saw last night, I can't marry you."

"Jody, don't be ridiculous!" Doug exclaimed. "I didn't hurt *you!*"

"Doug, you laid a man out cold across a bar table," Jody replied. "I've been trying to convince myself for over a year now that you're not violent, but you showed me last night just how violent you can be!"

Doug made an impatient motion with his hand. "I knocked out a drunk who was trying to run out the door with you," he said. "That's a lot different from abusing my wife."

"But Doug," Jody said softly, "don't you see? You got mad last night and you hit him. Twice. Hard enough to knock him out cold. And if you got that angry with him, what's to stop you from getting that mad at me someday?"

"Jody, even if I got that mad at you someday, I wouldn't hit you!" Doug protested.

"How do I know that?" Jody asked miserably. "How do you know that? How do you know you wouldn't get angry or frustrated and take it out on me?"

"Because I love you," Doug said.

"Oh, Doug, I don't doubt that you love me," Jody said sadly. "But that's just it. Larry never stopped loving me, even when he was cruel. Sometimes people can be very unkind to the people they love. I love you, Doug, but I'm too scared to marry you now."

"That's totally ridiculous!" Doug snapped. "You're planning to throw away everything we have together just because I got into a barfight? Good grief, that's only the second time in my life I've ever even done that."

"Doug, I'm sorry," Jody said helplessly. "But I can't help it—I'm scared to death to marry you now. Maybe I am being ridiculous, but that's the way I feel."

Doug threw up his hands in frustration. "Jody, I can't do or say any more to convince you that I'm not going to abuse you like Larry did. You either believe in me or you don't. I'm tired of trying to prove to you that I'm not going to mistreat you. Because that's the problem, Jody—I simply cannot prove to you right now that I wouldn't hurt you. The only way I can do that is for you to marry me, and live with me, and let me show you that I'm different. You have to have some faith in me, enough faith to overcome your fear."

Tears welled in Jody's eyes and ran down her cheeks. "I'm sorry, Doug," she said quietly. "But I don't have that much faith."

"Thanks a lot," Doug said as he got up off the couch. "Thanks a whole damn lot."

"Doug, I'm sorry," Jody said brokenly.

"Yeah, that makes two of us," Doug said as he slammed out of the house, leaving her standing in the middle of the room with tears running down her face.

Jody locked the store and got into her car. Doug had invented an excuse to leave early today, as he had for the last three days. She was intensely relieved that he hadn't tried to talk to her again. He had thrown the ball in her court, and he was obviously waiting for her to make the next move.

And oh, she wished that she could make it! She wished with all her heart that she could say the words he wanted to hear and take the hurt from Doug's eyes and make him smile again. But every time she would start to say or do something, she would remember the rage on Doug's face as he had hit the young punk, and she simply could not overcome her fear. It was breaking her heart to call off the wedding, but she felt that she had no other choice.

Jody picked Scott up and made him a light supper. He had been very quiet ever since she had told him that the wedding was off, and she sincerely hoped that this would not set him back. His visits to Dr. Blundell were on a monthly basis now, and she hoped that they could be discontinued by the summer. She had called and advised Dr. Blundell of the broken engagement, in case Scott brought it up with him.

Jody cleaned up the kitchen and was ironing a blouse when she heard a knock on the door. She turned off the iron, afraid that it was Doug, and found Hunter and Marilyn waiting for her.

"Have a few minutes to talk?" Hunter asked quietly.

"Sure. Where are the girls?" Jody asked as she let them in.

"Doug's watching them for us," Marilyn said.

"Did he ask you to come?" Jody asked quietly.

"Yes. Do you mind?" Hunter asked.

"No, of course not," Jody said. They sat down in the living room. "I guess he told you what happened."

"Yes, he did," Marilyn said. "And he didn't try to gloss it over. He admitted that he knocked that kid out cold."

Hunter laced his hands around his knee. "You know, Jody, I saw a lot of barfights during my days in the navy. I was even in a couple. I saw a lot of black eyes and bloody noses. And I'm willing to bet that none of those guys ever beat their wives later. There's a vast difference between fighting in a bar and abusing a woman."

"I know that," Jody admitted. "But you should have seen his face, Hunter! He was absolutely furious!"

"Most men in that situation would be," Marilyn pointed out. "He was only trying to protect himself and you."

Jody took a deep breath. "In my head I know that. But down here"—she pointed to her heart—"down here, I'm scared to death of him now. He was in a rage, Marilyn." She shuddered slightly. "He looked like Larry looked that last time when he hurt me so badly."

"But the anger wasn't directed at you, Jody," Hunter said.

"No, it wasn't, this time. But who's to say that it might not be at some point down the road?" Jody said.

"Jody, do you love Doug?" Marilyn asked.

Jody's eyes filled with tears, and she dashed them

away impatiently. "Yes, I love him. Don't you think this is killing me inside?"

"But do you love him enough to have some faith in him?" Marilyn pressed on.

"I've tried, Marilyn!" Jody's voice was full of anguish. "You don't know how many times I've tried to walk across that street and tell Doug that I'll marry him after all. But I can't—I just can't." She buried her face in her hands and sobbed. "I guess I don't have that faith you and Doug keep talking about."

Jody felt Hunter's gentle hand on her neck. "Hush, Jody, we didn't mean to upset you," he said. "But Doug's dying on the inside. He loves you so much."

"And I love him," Jody said dully. "I love him with all my heart. But that doesn't stop me from being scared at the same time."

"Jody, what are you going to do about Doug?" Marilyn asked. "Are you going to keep on with the affair? And what about the store?"

"I haven't even thought that far ahead," Jody admitted. "And he hasn't brought either issue up."

"I was afraid when we came over here that we weren't going to have any magic words of wisdom for you," Hunter admitted. "Just know that we love you, and that we'll do anything we can to help."

Jody's eyes were swimming with tears as she hugged her two friends. "Thanks. I don't know where I would be without you two sometimes."

"We just wish we could do more," Marilyn said, sharing just a little of Jody's burden.

Jody stared out the window of the store at the bright bluebonnets across the street. Everyone said it was one of the prettiest springs they could ever remember, but Jody hadn't really noticed. She had felt herself growing more and more depressed as the weeks passed, and she still didn't know what to do about Doug. She knew that her fear of him wasn't entirely rational, but she still could not bring herself to change the stalemate that had grown up between them. They had not spoken of the broken engagement since that night three weeks ago at her house, but she could feel him looking at her with a question in his eyes, and she would see the question turn to hurt when she had nothing to say to him. He had not asked her if she wanted to resume their affair, and she wasn't sure she would have wanted to even if he did.

Jody helped a young couple from Austin pick out a brass bed, and she was just ringing up the sale when Doug came in the back door with a manila envelope in his hands. "Jody, I need to see you in the office for a minute when you're through there."

Jody and the couple agreed on a time when they could pick up the bed, and Jody joined Doug in the office. "Here, these are for you," he said as he handed her the envelope. "I had Sam Adamson draw them up."

With trembling fingers, Jody removed the legal documents. "Doug, you can't do this!" she said as she scanned the papers. "This store is your whole retirement! You can't just give your half to me!"

Doug shook his head. "I can't do anything else, Jody. I love you too much to stay here and be around you all the time and not have you as my wife. I'm leaving town."

"You can't!" Jody protested. "This store is your future."

"You were my future," Doug said. "You and Scott were everything I wanted in life. But that's gone now. You've made up your mind, and it's tearing my guts out to see you every day and work with you and

263

not be able to go home with you in the evening and love you as my wife."

"But what about the store?" Jody asked. "I need you here. And what will you do for a living?"

"You can hire help," Doug said harshly. "And I can get a job doing something in Houston. I'm sorry, Jody. If I stay here I'm going to go crazy."

Doug left and Jody stood staring down at the papers. He was leaving her and Scott, removing himself completely from their lives. Jody knew that she ought to run after him, to beg him to stay and tell him that she would be his wife, but the same fear that had held her in its grip for so long held sway yet again, and she didn't move. She heard the back door open and close, and in a minute Doug's car roared out of the parking lot. Jody sat down in a chair and stared straight ahead, too numb to even cry. The man she loved was walking out of her life, and she had no choice but to let him go. Some time later, the bell on the front door tinkled, and with a heart that was breaking she got up and took care of her next customer.

CHAPTER FIFTEEN

Jody looked out her living-room window, hoping to see Doug's car in his driveway. He had gone to Houston three days ago to look for a job, and Jody was beginning to get worried about him. He had said he would call her, but she had heard nothing, and she was beginning to wonder if he had gotten sick or hurt.

Doug's car was not there. Jody stifled a sigh of disappointment and returned to the kitchen where she was dying a batch of Easter eggs for Rachel and Scott. Although Scott was long past the Easter Bunny age, he still loved to hunt for the eggs, and this year they had offered to fix and hide Rachel's for her, since Marilyn was so busy with Ruth, who had developed colic. Jody was just putting a pretty violet egg in the drainer when she thought she heard a car come down the street. Telling herself that she was being silly, she ran to the window.

Jody watched as Doug got out of his car and carried his suitcase to the front door. His shoulders were slumped and even from as far away as Jody was, he looked tired. She fought the urge to run across the street and put her arms around him. Under the circumstances, he probably wouldn't appreciate the gesture very much. But she would go over when she was through with the eggs and see if he had been able to find work.

Doug threw his suitcase on the couch and opened the back door, whistling for Goldie. The big dog ran to him and almost knocked him down in her eagerness to see him.

"Yeah, I've missed you too, Goldie," he said as he stroked the animal's luxurious coat. "You're the only woman I've ever met that I can figure out."

Doug checked her food and water, mentally thanking Scott for taking such good care of her. His chest tightened when he thought of how much he was going to miss that boy when he moved to Houston. Scott and his mother meant the world to him, but try as he might, he simply couldn't break down the wall of fear that Jody had built around her. He had hoped that presenting her with his half of the store might shock her into changing her mind about him, but Jody had mutely accepted the store and the fact that he was getting out of her life completely. Doug knew that she cared about him—he could see it in her eyes every time she looked at him—but fear had her in a stronger grip than love.

Doug got a beer out of the refrigerator and sat down on the back porch. He didn't hear Jody knock at the front door, but she called to him a moment later from the side fence.

"Hi, have a minute?" she asked.

Doug nodded. Jody unlatched the gate and wandered up to the porch. "Have another one of those?" she asked, pointing to the beer.

Doug started to get up, but she quickly said she would get it herself. Pain shafted through Doug as she went in his kitchen. He loved her so damn much.

Jody bit her lips to keep from crying as she opened

266

the refrigerator. Doug had looked at her with such love and hurt. *Oh, why couldn't he have been a different kind of man? Why did he have to have that same violent nature that Larry had?* Taking a deep breath, Jody got a beer and went back out onto the porch, sitting down on the step and leaning against the post. "Did you find a job?" she asked quietly as she sipped the beer.

"Yes, I got a job at an upholstery shop," Doug said. "The pay's not that great, but I figure that with the navy retirement, I won't do so badly. I start the middle of next month."

"Doug, there's no reason that you can't stay a partner here," Jody said. "We could agree on a percentage for me to send you every month."

"Don't be ridiculous—you're going to have to pay for all the things I was doing," Doug said harshly. "You and Scott should have a decent life-style."

"Do you have to go?" Jody asked softly.

"What do you think?" Doug asked. "I told you, Jody, I can't stand living here and not having the freedom to love you as I need to. Just sitting here with you is pure torture."

"I—I'm sorry," Jody stammered. "I'll go."

She started across the yard, tears swimming in her eyes, but a flash of reddish-gold ran in front of her and beat her out of the gate, running toward the street.

"Goldie, no!" Doug yelled as he jumped up and started across the yard.

Jody ran too, but neither of them could get to the dog in time. She darted out into the street, right in the path of an oncoming car, and the young driver couldn't stop in time. Jody heard a sickening snapping of bones as the car collided with the dog.

Doug pushed past Jody and knelt beside his dog,

whose eyes were glazed with pain. "Goldie," he murmured as the dog whimpered pitifully.

The young girl who was driving the car got out. "Oh, God. I tried to stop," she said. "She ran right out in front of me."

"I know that," Doug said. He turned to Jody, and she gasped at the sheer fury she saw on his face. "You left the gate open," he said accusingly. "Dammit, do you have to take away everything I love?"

Instinctively, Jody threw up her arms and started to back away. "I—I'm sorry," she stammered, stumbling on the curb. She couldn't stop her fingers from trembling as she stared into Doug's face, rage contorting his features into the same mask that Larry had worn.

Doug gulped at the terror on Jody's face. For the first time, he was fully able to comprehend the fear she had of him and his temper. She had instinctively thrown up her hands to ward off a blow. Doug reached for her, wincing when she cringed, and gently lowered her arms. "It's all right, Jody. You didn't mean to let the dog out. Go call the vet, and we'll see if he can save her. I'll talk to the woman in the car so she can go."

Jody swallowed and ran for the house. She flipped open the telephone book and punched in the number of Dr. Kingsley, the veterinarian she had always used for the ranch, and grabbed an old blanket and a board out of the garage. "Here, let's slide her onto this and wrap her up," Jody said when she returned to Doug and Goldie. "If we pick her up, we might hurt her more."

Jody laid the board on the street. With gentle movements, she and Doug inched the dog onto the board and Jody tucked the blanket around her. Doug held her in the backseat while Jody raced through the streets to Dr. Kingsley, who had just seen his last patient of the day and was waiting for them. Doug carried Goldie in, and the vet laid her out on the examining table.

Doug gripped Jody's hand tightly as Dr. Kingsley ran trained fingers over Goldie. When he turned to them, his expression was solemn. "I can save her, but it's going to cost a lot of money, more than it would cost to buy a new animal. And even if she recovers completely, she'll never be able to carry a litter."

"Save her," Doug said instantly.

"Don't worry about the cost—I'll pay whatever it takes," Jody said.

Dr. Kingsley smiled. "I thought you would probably want to save her, but I had to be sure. Why don't you folks make yourselves comfortable in the waiting room while my assistant and I fix this lady up?"

Doug and Jody sat down in the waiting room, and Doug lit a cigarette with fingers that trembled. "I haven't seen you smoke in ages," Jody said.

"I only do it when I'm under stress." Doug puffed nervously. "And God knows, I've been under enough lately."

Yes, Doug has been under a lot of stress lately, Jody thought with a start. He had suffered the loss of his fiancée and his business, and now he ran the risk of losing his beloved dog. He had lost—or nearly lost— just about everything that was important to him, just as Larry had. Actually, Doug had lost more, she realized. Larry had still had his wife and son. He had only lost his ranch, not the woman he loved too.

"I'm sorry I left the gate open," Jody said quietly.

"Don't torture yourself about it," Doug said. "It was an honest mistake. And you don't have to pay the vet bill. I can afford it."

"It's my fault, and I'll pay," Jody said stubbornly. "You helped pay for Dr. Blundell."

They argued for a while and finally agreed that they would split the bill. Doug filled an ashtray while they waited, and finally Dr. Kingsley came to the door. "She's ready to go home now," he said. "But she's going to need a lot of nursing for the next week or so."

"We'll take care of her," Jody said.

"What do we need to do?" Doug asked.

Dr. Kingsley gave them detailed instructions, and they carefully loaded the sedated dog into the backseat of Jody's car. She had casts on three of her legs and a long row of stitches on her stomach where Dr. Kingsley had repaired some internal injuries. "Your Dr. Kingsley seems very talented," Doug said as they made Goldie a bed in his kitchen. "Does he specialize in small animals?"

"No, he takes care of cows and horses too," Jody said. "He was Larry's vet on the ranch."

They settled Goldie into her bed in the kitchen, and Jody sat down cross-legged on the floor beside her. She ran a gentle finger down Goldie's row of stitches. "I'm sorry she can't have puppies now."

Doug shrugged. "I wouldn't have been able to breed her in Houston, anyway," he said glumly.

Goldie whimpered, and he was immediately by her side. "What is it, girl?" he crooned.

"Here, she might be thirsty after all the sedation," Jody said. She handed Doug the water bowl, and he held it so that Goldie could drink a little.

Goldie laid her head down and went back to sleep, but Jody couldn't tear herself away from Doug and the dog. She watched as Doug stroked the dog's side, incredible tenderness on his face as he stared down at his sleeping animal.

"I don't know what I would have done if he hadn't been able to save her," he murmured. He turned solemn eyes on Jody. "She's about all I have left." Jody tried to hide the wince but couldn't.

Scott came in the front door a few minutes later. "Uncle Doug, have you seen Mom? She wasn't there when Ryan's mom dropped me off."

"I'm in here, Scott," Jody called.

Scott stopped and stared when he saw the splinted, bandaged dog. "What happened?"

"I left the gate open and she got out," Jody said quietly. "A car hit her."

"Boy, I bet you were mad, weren't you, Uncle Doug?" Scott said.

"Yes, I was for a moment," Doug admitted, remembering the extreme anger he had felt and the terror on Jody's face when he had looked at her like that. He cursed inwardly at the hopeless position he was in. If she was honestly that frightened of him, there was no way she would ever marry him. And the irony of it was, he not only wouldn't ever hit her, he didn't think he could hit her, even if somebody was holding a gun to his head.

Scott joined the vigil and made the three of them sandwiches for supper when both Jody and Doug declined to leave Goldie. Jody and Scott stayed until Scott's bedtime, helping Doug when they could but mostly just watching Doug take care of his dog. His hands and his voice were incredibly gentle as he held her head so that she could drink the milk that Jody warmed up on the stove. It was as if Doug were willing his dog to get better, hoping his incredible love for her would pull her through and make her well.

Finally, Doug shooed them out, saying that Scott needed to go to bed. Scott went on to bed and was soon asleep, but after her shower Jody sat down on the living-room couch and curled her feet up under her. Scott had been right—Doug had been furious with her this afternoon. If his expression had been anything to go by, he had been far angrier with her than Larry had ever been. Her carelessness had almost cost him the dog that he loved so dearly. Yet he hadn't hit her or even come toward her threateningly. He hadn't even yelled at her.

Jody replayed the scene in her mind over and over. He had pulled her hands from her face, told her it was all right, and found her something constructive to do. And later, he had told her not to feel badly about it, that it was an honest mistake on her part. He had controlled his anger with her and channeled it into getting Goldie to the vet. Jody cringed when she thought of what Larry probably would have done under similar circumstances.

She went upstairs and slept for a little while, but she woke up about two and saw that Doug's kitchen light was still on. Afraid that Goldie had taken a turn for the worse, she wrapped a thick terry bathrobe around her and darted across the street, going around the back and lightly rapping on Doug's back door.

"Jody, what's wrong?" he asked as he opened the door.

"I was about to ask you the same thing," Jody said as she stepped inside. "I saw the light on, and I was afraid that Goldie was worse."

Doug looked a little sheepish. "I made me a pallet on the floor. I was worried about her."

Goldie whined and thumped her tail. "Hungry, girl?" he asked as he quickly knelt beside the dog.

"Here, let me make her something she can eat," Jody said. She carefully mashed some dog food with a little warm milk, and Doug held it for Goldie. The dog ate a few bites before exhaustion overtook her and she laid her head back down.

"You can warm this up and feed her again in about an hour," Jody said.

"You seem to know a lot about taking care of sick animals," Doug said.

"A rancher's wife learns," she replied. She sat down beside Goldie and stroked her side. "I'm so sorry, Doug," she said quietly. "I never meant to hurt either you or her."

Doug's gentle fingers touched the top of Jody's head. "I know that," he said softly. "I guess there are some things in life that can't be helped." He got out another cigarette and lit it. "I'm glad she's going to be all right. I sure would have hated to lose her."

"I guess you feel like you've lost everything, don't you?"

"Yes, Jody, I really do," Doug admitted. "You don't know how many times I've cursed the fates that took us into that bar in San Antonio." He shrugged and ground out his cigarette. "Well, I guess neither of us can help being the way we are."

"No, I guess not," Jody said, but she was thoughtful as she walked across the street and climbed back into bed. She had seen Doug's reaction to both anger and stress today, and the way he was didn't seem that terrible to her anymore.

Jody and Scott spent a lot of time in Doug's kitchen over the next few days. Doug spent all of his time with the injured dog, feeding her and stroking her and talking to her, and Goldie responded to his tender care. She tried to sit up the third day, and managed to in spite of her casts on the fifth. Jody marveled at Doug's unceasing tenderness. She had never in her life seen a man so gentle and kind with an animal, and the sight was so beautiful that it brought tears to her eyes. *He would be that way with a baby,* she thought one afternoon while she watched Doug coax a little more food down Goldie. She shivered as she remembered their lovemaking. He had been that way with her, and she hadn't even realized it.

Jody offered to drive Doug and Goldie to Dr. Kingsley's to have her stitches removed. She laughed when the big dog squirmed all over the backseat and licked Doug in the face. "That's some baby you have back there," she teased as Doug tried to control the wiggling dog without hurting her.

"Some baby," he laughed. "This little baby weighs sixty pounds. Oh, Goldie, stop that," he said as the dog licked his face again.

"Come on, you know you love having her feeling good again," Jody said.

"Yeah, I sure do," Doug agreed.

Doug struggled with Goldie all the way to Dr. Kingsley's office. When Goldie realized where she was, she set up a terrific struggle, and it took both Doug and Jody to control her in the waiting room until the vet could see her. Dr. Kingsley laughed when he came to the door and saw the two of them trying to subdue the frightened animal. "She remembers this place well." He laughed as they carried her into his office, struggling with every step they took.

Doug held her head and Jody her feet while Dr. Kingsley examined her and gently removed her stitches. "Those casts need to stay on for a few more weeks, but there isn't any reason she can't hobble around on them a little."

"Are puppies still out?" Jody asked. "I know that Doug wanted a litter."

"I'm afraid so," Dr. Kingsley answered.

Doug laid his hand on Jody's shoulder. "I told you it didn't matter, hon," he said.

"But other than that, she'll be as good as new," the doctor assured them.

They pulled out their checkbooks and split the bill to date, then Jody dropped Doug and Goldie off. But instead of going to the store, she gathered up the legal papers that Doug had presented her with in her office that afternoon earlier in the week and paid a visit to Sam Adamson's office. She emerged an hour and a half later with a new set of papers that she would take over to Doug's tonight. They needed to talk, and the papers would convince him that this time she was sure of what she was doing.

Doug sat on the back porch and watched Goldie hobble a few steps on her casts before she stumbled to the ground. "Girl, I don't think you're ready for this yet," he said as he rose to help the dog to her feet. She swayed uncertainly but righted herself and wobbled across the yard slowly, her tail wagging as she savored her regained freedom.

"Good for you, Goldie," he said as she sniffed her favorite bone hole. He would have to try to rent an old house in Houston, one with a big yard for her to play in, he thought.

Doug gazed around the yard as an aching sadness gripped him. He was almost tempted to call Houston, decline the job offer, and stay in New Braunfels in spite of Jody's refusal to marry him. But he couldn't do that. He couldn't stay trapped in a no-win situation with her. He would move to Houston and leave them both to get on with their lives. Jody would meet someone someday, someone who didn't frighten her. Maybe he'd meet someone too. But he knew that it was going to take him a long time to get over her.

Doug let Goldie play until it was almost dark and helped her back up the steps and to her bed. He went upstairs, took a shower, and was rubbing his hair dry when he heard a knock on the door. He pulled on a pair of jeans and loped down the steps just as Jody opened the front door and poked her head in. "Doug? Are you here?"

"Right here," he said. "Come on in."

Jody stepped in. Doug glanced at her darkened house. "Has Scott gone to bed yet? He usually comes with you to check on Goldie."

"He's spending the night with the Bohannons." Jody clutched a manila envelope in her hands, and Doug thought she seemed a little nervous.

"Goldie actually wandered around out in the yard for a little while," Doug said proudly as he followed Jody to the kitchen.

"I'm glad," Jody said. She knelt down and patted Goldie's flank. "She'll be running around as good as new before you know it," she said.

Goldie thumped her tail on the floor. "That dog really likes you," Doug said as Jody stood.

"She's one of the best-natured dogs I've ever known," Jody said. She licked her lips nervously. "I have something for you," she said quietly. "Could we sit down for a minute?"

Jody handed Doug the manila envelope, and he sat down at the kitchen table. Jody poured herself some iced tea while she waited for Doug to scan the contents.

"Why?" Doug asked as he lifted his head. "Why are you deeding half the store back over to me? I don't want it anymore."

"Call it a wedding present," Jody said quietly as she sat down across from him. "Only this time I'm not going to change my mind."

Doug thrust the papers back across the table. "Jody, I appreciate what you're trying to do, but you don't have to marry me to ease your guilty conscience. Keep your store and raise your son. I'll be all right."

"I'm not doing this because I have a guilty conscience," Jody said. "I don't think I have anything to feel particularly guilty about," she added, more tartly than she had intended.

"Oh? Then why have you changed your mind again? You and I are still the same people we were back in the bar in San Antonio. I still have a temper, and you're still afraid of it."

"But that's just it—I'm not afraid of it anymore," Jody said. "Remember when we were talking and you said that you couldn't prove that you would never hit me? Well, you did prove it to me, Doug. You proved to me beyond a shadow of a doubt that you're different from Larry."

"When did I do that?" Doug asked, puzzled.

"Over the last week," Jody said. "Really, I guess on the day Goldie was hurt." Jody stood up and put her hands into the pockets of her jeans. "You had been under incredible stress—I'd broken it off with you, and you'd given up your share of the business. And then I left the gate open and Goldie ran out and got hit. You were furious with me that afternoon, Doug. You were angrier with me than Larry ever was. But you didn't hit me—you didn't even yell at me. And later you told me not to worry, that it wasn't my fault." She turned around to face Doug. "Do you have any idea how Larry would have reacted under similar circumstances?"

277

"Violently, I suppose."

"You suppose right," Jody said. "I hate to think what he would have done to me." She stood before Doug and stared down into his eyes. "But you didn't. You didn't take your anger out on me."

"And that's what made you change your mind?" Doug asked.

"Not entirely." Jody looked over at Goldie. "I've watched you nurse Goldie. I've seen up close how you treat the animal that you love. And if you treat her that well, you'd treat me and Scott that much better." She looked down at Doug anxiously. "Have I destroyed everything you felt for me? Have I ruined what we had before?"

Doug stood up and framed Jody's face between his palms. "No, you haven't destroyed what I feel for you. But, Jody, I don't want to get my hopes up and then have you change your mind again. I couldn't take it a second time."

"Doug, I'm not going to change my mind again. Before, when I told you I'd marry you, I did so in spite of the fact that I wasn't sure of you. But this time I am. I know that you're not going to abuse me."

"Are you sure? You looked so frightened of me in the bar and on the day that Goldie was hurt."

"Look at me now, Doug. Do I look frightened? Do I look unsure of you?"

Doug looked down into Jody's eyes. There was no doubt or fear or apprehension in them, only love. "You trust me," he whispered. "You finally believe that I'm not like him."

"Yes, I finally believe it," Jody said, reaching up to put her arms around Doug's neck.

Doug slid his arms around Jody and folded her into his warm embrace. "Oh, Jody, thank you."

She held him tightly to her as sobs of joy shook his body.

"You've given me back the world," he said.

Tears flooded her eyes. "Doug, I'm so very sorry I hurt you," she said. "Please forgive me for the pain I've caused you."

Doug wiped his cheeks on her hair. "There's nothing to forgive," he said quietly. "My brother put you through hell. It's only natural that you'd think I might be like him." He moved away from her and looked into her eyes. "You're sure of me now? Absolutely sure?"

"Absolutely," she said, love and trust shining from her eyes. She stood on her tiptoes and kissed the tears from Doug's cheeks.

"I feel like a fool, crying in front of you," he said. "I hadn't cried in years, not until I met you, and now I feel like I'm doing it all the time."

Jody smiled tenderly. "You better get used to it. You may shed quite a few in the future—at our wedding, when your children are born, when they marry."

"And when I look into your eyes and see the love you feel for me," he added. "Jody, I feel like I've gone from hell to heaven in the last few minutes."

"I know. This is the first time in years that I've felt completely happy," Jody admitted. She leaned her head against Doug's chest. "Even before, when we were going to get married, I wasn't completely happy, but now . . ."

"I know," Doug said simply, and Jody knew that he did.

"I've missed you," she said quietly, feeling his powerful heartbeat against her face.

"We've been together a lot recently," Doug said as he ran his hand down her back.

"Yes, but there's been a barrier between us. We haven't laughed together or talked about all the things that we used to talk about." She blushed as she looked up at Doug. "We haven't made love."

Doug smiled as he scooped her into his arms. "We can remedy that. We can talk and laugh after we make love." He started out of the kitchen with her.

"Doug, we can't! What about—"

"To hell with what about," he said as he grinned wickedly. "Scott's away for the night. Besides, I'm making an honest woman of you the minute I can."

"But the neighbors—"

"To hell with the neighbors too," Doug said. He carried her to the living-room door. "I feel like yelling it to the neighbors."

"Doug!"

"You're right. We'll tell 'em in the morning," Doug said as he shut the front door with his foot.

Jody laughed as he carried her up the steps, but her laughter faded when Doug set her down in his bedroom. Several boxes were already packed, and Doug's suitcases were out on the bed.

"You really would have left," she murmured as Doug took the cases off the bed.

"Yes, I would have had to," Doug said as he turned back the cover. "I love you too much. It would have torn me apart to do anything else."

"Praise God that didn't happen," Jody said quietly. She sat down on the edge of the bed and Doug joined her there.

"Yes, we have Him to thank, and I suspect those two across the street did some powerful pleading with Him on our behalf," Doug said as he took her hand. He kissed the finger where she still wore her cameo ring. "I can hardly wait to put your other ring there."

Jody picked up his hand and kissed it. "I can hardly wait for you to make love to me on our wedding night," she said. "The affair's been beautiful, but I want to make love to you as your wife."

"Would you rather wait?" Doug asked.

"Heavens, no," Jody said as she ran her hand up Doug's bare chest. "It will be so beautiful tonight, now that we have nothing between us."

"That's right," Doug said as he unbuttoned the top button of her blouse. "No doubts, no fear, nothing but love." He pushed her blouse from her shoulders and kissed her bare throat.

"I need you, Doug," Jody said as she placed gentle kisses along his jawline. "I almost went crazy wondering what I would do, once you were gone. You don't know how much I missed you when you were in Houston." She grinned sheepishly. "I kept running to the window to see if you were back yet."

"I'm glad." Doug grinned wickedly, but there was a tender expression in his eyes. He unhooked her bra and dropped it onto the floor, then they shed the rest of their clothing. His tender fingertip grazed one of her nipples. "I can hardly wait to see our child nurse here."

"Soon," she promised him as his lips captured the tender tip. "Very, very soon."

They lay back as his lips caressed her rosy nipple. "I want to see you big with my child," he said. "And I want to be a father to Scott, if he'll let me."

"He looks on you as a father already," Jody said. "He's going to be so happy we're back together."

"He's not the only one," Doug said as he bathed her breast with his moist tongue. Jody quivered underneath him with the pleasure he was giving to her. He caressed the other one in the same manner, groaning with pleasure when Jody turned him over

281

and touched him in exactly the same way. The hair on his chest tickled her mouth as she nibbled at his flat male nipples, turning them into hard little buds.

"Remember how shy you were about your body the first time we made love?" Doug asked as Jody moved to lie beside him, totally comfortable in her nudity.

"And you made me feel like a desirable woman again that night," Jody said. "Make me feel like that again, Doug. Make me feel sexy and desirable."

"Jody, you *are* sexy and desirable," Doug assured her as he covered her face with tender kisses. "So sexy," he assured her as his fingers splayed over her stomach. He rubbed tender circles there before his hand strayed lower. He stroked her hips with his palm, touching and caressing a tender circle around her femininity. "And desirable." He stroked her thighs, gently parting them, and caressed the insides gently, still not touching the heart of her womanhood. "And so very womanly." He continued to touch and stroke her hips and stomach, drawing near to her passion but never quite getting there.

"Doug, you're driving me crazy," Jody moaned as he continued to tease her with his fingertips. He grinned at her, and ever so lightly he grazed her womanhood. Jody sucked in her breath, but Doug's fingers withdrew and caressed the insides of her thighs.

"Good. I'm going to have you so on fire for me that you won't be able to stand it."

Jody blinked as her hands drifted down past Doug's waist. "Two can play at that game," she said as she caressed his stomach.

Doug and Jody ministered to one another for long moments. She stroked his stomach and his hips, only occasionally letting her fingers trail across his throbbing masculinity, and Doug continued to touch and to tease her. But there was love in each caress. Their loveplay was designed to stoke the flames of passion so that when they did come together, it would be cataclysmic for them both. They kissed and caressed long past the point of simply being ready, until Jody thought that if Doug did not take her soon she would cry out with longing. Doug felt the tightness in his body and knew that he was almost to the point of no return. He pushed Jody's hand away, and she wrapped her legs around him and took him into her warmth.

They had made love before, many times, but it was different now that there were no doubts or fears between them. Jody gave herself fully, no longer holding anything back. She gave herself over to Doug's passion without reserve, arching herself so that they were fully united in love. Sensing the change in her, Doug held back nothing, making love to her with fierce tenderness. His unbridled passion would have frightened Jody at one time, but now she reveled in it, matching it with loving aggression of her own. They soared together quickly and reached a tumultuous peak together, their bodies stiffening in unison as a powerful release of pleasure exploded in them. Jody gasped, and she heard Doug cry out her name as passionate release overcame him too.

They lay still for a moment, a damp tangle of arms and legs, too tired even to move.

"And to think that we have this for the rest of our lives," he said with wonder. He kissed Jody's temple. "How soon can we get married?"

Jody thought a minute. "We have to start over on the arrangements, I guess. And I have to find another dress."

"No, you don't." Doug got out of bed and opened

his closet, pointing to the piled boxes in the corner. "I couldn't bring myself to take them back. I kept putting it off, even when I'd given up on you."

"I'm so glad," Jody said. "Well, I guess we could still get married next month, if Hunter doesn't have another wedding that night."

"Let's ask him," Doug said as he sat down on the edge of the bed.

"Doug, it's late," Jody protested, but Doug dialed anyway, and with real happiness in his voice he told Hunter that his services would be needed after all.

Since they had no champagne, they toasted one another with a glass of wine and made love again before Doug drifted off to sleep in Jody's arms. Jody stared down into his tender, gentle face, and she said a little prayer of thanksgiving before she too shut her eyes and went to sleep.

Now you can reserve April's
Candlelights
<u>before</u> they're published!

♥ You'll have copies set aside for *you*
    the instant they come off press.
♥ You'll save yourself precious shopping
    time by arranging for *home delivery.*
♥ You'll feel proud and efficient about
    organizing a system that *guarantees* delivery.
♥ You'll avoid the disappointment of not
    finding *every* title you want and need.

ECSTASY SUPREMES $2.75 each

☐ **117 DESERT PRINCESS**, H. Monteith 11895-6-22
☐ **118 TREASURE FOR A LIFETIME**, L. Vail 18758-3-15
☐ **119 A DIFFERENT KIND OF MAN**, B. Andrews . . 12039-X-19
☐ **120 HIRED HUSBAND**, M. Catley 13646-6-12

ECSTASY ROMANCES $2.25 each

☐ **418 GYPSY RENEGADE**, M. Lane 13280-0-13
☐ **419 A HINT OF SPLENDOR**, K. Clark 13610-5-14
☐ **420 DOCTOR'S ORDERS**, P. Hamilton 12074-8-15
☐ **421 RACE THE WIND**, V. Flynn 17232-2-39
☐ **422 FORTUNE HUNTER**, C. Kenyon 12665-7-28
☐ **423 A WOMAN'S TOUCH**, K. Whittenburg 10513-7-26
☐ **424 MIDNIGHT SECRETS**, K. Daley 15619-X-10
☐ **425 TONIGHT YOU'RE MINE**, E. Delatush 18988-8-17